Praise for The Books of Umber:
HAPPENSTANCE FOUND

★ "Catanese dazzles in the first of the planned
Books of Umber series . . . rich characterizations . . .
well-choreographed action sequences and
genuinely surprising twists at the end."
—*Publishers Weekly*, starred review

"Rife with grisly horrors and absorbing wonders,
Umber's coastal kingdom exerts a fascination that lingers
after the last page is turned." —*BCCB*

"Try this with fans of Eragon or Jeanne DuPrau's
Ember books, or readers seeking an engaging
and deftly written fantasy." —*Booklist*

"Cinematic quality . . ." —*Horn Book Magazine*

Also by P. W. Catanese

The Books of Umber
Book 2: Dragon Games

The Thief and the Beanstalk

The Brave Apprentice

The Eye of the Warlock

The Mirror's Tale

The Riddle of the Gnome

P. W. CATANESE

THE BOOKS OF UMBER

HAPPENSTANCE FOUND

ALADDIN

NEW YORK   LONDON   TORONTO   SYDNEY

ALADDIN

An imprint of Simon & Schuster Children's Publishing Division

1230 Avenue of the Americas, New York, NY 10020

First Aladdin paperback edition December 2009

Text copyright © 2009 by P. W. Catanese

All rights reserved, including the right of reproduction in whole or in part in any form.

ALADDIN is a trademark of Simon & Schuster, Inc., and related logo is a registered trademark of Simon & Schuster, Inc.

Also available in an Aladdin hardcover edition.

For information about special discounts for bulk purchases, please contact Simon & Schuster Special Sales at 1-866-506-1949 or business@simonandschuster.com.

The Simon & Schuster Speakers Bureau can bring authors to your live event. For more information or to book an event contact the Simon & Schuster Speakers Bureau at 1-866-248-3049 or visit our website at www.simonspeakers.com.

Designed by Karin Paprocki

The text of this book was set in Bembo.

Manufactured in the United States of America

1112 OFF

6 8 10 9 7

The Library of Congress has cataloged the hardcover edition as follows:

Catanese, P. W.

Happenstance found / by P. W. Catanese.

p. cm.

(The books of Umber)

Summary: A boy awakens, blindfolded, with no memory of even his name, but soon meets Lord Umber, an adventurer and inventor, who calls him Happenstance and tells him that he has a very important destiny— and a powerful enemy.

ISBN 978-1-4169-7519-9 (hc)

[1. Adventure and adventurers—Fiction. 2. Identity—Fiction. 3. Magic—Fiction. 4. Imaginary creatures—Fiction. 5. Fantasy.] I. Title.

PZ7.C268783Hap 2009

[Fic]—dc22

2008045966

ISBN 978-1-4169-5382-1 (pbk)

ISBN 978-1-4391-5337-6 (eBook)

FOR MOLLY McGUIRE WOODS

CHAPTER I

The boy felt as if he'd emerged, fully conscious and wholly formed, out of nothing. Not out of darkness, or chaos, or mist or murk. He was sure he'd sprung from *nothing*, and now he was lying in a strange place with rough stone pressing against the back of his skull.

He began to notice peculiar things. A strange taste painted his throat. His clothes were damp, especially the thick cloak. And he couldn't see, because something was across his eyes: a cloth, tied behind his head. When he reached for it, someone spoke.

"Don't touch that."

The voice was unfamiliar. Of course it was—it was the first the boy ever remembered hearing. The man had spoken briefly, but the boy detected something in those three words. Amusement. Or eager anticipation.

"Who is that? Who are you?" asked the boy. He pushed himself up until he sat on the stone floor.

"Never mind about me," said the man, nearly singing the words. The boy heard a patter of stealthy feet, a scuffle of shifting cloth. When the man spoke again, his voice was closer. He'd been standing before; now he must have been kneeling. "I'm curious about you, though," the man said. "How do you feel? What do you know?"

"What do I *know*?" the boy asked. The question was strange, the answer even stranger. Because, in fact, he knew very little. At the moment, anyway, knowledge seemed to arrive bit by bit, as he needed it. *What is this I'm sitting upon? A stone floor. What is around my eyes? A blindfold. What is on my feet? Boots. What is it called when I open my mouth and draw in air? Breathing.* A spring inside his mind surged forth and filled his head with words and notions. But when he called on the spring to tell him one particular thing, there was no response. The boy gasped.

"My name!" the boy cried out. "I don't know who—"

"Hush!" cried the man. "Listen!"

The boy heard nothing at first. He turned his ear, searching. His senses hinted that he was in a confined space, surrounded by walls. But the space wasn't entirely enclosed, because a sound came from one direction, distant but growing.

"Best be quiet for a moment. Until the worm passes," the man whispered, so close that the boy felt warm breath on his ear.

Worm? That word had more than one meaning, the spring of knowledge told him. There were the worms in the ground, the tiny, wriggling things that were feasted on by birds and in turn feasted on all things dead. Then there were the other worms. Beastly and dangerous.

He heard the thing coming—but was it one thing, or an army of things? A massive bulk scraped across a rocky surface, and there was an incessant clacking, as if hundreds of talons scrabbled over the ground. The noise grew until it became a roar as the creature passed a narrow window or door, just a few strides away.

The boy felt a single finger across his lips, and the knowledge came to him: It was a sign that he should be quiet. His shoulders quivered as the scraping, tapping sounds went on for longer than he could believe. Finally, they began to fade. The worm was gone, propelling its vast bulk—a many-legged bulk, the boy decided—through the adjacent corridor or passageway.

When the sound died, the man spoke. "Well. I hope the worm doesn't eat them."

"Eat *who*?" asked the boy.

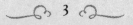 3

"The ones who are coming for you. Where are they, by the way? They should have been here by now. Hold on—they're getting close. Yes, that's them. And *he's* with them. I knew he would be." Something in the tone of the voice made the boy think the man was grinning. "Don't be afraid. I want you to trust them."

"I don't understand. Who are these people?" asked the boy. The man didn't answer. "Hello?" The boy pushed the blindfold over his forehead. The room was dark, but his eyesight pierced the gloom. The man was not there.

As he'd guessed, the room was small. The walls were chiseled blocks, fitted tight, and the floor was made of paving stones. At the near end of the room a narrow archway led to a broad corridor where the worm had slid by. He turned to the opposite end. There, a wider archway opened into another gloomy space.

The boy pushed himself to his feet. His short leather boots squished when he stood, and water dripped from his cloak. He wondered why they were so damp, and why he wore such a heavy garment at all—it was warm in this place, almost uncomfortably so. He shrugged the cloak off, revealing a dull red tunic and brown trousers underneath.

He turned to the far end of the room again because a dawning orange light was filling the archway there. There were footsteps and voices. Faint echoes bounced off the walls.

The first voice he heard was deep, as if born from a thick and powerful chest. "Is this the place? Fine. Get the thing, whatever it is, and let's get out of here."

Another man spoke in quick and eager tones. "Hush, Oates. Where's your sense of adventure?"

"I think this is it, Lord Umber." That was a third voice, female and young. The light flickered, disturbed by their shadows. *One of them has a lamp,* thought the boy.

A trio appeared in the archway. They froze and stared at the boy. The largest was a towering, slab-jawed, burly man who scowled down with dark, narrowed eyes and tightened his grip on the long spear that he carried. *That's the deep-voiced one—Oates,* the boy guessed. On the other side was the young woman. A girl, really—surely not yet seventeen. She was tall and gangly, with hair pulled back from a fragile face. The boy felt a pang in his heart when he saw that her right arm ended at the wrist. Where a hand should have been, there was a three-pronged piece of metal holding the lamp.

The man in the middle, who had to be Lord Umber, held a parchment in two hands. He was slight of build, with a wide-eyed, small-chinned face under a mess of sandy hair. His eyebrows wandered toward his scalp, and he tilted his head to one side and smiled. The smile showed every tooth, and it formed effortlessly; the boy got the feeling that it always did for this man.

"Well," Umber said, chuckling. "We didn't expect to meet anyone down here." He looked back at the corridor. "This is the place. The map couldn't be clearer." Umber let go of the parchment with one hand. It was inclined to curl, and so it rolled up instantly. Umber stuffed it into one of the bulging pockets in his vest.

The big fellow, Oates, jabbed his elbow into Umber's side, hard enough to make the smile falter for a moment. "Umber . . . his eyes!" Oates whispered.

"Oates, your manners," Umber hissed at the big fellow.

The boy touched the corners of his eyes, wondering if he was injured. "What's wrong with them?"

"Nothing, young friend," Umber said, shooting a peeved look at Oates. "They're remarkable, actually. Quite striking."

"They're weird. I don't like them," said Oates, thrusting his sizable jaw forward.

Umber pinched the bridge of his nose. "That'll do, Oates," he said grimacing sideways. "One more comment like that and you'll be muzzled. I'm serious." His expression brightened again as he turned toward the boy. "Actually, young man, we came here looking for something." Umber's gaze darted around the barren room. "I don't see anything, though, except for you. What's your name?"

The boy opened his mouth to reply that he didn't know, but the question was answered for him. "Call him Happenstance," the voice said, from somewhere out of sight.

Oates gripped the spear with both hands and raised it. "Who's that? Who's there?"

Umber put his hand on Oates's heavy shoulder. "Let's not make primitive threatening gestures at every stranger we meet, Oates." He peered around, trying to find the source of the voice. "Hello, stranger. Come out and talk to us. You have nothing to fear."

"Nothing to fear but something to lose," the singsong voice replied. "Happenstance himself is what you came for. Take him, Umber. Keep him with you. You'll need him, if you're serious about that task you have in mind."

The girl looked at Umber. "What task is that, Lord Umber?"

Umber shrugged. "I haven't the slightest," he said, but for an instant the boy saw an uncertain look in the man's eyes. Umber raised his voice to address the stranger again. "You know me, but your voice is unfamiliar. Do I know you, sir?"

"Not by name or face," came the reply.

Umber scratched the back of his head. He turned as he spoke, not sure where the stranger hid. "I don't think I understand. Tell me, sir—was it you who sent me that note, about the treasure I'd find in the buried city?"

"The chance exists," the stranger sang. Every time he spoke the three of them looked in different directions, trying to find the source of the voice. Oates looked ready to hurl the spear if the stranger showed his face.

"No time for questions now. There's a note in the boy's pocket," the stranger said. "You'll find some answers there. As for you, Happenstance—farewell! Good fortune!" The stranger didn't stop speaking; instead, the voice faded until it could not be heard.

Oates glowered, and the girl shifted nervously from foot to foot. Umber pursed his lips and finally cleared his throat. "So," he said to the boy. "Your name is Happenstance?"

"I . . . I guess so."

Oates grunted. "You guess so. You call that an answer? Umber, I told you the boy was weird."

"Oates!" snapped Umber. He clenched his fists, and then shook the fingers loose and pointed toward the archway that they'd entered. "Sophie, take Mister Loose-lips and step outside for a moment. I'd like to talk to . . . er, *Happenstance* before Oates makes a permanent bad impression."

"Come, Oates," Sophie said, tugging his sleeve. When they turned, Happenstance noticed the other weapons they carried. The girl had a quiver of arrows on her back, and a short bow strapped there as well. Oates had an ax dangling on one side of his belt, and a thick-headed club on the other. They left the chamber, taking the lamp with them.

"Don't mind the dark, Happenstance," said Umber. He had a pack slung over one shoulder and he opened its flap and reached inside. "I have my own light."

"It's all right. I can see," said Happenstance. He wondered why Umber needed more light. Everything was plainly visible to him.

Umber froze with his hand inside the pack. "You can? But it's pitch-black in here."

Happenstance nodded, and then realized that Umber couldn't perceive the gesture. "I can see very well."

"How many fingers am I holding up?" said Umber.

"Five, if you count the thumb," said Happenstance.

An expression came to Umber's face, one that Happenstance would see many times in the days to come. Umber's eyes grew wide and round, and his mouth burst into a toothy, delighted smile. "Nocturnal vision!" Umber cried. "What a world! But I'm blind as a bat down here." He pulled a jar from his pack. It held a dozen fat wormy things, each gleaming with soft light in shades of yellow, orange, and red, while feeding on a scattering of leaves and mushrooms. Using them to light his way, Umber sat with his legs folded, face-to-face with Happenstance. "Glimmer-worms," Umber said, tilting the jar. "Now then, Hap—do you mind if I call you that? *Happenstance* takes so long to say."

Hap shook his head. "It doesn't matter." Neither name had any meaning or felt familiar. He looked toward the corridor where the others waited. "Would you tell me something, please? What's the matter with my eyes?"

Umber smiled. "Ah. That's one of the things I wanted to discuss. Nothing's wrong with your eyes, Hap. But I've never seen a pair quite like them, and I've seen a lot. They're an unusual shade of bright green. And they practically sparkle, here in the dark." He put the jar of glimmer-worms on the ground between them and rested his elbows on his knees. "That big fellow, Oates? Let me apologize for him, Hap. He—how do I explain this?—has this compulsion. He's compelled to speak his mind, with absolute honesty, at all times. Sometimes he has to muzzle himself, believe it or not, for his good and ours. However, this compulsion—well, it's a *curse*, really; I'll explain it some other time—makes him a most trustworthy servant. On the other hand, it makes him nearly unbearable to be around much of the time. I don't recommend a steady diet of pure honesty, frankly. You'll be out of friends by the end of the week."

Hap nodded. He wondered if all people were as odd as this trio.

"Anyhow, I hear you have a note?" Umber said. His fingers waggled.

Hap patted his tunic and leggings, but found nothing. *The cloak*, he thought. He picked up the soggy garment, ran his hands along its sides, and then found a pocket in its inner lining. A short scroll was tucked inside. It was rolled tight and sealed with a green glob of wax, with words in dark brown ink under the seal:

For the Eyes of Umber Only.

"I've seen that seal before. Notice the letters, WN? That was on the scroll that brought me here," Umber said, patting the pocket where he'd stuffed his parchment. "May I?" He held out his hand. Hap looked at the scroll for a moment, and then gave it to Umber.

"So intriguing," Umber said. He sniffed the scroll and peered into one of its rolled ends. "Do you know who that fellow was, who spoke to us just now?"

Hap shrugged. "I don't even know who *I* am."

One of Umber's eyebrows vaulted high. "That is *also* intriguing. Well, let's have a read." Slipping a finger under the edge of the parchment, he broke the wax seal. He unrolled the scroll and gazed at it for a while, with his lips moving now and then, mouthing words. Hints of emotion flickered over his face. He seemed amused, then surprised, and gradually went pale. He licked his lips as if his mouth had gone dry.

"What does it say?" Hap asked, craning his neck.

"If you don't mind, I won't tell you right now," Umber said. "I'd like some time to . . ." His voice faltered, and he stared at the parchment again.

"What?" said Hap. "Is something wrong?"

Umber pinched the note at opposite corners, holding it with the nails of his thumb and forefinger. "Curious. The parchment feels warm. Almost too hot to hold." Wisps of smoke streamed from the paper. Umber blew on it, but the note abruptly burst into flame. He squeaked and dropped the parchment. It turned white-hot and disintegrated into ash before it touched the ground.

Umber stared at the snowy remains. "Well, there's a trick. I have to learn that one." He used the edge of his hands to sweep the ashes into a pile. He scooped them, along with the broken seal, into an empty envelope that he extracted from one of his pockets. After he tucked the envelope away, his gaze fell on Hap again. Something had shaken his high spirits momentarily, but the smile soon came back.

"Well, Hap. I don't think we have a choice about this. You'd better come with us. We can't leave you alone in this tomb of a city. Is that all right with you? Will you come with me?" Umber stood and extended a hand to Hap.

Hap took a deep breath. He looked at Umber's pleasant, almost giddy, face and the kind hazel eyes that crinkled at the corners. "I don't know what else to do," Hap said. He clasped Umber's hand just as a deep rumbling shook the room and dust and rock started to rain down.

CHAPTER
2

The shaking stopped a few heartbeats
later. Umber coughed and used his fingers to comb a pebble
from his hair. "Just a tremor," he said. "Nothing to fear. We've
felt a few since we arrived. Not as strong as that one, though.
Come on." He led Hap through the archway, where the others
waited.

"Did you feel that?" asked Oates.

"No, Oates," Umber said gravely. "All of my senses suddenly
departed me, leaving me unable to detect an earthquake."
Sophie laughed, but dropped her brown-eyed gaze when Hap
looked her way.

Hap stared at his new surroundings. Until that moment,
all he consciously remembered was what he'd seen in the

plain little chamber. Now as he looked around, the fountain of knowledge bubbled to life again and eagerly supplied the names for the strange sights before him.

There was a long, wide tunnel, crudely hacked from porous rock. The roof was so low that Oates had to move in a perpetual crouch. On each side the rock had been gouged away to uncover doors, windows, and alleys. Hap peered into the gloom and saw other, narrower tunnels intersecting this one, creating a—he waited for the word to come—*maze* in the stone.

"Do you know where we are, Hap?" Umber said.

Hap shook his head. "You called it the buried city."

"Yes, but it has another name: Alzumar. Sophie, why don't you tell Hap about it?"

The girl saw Hap looking at her and hid her damaged arm behind her back. "That's all right," she said, so softly it was hard to hear. "You do it, please."

Umber smiled at her and nodded. "Of course, dear. Hap, Alzumar was the wonder of its age, centuries ago; a thriving city of dazzling wealth, peopled by artisans who imported precious metals and jewels from the corners of the world and wrought them into all manner of glorious things. Kings and queens still wear crowns and wave scepters that were crafted here. But sadly, its founders built Alzumar in an ill-fated location—in a valley, at the foot of a volcano called Mount Ignis. Do you know what a volcano is, Hap?"

Hap waited for the knowledge to come. "A mountain of fire," he replied. The moment he said the words, a stronger tremor shook the underground city, echoing down the intersecting tunnels. Somewhere out of sight, a chunk of rock fell.

"We should get out," said Oates, eyeing the rough-hewn ceiling.

"I suppose," Umber said, pulling a loose thread from his vest.

Oates raised a finger and jabbed it Umber's way. "Hold on—you're wasting time on purpose! You're keeping us here because you want to see that worm."

Umber pretended to cough, but Hap saw him cover his grin with one hand. "Well, I was hoping to catch a glimpse. But I don't think the beast is here after all."

"It *is* here," Hap said. He bit his lip when the others spun their heads his way. "Something's here, anyway. It's big. With a lot of legs."

Umber gave a happy squeal and clapped his hands. "Wonderful! You actually *saw* the worm?"

"I heard it," said Hap. "Just before you got here."

"Now I'm sure we should go," said Oates, turning to look over his shoulder.

"It sounded . . . scary," Hap said.

"I should think so!" Umber rubbed his palms together. "Still, I suppose Oates is right. These quakes do rattle the nerves. We'll go—but who knows, perhaps the worm will pop up before we reach the light of day. If we're lucky."

They walked down the craggy tunnel. The glow of Sophie's lamp washed over half-exposed walls. Hap saw parts of columns and hints of friezes with images of men and women dancing and leaping.

"Hap, I didn't tell you about the terrible fate of Alzumar," Umber said. "When Ignis erupted, tons of ash fell, filling the valley to the brim and burying the city. Some folk managed to escape, but many were trapped here, along with Alzumar's legendary wealth. The whole city was hidden under solid ash, intact but entombed. Before long, men returned to recapture the gold and jewels. They excavated the streets and tunneled into the doorways. It took hundreds of years, but finally almost every byway had been explored, and most of the wealth was found again. Still, people came searching for more. But sometime in the last fifty years, something else made its home here."

"The worm?" asked Hap.

Umber nodded. "The *tyrant worm*, to be precise. Alzumar is a perfect lair for a creature that can't stand the light of day.

Quite a few fortune-seekers have met their doom in the tyrant worm's jaws. It's a legendary man-eater."

Hap stared. "So why do you want to see it?"

Oates snorted. "Because he's crazy, that's why. He'll go to the end of the world to get a peek at a monster."

"Everyone needs a hobby," Umber said. "I've heard the tyrant worm described as a cross between a dragon and a centipede. I'm beside myself with curiosity, Hap. How long is it? I've heard a hundred feet or more. And is it true that it's blind, and finds its prey by sound alone?" Umber's face was radiant, and he waved his hands in the air as he spoke. He would have gone on, but Sophie cut him off.

"Listen!" she cried.

They stopped walking. Umber put a hand to his ear. His mouth was reduced to a tiny, puckered circle. From somewhere in the distance, meager sounds wandered down the tunnel: soft thumps, like fingers drumming on stone.

Hap squinted so his keen sight better pierced the gloom, and he saw the worm—part of its long body, at least. Hundreds of paces away, well beyond the flickering yellow light that the lamp cast, the creature was crossing the main tunnel, going from alley to alley. It was immense, with a round body that nearly touched the stone roof, propped up on pair after pair of short, churning legs.

"It's there," he said.

"You can see it?" Umber whispered, tugging at Hap's sleeve.

Hap nodded. At first he'd felt relieved that the worm wasn't coming directly at them—perhaps it didn't know they were there. But the hairs on his arms stood when he remembered how, when he heard it pass before, it sounded as if the creature was dragging its body while its clawed feet raked the stone. Not this time, though. Now it moved in stealth, with its body raised on its multitude of legs. The claws were retracted, so that only the leathery pads of each foot touched the stone and every step was muffled.

Umber tugged again. "What does it look like? What is it doing?"

"I don't see the head. Just the body. It's like a . . . serpent with a thousand legs," Hap said. "And I think it's hunting us." He heard movement behind him, and when he'd turned around, the lamp was on the ground and Sophie had strung an arrow in her bow. The weapon had been cleverly designed so that the metal prongs at the end of her wrist slid into holes drilled in the bow. She aimed the arrow down the main passage.

"It's not coming right at us," Hap said. He pointed. "It's crossing over, that way. I think it will come at us from the side, to surprise us." The creature was still sliding across the intersection. Hap thought it would never end. But finally the body tapered. Every pair of legs grew smaller until he finally saw a slender tail with a barbed and lethal point.

"How can you see that, boy? I can't see a thing!" said Oates.

"We're being stalked! Isn't it exciting?" cried Umber.

"Should we run?" asked Sophie.

"Oh, let's move toward the exit, by all means," Umber replied, grinning. "If it pounces, we'll just dodge into one of those narrow doorways, easy as pie!"

Oates looked at Hap and shook his head gravely. "Umber's out of his mind. Get used to it."

Oates led the way with his spear pointing right, where the worm might lunge out. Hap glimpsed down the dark alleys and byways that they passed, where more hints of lost buildings were revealed. At the far end of the corridor he saw a tiny rectangle of bright light. *The sun,* his growing knowledge informed him.

Umber tugged Oates's arm from behind. "Slow down—I need to get a look at it!"

The rectangle of light was blotted from sight as the worm shot out from another crossroad ahead of them. It plunged down the opposite byway, blocking their path. Hap caught a glimpse of a monstrous head. The reptilian hide kept sliding by, propelled by endless pairs of lizard legs.

"How long is this thing?" shouted Oates.

Umber shook his head, amazed. "Hundreds of feet. Look—I think it's circling us, cutting us off in every direction! Brilliant! I'll bet it comes from behind next. Ha! I was right!"

The head of the worm emerged from an alley just a few strides to their rear and poised there. The strange face was covered by scaly armor. Spiny whiskers, each longer than a man's arm, bristled from both sides of the head. There was a thin line where its mouth was clamped tight, topped by a row of holes that might have been nostrils or ears. There were no eyes that Hap could see, only an odd domed structure like a beetle's shell on its forehead. The two legs nearest the head were thick and powerful, with five wicked claws at the end of its fingers.

There was a moment of shocked silence, until Sophie gasped aloud. The thin horizontal line on the worm's face cracked apart, the whiskers folded flat against the head, and the mouth opened with a roar. Row upon row of jagged teeth lined its jaws. The cavernous throat could swallow any of them in a single gulp. The tongue was slick and pale with plum-colored veins.

The legs of the worm churned like the oars on a galley,

propelling it forward. The mouth snapped with terrible speed, and the teeth clashed so hard, Hap thought they would crack into pieces. Oates seized Sophie and Umber by the shoulders and pushed them through the nearest doorway before plunging in behind them. Hap bent his legs and sprang after them in a broad leap that carried him into the room, just ahead of the gnashing jaws.

"You're a nimble one, aren't you?" said Umber as Hap straightened out of the froglike stance in which he'd landed. Oates and Sophie shook with fear from the narrow escape, but Umber grinned wider than ever. As the raging creature hammered its head against the door, he looked at it like a beloved pet. The heavy blocks of stone on either side of the threshold shook but did not budge, even when the worm turned sideways and tried to squeeze inside. Hap was glad to see that the head was too bulky to slip through.

"It can't get in, so we're perfectly safe. We'll just wait it out here," Umber said.

"Wait it out like that fellow did?" grumbled Oates. He jabbed his thumb toward the corner of the room. Hap saw the slumping remains of some earlier fortune-seeker, now just a skeleton in a moldy tunic, with a rusted sword and shield at his side. The skull grinned from inside a battered helmet.

"Not necessarily," said Umber. "It's called optimism, people. Try it, I beg. Here's the secret: Everyone, stop talking and don't move. It's said that the worm hunts by sound, not sight. In time it should lose interest and go. If not, I have the means to knock it out, remember?" He patted a bulging pocket in his vest. "But let's try the silent treatment first."

"Should I douse the lamp, Lord Umber?" Sophie whispered. Umber shook his head and tapped his lip. They stood perfectly still, scarcely breathing aloud. Hap looked around the room, which wasn't so different from the one where he'd been found. Aside from the ancient corpse it was barren, stripped of valuables long ago. There was another doorway at the other end, thankfully just as narrow as the one that held the tyrant worm at bay.

Hap felt a tap at his shoulder. Umber pointed at the worm's head, where something odd was happening. The shell on the creature's forehead opened in the middle like shutters, and something emerged from the dark hole inside. It was a moist, twitching, globular thing, drooping at the end of a long stalk. As Hap watched, a black disc appeared within the globe and spread like oil on water. He heard Umber draw a quick excited breath.

Hap's blood turned cold as the globe swiveled left and right before facing their small group. The black circle expanded and contracted, and Hap knew it was *seeing* them, bringing them into focus. The worm hissed.

"You said it couldn't see!" shouted Oates, forgetting Umber's instruction to be silent. He shook a fist. "We all heard it, Umber! You specifically said, it couldn't see!"

"I know—isn't it wonderful to learn something new?" Umber laughed. He reached into a pocket and drew out a bottle made of red glass and sealed with wax and cork. A dark liquid sloshed inside. "I hate to do it, really, but we have to put this specimen to sleep for a while."

He cocked the vial over one shoulder and threw it toward the threshold. It struck the ground under the jaw of the beast, and a purple cloud billowed up from the shattered glass. The worm shook its head. It drew in a great breath and sneezed. Hap put his elbow across his face as a spray of noxious liquid spattered the room. Sophie wiped her cheek with her sleeve and looked as if she was going to be ill.

"Don't fight it, you beautiful creature," Umber whispered to the worm. "Let sleep come."

The dangling eye wavered, and the black circle shrank to a dot. The creature's head slumped until it touched the floor, where it rocked back and forth. For a moment, Hap thought the creature was going to sleep, but it suddenly snapped its head up and hammered it against the sides of the door. It opened its mouth wide and roared, louder than thunder. Hap felt hot breath ruffle his hair.

Umber puckered his lips and scratched his chin. "Huh. Should've brought the bigger bottle after all."

"What's that smell?" said Sophie. She pulled the collar of her shirt up to cover her mouth. Hap caught the scent as well. It was sharp and disagreeable.

"Wasn't me," said Oates. "Is it the worm?"

Umber's nose wrinkled. "That's sulfur, I believe. Not what you want to sniff when you're at the foot of an irritable volcano. I think we ought to get out of Alzumar, very soon. We'll have to find a way around the worm." He headed for the rear archway, and the others followed. As Umber approached the threshold he took a final look back at the worm. Its eye hovered, watching them, but its head did not move.

"Interesting," Umber said. "You'd think it would come around after us—" His eyes widened as if a thought had come to him, and he turned and dropped to the floor just as something whipped into the room through the threshold, slicing the air over his head with a *whoosh*. It was the narrow tail of the worm. Umber scrambled back as the barbed tip lashed at him. "Oh dear," he said. "That could do some damage."

The tail slithered into the room, driving them toward the gaping jaws at the other door. Oates growled and stepped in front of Umber, jabbing at the tail with his spear. "Do something, Umber!" he shouted.

"Yes," Umber said, rubbing the back of his neck. "Think, Umber! The trouble is, it can see us. Didn't expect that." Sophie readied an arrow, and she turned to point it at the dangling eye.

"Hold on, Sophie," Umber said. "Really, an arrow in the eyeball? Perhaps we don't need to be so cruel." He kneeled and pushed together a small pile of dirt. He lifted the pile in cupped hands, stepped toward the worm, and slung the dirt at its eye, coating the watery globe with grit. The beast let out an earsplitting howl and shook its head. The eye-stalk shrank back and the halves of the shell clapped shut over it.

Umber put a finger to his lips and gestured for the others to follow. As the tail stabbed blindly around the room, he edged around it and slipped through the narrow space between the tail and the threshold. Sophie followed, and Hap went next, prodded by Oates.

They moved with their backs pressed against the wall of the building they'd departed. Hap saw the body of the worm stretch down the narrow road and disappear around the corner. He looked at Umber, wondering where this reckless man would lead them next.

A louder, stronger tremor shook the entombed city. Hap

felt the ground vibrate under his feet. Chunks of rock fell all around. At his back, the wall grumbled. Already, this quake had outlasted the others, and he had the feeling it wasn't going to end.

The legs of the worm churned, scrabbling in unison against the stone. As the end of the worm slid by, the group ducked under its waving tail. Hap couldn't tell if the worm was frightened by the tremor or on its way to hunt them down.

Umber didn't hesitate. He smiled brightly, waved for them to follow, and ran after the monster.

...he creature survives, since prey ...not be plentiful in its subterranean lair. Perhaps it emerges at night to hunt, although such a thing has never been witnessed. Nor is it understood how the tyrant worm finds its habitat. Alzumar, for example, is hundreds of miles from any known

CHAPTER
3

The barbed tail swept before them as they ran past black alleys and doorways, turning left and right through the buried maze. Umber suddenly broke off from the pursuit of the tail. "Run for it!" he shouted. Hap saw that they'd found the main tunnel again. The rectangle of daylight was ahead, closer than before. He risked a look behind him, and it felt like a fist had tightened around his heart. The head of the worm shot out from a side street and turned in pursuit.

"Faster!" shouted Umber. Hap's legs churned, and before he knew what he'd done, he was ahead of all of them. He looked back and saw their nostrils flaring and their cheeks puffing, and he wondered why they couldn't keep up. It wasn't from lack of effort; Sophie ran like a deer, and Oates charged like a bull. Umber was the worst runner by far. His knees rose awkwardly high, and his arms flailed. Sophie went by him easily, but Oates refused to pass Umber. The big man tightened his grip on his spear and looked over his shoulder, ready to fight. The worm was only a few strides back, and gaining.

Hap looked ahead and saw the opening, so bright with daylight that it stung his unaccustomed eyes. Umber had said that the tyrant worm could not stand the sun. But while Hap knew he'd make it to safety, he wasn't sure about the others. The worm's long whiskers reached forward, probing. One brushed Umber's heel, and the creature's mouth cracked wide in response. Its jaws would have snapped shut with Umber inside if Oates hadn't heaved his spear into the worm's throat. The creature paused to whip its head from side to side, flinging the weapon loose.

They spilled into the searing light of day, where the reek of sulfur was strong and the rumbling soared in pitch, no longer conducted through surrounding rock. They ran away from the dark tunnel opening until Umber wheezed, "Enough! That's far enough!"

Umber bent at the waist and grabbed his stomach. He managed to laugh and pant at the same time. Sophie threw herself on the ground. Oates turned to make certain the worm hadn't ventured outside. Then he pointed a thick finger at Umber. "You won't be happy till you get us killed, will you? I almost wet my trousers! You know what I think, Umber? I think—"

The rumbling grew and the ground quivered. Hap craned his neck to see the steep, headless mountain that loomed over the buried city. It belched black smoke and vomited molten rock out of the cauldron at its peak. An orange river oozed down the mountainside, forking into streams. One of them looked sure to engulf the mouth of the tunnel and the place where they stood.

"I think it's time to leave these ghostly shores," Umber said, raising his voice to be heard. Hap looked behind them and saw that the land sloped gradually down until it reached a sparkling sea.

They walked swiftly until they reached a rocky beach where pocked volcanic boulders littered the sand. The sea was serene, with the smallest of waves caressing the shore.

"Would you mind fetching the jolly boat, Oates?" Umber asked.

Oates muttered something and stalked off toward a jumble of rocks. Umber stared back at the mountain, tapping his chin with a fist. "Will you look at that? The lava will cover the entrance and seal off the city again. And the tyrant worm with it, I suppose. Poor thing—I barely had a chance to study it." His lips formed a pout and he turned to Hap. "And Happenstance, why do you suppose we met you at this precise moment, just before Ignis blew its top? A few minutes later and you'd have been trapped inside, doomed for sure. Do you think that was a coincidence?"

"I guess," Hap replied.

Mount Ignis rattled and fired a glowing jet of molten rock out of its throat. Umber watched the mouth of the tunnel disappear. "Awfully convenient, if someone wanted to cover his tracks. But who could know when such a thing was going to happen?"

"Let's go!" Oates shouted over the roar. Hap turned, and his mouth dropped open when he saw the big fellow coming back to the beach balancing a boat over his head with both hands. The boat was long and wide enough for eight people to sit in pairs, but Oates bore it across the sand like a wicker basket.

"He's that strong, all right," Umber said, stepping beside Hap. "Put it in the water, Oates!"

"And where else would I put it?" grumbled Oates.

Oates stood behind the boat, ready to shove off, while the others got inside. It was Hap's turn, but he froze on the sand

and stared at the water, wondering why his throat was knotting up inside his neck.

Umber's hand rested on his shoulder. "Something the matter, Hap?"

Hap's tongue stuck on the roof of his mouth when he tried to answer. "The water. It scares me."

Ignis spoke next, with a fiery explosion that made Hap jump. He turned to see chunks of stone spewing out of the volcano's top. Oates cleared his throat loudly and shoved the boat a foot deeper into the sea.

Umber frowned at Oates before giving Hap an encouraging smile. "You're not the first person to fear water, Hap, but I think we'd better put some distance between us and the volcano. Would it help if I held your hand?"

A smoldering boulder thumped into the sand nearby. Hap shook his head. "Thank you. I can do it." With his legs quaking, he stepped into the narrow craft, took a seat on a low bench, and closed his eyes. His other senses told him what happened next: Umber hopped in and sat beside him. Oates grunted and the boat ground across the sand, then bobbed in the shallows. The water behind them sloshed as Oates waded for a stride or two, and then the boat rocked as he jumped into the stern.

Hap thought he might have to pry his eyelids apart with his fingers, but he willed them open at last. And that was good, because he didn't have to break his iron grip on the edge of the bench. He sat facing the back of the boat where Oates paddled hard, propelling them away from the raging mountain. Black smoke billowed across the sky.

"How long have you been afraid of water, Happenstance?" asked Umber.

"As long as I can remember," Hap replied.

Umber chuckled. "Funny, Hap." The smile faded by half. "Did you mean to be funny? Because you don't remember anything, do you?"

Hap shook his head. "Not before I woke up. No." He looked over his shoulder and saw the open sea. The strange nature of his memory struck him again. He couldn't remember ever being at sea, yet he knew that *sea* was the name for this watery body, and he knew that it swarmed with *fish*, and he knew that he'd taste *salt* if he put a drop in his mouth. Instinct told him that the sea wasn't always this placid, and that it could heave up lethal, towering waves when its ire was raised. He glanced over the side and wondered how far he'd sink if the boat capsized. The thought made his breath stop, and he dug his nails into the wood of the bench.

"Where are we going?" Hap asked, forcing the words out of his tight throat.

Umber leaned closer. "Back to Kurahaven, Hap. It's where

I live. I honestly don't know where else I'd bring you. Besides, it's not as if we're taking you away from your home. I don't know where you came from, but it wasn't this deserted land."

Hap looked again at the endless expanse of water. "How far is Kurahaven?"

"Far," Umber said. "In the kingdom of Celador. But don't worry, Oates won't paddle us the whole way." He reached down and lifted a long brass tube with a fat bulb at one end. It ran nearly the length of the boat. Umber lowered the bulbous end into the water, letting the rod slip through his hands until most was submerged. Then he lifted a mallet made of the same metal. "Oates, do you suppose it's deep enough?"

Oates leaned over and stared into the depths. "Ought to be."

Umber hammered on the tube with the mallet, playing a song with only one note. It rang like a bell with every strike and still hummed when he was done. Umber whistled as he pulled the tube out of the water and stowed it.

Mount Ignis exploded again. A hundred gray plumes shot skyward as rocky debris peppered the sea.

"Keep paddling, Oates," Umber said, miming the motion. "No need to cut it close." Oates grunted and dug deep with the oar, and the boat picked up speed.

Hap was about to ask Umber what the purpose of the

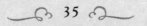

tube was, when something off the bow caught his eye. A swell came toward them from the open sea. It was wide and long, like a low hill of water, approaching fast. For the first time since he'd boarded, Hap let go of the bench with one hand. He pointed at the swell. "What *is* that?"

Umber laughed. "Nothing to fear, my boy."

The swell passed directly under them. Hap's stomach turned upside down as the boat crested and fell. He watched the bulge in the sea die down, and then the water swirled and bubbled. His eyes widened to the point of pain as he saw the water beside the boat darken—not because it was reflecting the dark volcanic cloud above, but because something enormous rose from the depths below.

A strange craft made of oily black wood, far larger than theirs, shattered the surface of the sea. It was rectangular, with a railing around its top deck and an enclosed hull below. Just as Hap wondered how the vessel could move underwater, the answer emerged in the form of a vast, knobby animal bulk. The craft was mounted on the back of a gargantuan creature with broad, powerful fins at its sides and a wide fluked tail that arched out of the water, flexed high in the air, and eased down. Water poured in sheets off the creature's speckled sides and was channeled in smooth, arcing jets from the corners of the craft.

Near the head, something bobbed momentarily above the surface. It was an eye, so large that Hap's hand could not cover it, with deeply etched lines above and below. The eye rolled and stared at the small boat before submerging again. Just in front of the craft, from a hole in the creature's back, a plume of water shot a hundred feet into the air.

CHAPTER
4

Hap felt as if the gears of his mind had disengaged. He barely heard Umber's voice: "Hap, this is the leviathan barge. And that is her captain."

Hap blinked fast to regain his senses. *That is her captain?* He saw a slender figure walk nimbly along the creature's back in front of the wooden barge. It was a woman, dripping water from slick-backed hair, and clad in a snug shirt and leggings made of oily, shiny material. She walked up a flight of steps onto the barge and shoved something over the side through a gap in the railing. It was a ladder made of cord and wood that unrolled as it tumbled to the water.

"Take us closer, Oates," Umber said.

"I'm already taking us closer," grumbled Oates. "Do I hate

when people ask me to do a thing I already started? Yes, I do."
He stabbed the water with his oar and paddled them to the
side of the leviathan. Hap stared down at the blue-gray flipper
that was just under the surface, gently stirring the water. The
crescent limb was a behemoth itself, twice the size of their
little boat. Even its subtlest motions made the water swirl and
peak.

The boat bumped against the slick hide. Sophie hopped
off her seat and went up the ladder, agile despite her missing
hand.

"Ready, Hap?" Umber said.

Hap stood and took a deep breath. He was happy to leave
the little boat, but he would have preferred dry land to a sea-
beast that might plunge back underwater at any moment. He
stared at the ladder.

"Don't worry, Hap," Umber said. "She's the safest craft
you'll ever board. Come, I'll be right behind you."

Hap nodded, seized a rung with two hands, and started
to climb. He didn't want to look down, so he kept his eyes
on the immense wall of speckled gray flesh before him. The
skin was dotted with hard shells that clung fast (the word for
them popped into his mind: *barnacles*), and water still trickled
down in wriggling streams. He counted the rungs to keep his
mind focused on anything but the deep sea. After twenty-six

he reached the top, where the captain put a hand under his arm and helped him onto the deck.

Umber bounded aboard next. He grinned broadly and held his arms wide. "Nima, my dear! How good to see you and Boroon again!"

The captain crossed her arms and bent her head to one side. "And you, Lord Umber." Her dark eyes went to the smoldering mountain behind them. "A close call?"

"What else?" Umber laughed. "I'll tell you later. There's an introduction to be made first. This young man is named Happenstance, but we already call him Hap. Hap, this is our esteemed friend, Captain Nima of the Merinots."

Nima closed her eyes and bowed at the waist. Hap mimicked the bow. When the captain opened her eyes again, she gave Hap a closer look, and her brow wrinkled as their gazes met. *My eyes again,* Hap thought. *Are they really so strange?*

"Boroon and I welcome you, Happenstance," she said. Hap looked around, wondering who Boroon was; he didn't see anyone else aboard. *Down below,* he figured, spotting a hatch that led into the hull. When he looked at Nima again, she was still staring, even as she gathered her long black hair in one hand and wrung the water from it. Hap's shoulders twitched as he noticed the thin sheets of transparent skin that bridged the spaces between her knuckles.

Ignis bellowed again, filling the sky with stone. "We should secure the jolly boat and go," Nima said, raising her voice.

"I'm already securing it!" Oates shouted. "Why must people tell me to do something I'm already doing?"

Umber brought Hap to the front of the barge, where Hap leaned uneasily on the rail and watched the sea. Even in this placid state it made Hap's chest tighten just to look at it. He almost wished they'd stayed at the foot of Mount Ignis and taken their chances with the molten rock.

Nima went down the stairs that led to the leviathan's vast back. Hap noticed she wore no shoes, and he thought the same kind of webbing that connected her fingers might also be there between her toes.

Nima walked up to the hole on the creature's back, not far from its head, and stood over it. She cupped her hands beside her mouth and called out: "Boroon! To Kurahaven!"

The leviathan sang a deep, booming note. Whirlpools appeared above its great fins. *So that's who Boroon is,* thought Hap.

"Look aft, Hap," Umber said, pointing behind them. The tail of the leviathan rose high out of the water, hovered ominously, and slammed down again, making a thunderous *pop.*

"Hold on!" Umber cried. He and Hap seized the rail just as the beast and barge surged toward the pale horizon. Nima somehow stayed on her feet despite the lurch. The leviathan's broad head plowed the sea, with waves foaming on either side. Hap felt suddenly dizzy. He released the rail and slumped until he sat on the deck. When he pressed his hand over his heart, it thudded against his palm.

Umber sat beside Hap and patted him on the shoulder. "Well, Happenstance. We're on our way."

Hap drew his knees to his chest and hugged them. Oates leaned on the rail at the stern and stared at the volcano in their wake. In the middle of the deck, Sophie opened the hatch and disappeared downstairs.

Hap turned and saw Umber watching him. He looked at the dark wood under his feet. "Everybody stares at my eyes."

"Well, they are something to see," Umber said. He reached into another one of the pockets on his vest, dug through its contents, and pulled out a palm-size brass object that was hinged on one side. He pried it open, revealing a mirror, and handed it to Hap. "Take a look."

Hap stared into the glass. Nothing about the reflection was familiar: not the prominent ears, or the narrow chin, or the straight brown hair, and certainly not the large green eyes that sparkled with faint points of light. He was looking at a face that he'd never seen before that moment.

"I don't know who I am," he whispered, handing the mirror back to Umber.

Umber sat for a while, tapping his temple with a pair of fingers. "Well. Do you remember anything at all from before we found you?"

Hap sniffed. "The first thing I remember is opening my eyes. Before that . . . nothing."

"And that fellow who was with you—do you know who he was? Anything about him?"

Hap shook his head.

Umber pressed a knuckle against his lips. "Bewildering. Hap, do those initials on the seal mean something to you? WN?"

Hap closed his eyes and concentrated. It was no use. He could trace his memories only back to when he'd awoken, and not a moment earlier. There was a barrier there he couldn't penetrate. "No," Hap said. "But . . . I would like to know what that note said, if you don't mind telling me."

Umber angled his head. "You mean the note that said 'For the Eyes of Umber Only'?"

"Oh. Right," Hap said quietly.

Umber stretched his arms and crossed his legs. "Tell me something, Hap. We're headed to Kurahaven. Ever heard of the place?"

Hap shook his head.

"No? How about Londria? Pernica? Norr?" Umber swept his hand toward the horizon. "The Rulian Sea?"

With every name, Hap shook his head again. He had a feeling he'd be doing a lot of that.

Umber looked right and left and leaned closer, dropping his voice so that only Hap might hear. He offered the names of five more places. As he spoke them, Hap saw a flash of sadness in Umber's eyes.

"I don't know those either," said Hap. He wondered why those names had to be whispered. He repeated them to himself, to preserve them in his memory.

"Well, can you recall the name of any place at all?" Umber asked. "A town, a city, a land, a sea?"

Hap didn't bother to shake his head. He simply let it hang.

"Now, Hap, don't be sad. Perhaps those memories will come back. After a good night's sleep, maybe. And dinner, too! Do you suppose you like seafood?"

CHAPTER
5

Umber showed Hap around the levia-
than barge, insisting that Hap would lose his fear once he saw
what a remarkable ship she was. He first pointed out how the
barge was affixed to Boroon. While the leviathan's sides and
belly had a slick, rubbery hide, his back was covered with a
natural armor that could bear the weight of the craft. Bony,
club-headed growths studded the armor, and thick ropes were
tied around those projections and secured to sturdy cleats. The
barge itself was perhaps eighty feet long, nearly half the length
of Boroon.

"There are two decks below," Umber said. "The bottom
deck, or the hold, is for cargo. The middle is for the captain's
cabin, the guests' quarters, the central cabin, and the galley. Ah,

the galley—are you as hungry as me?" He led the way down a steep staircase. The moment they left the open air, a pleasing fragrance seized Hap by the nose, so intense that he took a deep, audible breath.

"Smell that? The lingering scent of spices in the hold," Umber said, filling his slender chest with air. "Spice is a perfect cargo, compact and valuable. Ah, here we are: the central cabin." The bottom of the stairs opened into a spacious room in the center of the middle deck. "The captain's cabin is at the bow, unlike your typical ship. And the guests sleep in that room in the back. Hap, you remember the rest of our friends."

The room was lit by hanging lanterns that swayed gently, with their mellow orange light in constant motion. The teak walls were adorned with nautical maps and lined with barrels and cabinets that were lashed tight to keep from shifting as the barge rolled. A long table surrounded by chairs occupied one end. Oates was napping on a bench in a corner, with an elbow across his eyes. Sophie sat at a desk at the other end, scratching at parchment with a thin stick of charcoal.

"Smart girl, Sophie," Umber said, walking to her with Hap in tow. "Get it down while it's fresh in your mind. May we look?"

Sophie nodded and turned her work so that Umber and Hap could see. It was a collection of detailed sketches of the worm. There were large renderings of the ferocious head and its snaking body, and smaller studies of the creature's anatomy: the eye, the wicked tail, and the clawed feet.

"Lovely work as usual, Sophie," Umber said. He pointed to the drawing as he spoke. "Though I believe the body was a little fatter than you've shown here. And here, the claws had a joint near the bottom so it could raise them up and walk quietly on the pads of its feet. Take another crack at those and I think you can go to ink, dear. Thank you, excellent, excellent."

Sophie had kept her gaze cast down, but she nodded, and a smile teased the corner of her mouth. Without a word she pulled the drawing in front of her again and went on with her work, holding the parchment with her metal hook and sketching with her good hand.

"Sophie is a fine artist with an astounding memory for what she's witnessed," Umber whispered as they stepped away from her workplace. "You didn't think I brought her along just to shoot arrows, did you? And now," he said, raising his voice and rubbing his hands together, "let's see what we might whip up for dinner! I'm the best chef on board, Hap, I'll have you know. Isn't that true, Oates?"

"No," Oates said, without taking his arm off his eyes.

"Never mind him, Hap. Just because he believes it doesn't make it so. While I go to the galley, why don't you—"

A wooden door beyond the long table swung open. A small man of considerable age peeked out. He was bent at the shoulders, and moved as if all his joints ached at once. The old man squinted into the room, and then announced, "Ah. You're all here. And one more, I see. Well, supper will be ready in a bit."

"Balfour!" cried Umber happily. "Come out and meet the newcomer!"

Balfour had attempted a hasty retreat into the galley. But when Umber called, he sighed heavily and forced a smile. "My apologies, Umber, but I am busy with—"

"Yes, Balfour, and don't you worry, I'll be in to help in just a moment. You know how I love to assist in the galley!"

Balfour's posture deflated a bit, and he winced around the eyes, but still managed to hang on to the smile. "Yes, Umber. I know."

"Hap," said Umber, "this is Balfour, my trusted servant and friend, and while he's aboard this craft, also its cook. Balfour, this is our newfound friend, Happenstance."

Like everyone else, Balfour was transfixed for a moment

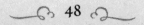

by the sight of Hap's eyes. Then he recovered, produced a more genuine smile, and bowed. "Very pleased to meet you, Happenstance." His gaze wandered over Hap's shoulder. Hap turned to see Nima descending the stairs from the upper deck.

"Lord Umber," she said. "There's something you should see."

Ahead of their course, the sun sank toward the sea. Umber and Nima stared the other way, past the relentless sweep of the leviathan's tail. Nima handed Umber a short, tapering brass tube, which he put to his eye and aimed at the distance. Hap had followed Umber onto the deck and he stepped to the back rail to see what had caught their attention.

There was a sail far beyond their wake, a triangular speck almost too distant to perceive.

"Not a large craft," Umber said. "Do you suppose it's following us?"

"It may be," Nima replied. "Should we turn around and see who it is? Surely we have nothing to fear."

Umber lowered the tube. He frowned at the distant ship, and his eye twitched at the corner. "Normally, curiosity would compel me. But not this time, Nima. I have a pressing engagement in Kurahaven and little time to spare. We'll outrun her eventually, won't we?"

Nima stared at the pursuer. "Most ships would have trouble staying with Boroon. Not this one, though. Even though the wind is light."

"Is she closing on us?" Umber asked.

"No. She keeps her distance and matches our speed. As if she only wants to know where we are heading. Is there a reason anyone would follow us?" Nima asked the question of Umber, but her eyes went to Hap.

Umber didn't answer. He clamped his bottom lip between his teeth. *Strange*, Hap thought. Umber seemed more nervous about the little ship than the monstrous worm that had almost killed them.

"What is that, Lord Umber?" Hap asked, pointing at the tube.

"A spyglass," Umber replied, holding it up. "Meant for getting a better look at things that are far away."

"May I try it?" Hap asked.

Umber wavered before offering it. "Er . . . of course. Take a look."

Hap pressed the narrow end of the spyglass to his eye as Umber had done. What he saw amazed him. Somehow, within that cylinder, the ship had magically leaped a mile closer. Under a yellowed triangular sail, he saw a slender ship made of pale wood, with a curving prow that ended in the carved head of a serpent. It was a simple craft with a low deck and a boxy structure in the center. A ghostly figure stood at the prow, wearing a strange loose garment that billowed around his legs. From this distance, it was hard for Hap to tell exactly what he was seeing, but it looked as if the man had a pale, hairless face covered with dark spots.

"There's a man dressed in gray," Hap said. "I think he's the only one there."

"You can tell that from here? Your eyes are amazing, Hap."

As Hap stared through the glass, he was sure the stranger's neck craned forward. Hap felt a chill sweep his arms. It seemed as if the same device that gave him a closer look at the stranger also allowed the stranger a closer look at *him*. The man reached into a pocket at his side and took out something that looked like a sack. He pulled it over his head, covering the face with only a single eyehole on one side.

Every muscle in Hap's body went taut as a bowstring. He tore the spyglass from his eye and thrust it into Umber's hands.

"I think *his* eyes are even better than mine," Hap said quietly.

Umber took the spyglass back. "Seen that ship before, Hap?"

"No, sir," Hap said, folding his arms across his chest and shivering.

Umber raked his hair with one hand. "Nima, I think we ought to throw this suitor off our trail, however ardent he may be. But without making a big show of it, if possible. What would you suggest?"

Nima raised her chin while she considered the problem. "We will alter our course gradually to the north. When this moonless night falls, Boroon will make a fast turn in the dark, and we will leave that ship behind."

Umber nodded. "Very good, my captain. Now come, Hap," he said, shaking off his concern and returning to his native enthusiastic state. "Back to the galley!"

Umber told Hap to make himself comfortable in the central cabin and plunged into the galley. Before the door closed behind Umber, Hap saw Balfour cast a quick pleading look toward the ceiling. Soon a steady stream of clattering pans and chatter drifted out from behind the thin wooden door: "Oh, you're a fine fish—look at the size of you, and fresh as anything! Come now, Balfour, I know perfectly well how to fillet a fish. I'm an absolute wizard with a knife, and—oh, did I nick you just then? Heavens, man, you're bleeding. Now, is that hot enough? Ouch! It certainly is. And tell me there's a lemon left—all is lost if there are no lemons! Ha, lemons galore!"

With Oates dozing, Sophie sketching, and Nima busy

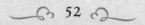

elsewhere, there was nothing left for Hap to do but find a place where he could sit and think. He took a seat at the long dining table near the galley. With his hands clasped before him, he closed his eyes, gathered his will, and took a headlong dash at the wall that blocked his memories. But his intentions shattered against it like an egg on stone. The barrier was impervious. Nothing came through, not the slightest hint of any history before he had opened his eyes in Alzumar. All Hap had to ponder was everything that had happened since that awakening. His life was still measured in hours, but it already sagged under the weight of unanswered questions.

One thing nagged at his mind, though it might have been the least of his puzzles. It was the way that, not long before, Umber had leaned close and whispered the names of those places, so careful to make sure the others didn't hear. He repeated the strange names to himself: *New York. Lon-dun. Paris. Toe-key-oh. Moss-cow.* Were they villages, cities, nations? Why were those a secret, Hap wondered, and not the others? *Why?*

Before he could dwell on the question, a booming sound penetrated the cabin. At first the pitch was so deep that Hap felt it in his bones more than heard it in his ears, but then it rose and grew stronger, like a horn signaling the end of all things. Every object in the cabin rattled. Sophie steadied the jars of ink so they wouldn't splash onto her drawings. Umber burst out of the galley, wide-eyed.

"What is that?" cried Hap.

"That is Boroon," Umber said, before springing up the stairs onto the deck.

objects in the world of the Dwergh, the Moltons may be the most remarkable. These are figures carved in stone, knee-high, that spring to life when heated in a fire or fed hot coals, which they eagerly devour. These animated statues serve their Dwergh owners with great courage and industry, and yet at the same time are fiercely independent. What it is that imbues them with life is a mystery. All Moltons are said to be centuries old

CHAPTER
6

Hap crept cautiously through the hatch, the last one up except for Balfour, who stayed in the galley. He looked at the ocean behind them and saw the ship, still in the distance. Everyone else was at the portside railing, staring down. When Hap joined them, he saw a thin stream of red trailing the leviathan's enormous fin.

"Boroon says something stung him," Nima said.

"Poor fellow," Umber replied. "Is there anything we can do?"

"It is a small cut. Normally I would not worry. It will heal quickly. But in these waters there are many . . ." Nima began. Her voice trailed off as she glared at something in their wake and clenched her teeth. Hap followed her line of sight and saw a black triangle in the water behind them, not far from Boroon's tail. The word for this thing rose into his consciousness.

Shark. Hap shivered. He knew this was a deadly, voracious creature. Worse still, a second fin appeared, farther off, and then a third.

"They smell the blood," Nima said.

"They're not very big," said Umber. "Can Boroon outswim them?"

"Perhaps. But more will come."

As if prompted by Nima's words, a fourth shark rose from the depths, close to the wounded fin. It surged forward and snapped at the limb, and suddenly the wound that was too small to see became a hand-size crescent of raw flesh. Blood billowed into the water. Hap gasped as more fins pierced the surface, closing in on the leviathan.

Boroon knew he was being pursued. He swept his tail faster, gaining speed. There were five sharks directly behind him when he lifted his great dripping tail high over the water and slammed it down again. The slap of his fluke was like a crack of thunder, and three of the sharks bobbed senselessly in the frothing water, belly up.

"Look at the size of that one!" shouted Oates. He pointed some twenty yards away, where a new shark knifed through the water. It was a blunt-nosed brute, longer than a man was tall.

The ugly predator closed in on the bloody wound, followed by what now seemed like a fleet of other sharks.

Nima dashed to a chest that was secured to the deck. She threw open a latch and swung the lid up. There was coiled rope inside, and a curved sword. She picked up both, wound one end of the rope around a cleat on the deck, and ran with the other end clenched in her fist until she'd drawn it taut, almost all the way to the prow.

"Nima, dear," called Umber, sounding alarmed. "What are you up to?"

"Hold on to something!" Nima cried. She cupped a hand beside her mouth and sang out a high note. Boroon responded by rolling gently. Hap and the others gripped the rail to keep from sliding along the steep tilt of the deck.

Nima twisted the end of the rope around her left wrist. Hap gasped along with the others as she hopped over the railing, pulling the rope behind her.

She slid down the side of the barge and landed on Boroon's back. With the rope in her left hand and the sword in her right, she ran across the leviathan's side and leaped outward, swinging in a wide arc that carried her directly over the largest shark just as it prepared to sink its jaws into Boroon's fin. Nima howled with rage as she slashed the sword across the back of the shark.

"Fancy that," Umber said, clutching the rail.

For a moment, Hap thought the stroke had done nothing. And then a gush of red flowed out of the cut on the shark's back. It thrashed in the water, lifting its head and snapping at the air with a frightening array of jagged teeth. The smaller sharks broke off the pursuit of Boroon and turned on their wounded brother. In moments, the sea exploded into a foaming pink mess, churned by gnashing jaws and thrashing tails.

Nima's momentum was slowed when she slashed at the shark. She continued to swing, but dropped until her feet dangled in the water. She tucked the sword into the belt at her waist and climbed the rope with two hands until she was close to the deck. Oates reached down, put two hands under her arms, and plucked her over the railing.

"Crazy woman," Oates said. "I could have speared that shark from here."

"Boroon is mine to defend," Nima said sharply. She stared at the wounded flipper and pinched her bottom lip between her teeth. Boroon seemed aware of what had happened; he rolled back to the horizontal and continued to swim.

"May I suggest?" said Umber. "You have needle and thread to repair the jolly boat's sails, and the hammocks, I presume. We could use them to close the wound. That is, if Boroon doesn't mind being stitched up like a pair of trousers."

Nima looked at Umber with her head inclined, and then nodded. "I will try. And Boroon will not mind, so long as I am the tailor."

Nima plunged into the water, bringing with her a long needle made of bone, and yards of heavy thread. She swam effortlessly down to the fin, where the shark's bite had left a dangling flap of skin. She stitched the flesh back in place while Boroon rested. Hap and the others kept an eye out for sharks, and Oates stood with a spear, ready to heave it.

Something strange was happening, Hap realized. Nima had gone underwater to sew the wound. But she had yet to come up for air, though minutes had already passed.

"How long can she hold her breath?" Hap asked.

"What? Oh, she's not holding her breath at all, Hap," Umber said. "And do you know what else is interesting? Even though we haven't moved, I don't believe our friend has gotten any closer."

Hap looked behind them. It was true: The pursuing craft was just as far, and just as close, as it had always been.

There was a splash below, and Nima surfaced. She gripped the dangling rope and held on while Oates hoisted her to the deck. "It worked well enough," she said, opening her mouth to breathe deep. "Only the tiniest bleeding remains, but not enough to cause trouble, I believe."

The light of day melted to red as Boroon continued to edge northward. The mysterious craft traced the same course. There was something maddening about this chase, where the distance between them never changed. Hap thumped the railing with his fist.

Umber's head popped out of the open hatch. "Dinner, Hap!"

"Are you coming, Captain?" Hap called to Nima, who sat on the leviathan's broad back, staring at the horizon with her chin propped on her fingers.

Nima shook her head. "I will dine later, Happenstance."

Hap went into the hatch, and his stomach reared like a horse when he saw the feast sprawled on the table. Balfour peeled silvery skin from an enormous, sizzling fish. There were platters with boiled crabs, clams, and oysters, loaves of hot bread that unleashed plumes of steam when the crust was broken, bowls of fruit, and pitchers of wine and cider.

"Let's not forget to thank Nima for the bounty of the sea," Umber said. "She caught all this herself, Hap. While we ran like ninnies through the streets of Alzumar, she secured dinner on our behalf. Oates, you cretin, you might have waited until everyone was seated."

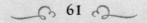

"I was hungry," Oates muttered through the quarter-loaf of bread he'd stuffed into his mouth.

Balfour's mood brightened once he'd gotten Umber out of his galley, and Umber was thrilled to have a willing, curious audience for the recounting of the day's events in Alzumar. Umber spun the tale while Oates bluntly corrected the slightest exaggeration. Sophie didn't speak at all, though she smiled at every joke. Hap said little; he was still trying to understand the world and the company he'd been thrust into. As he listened to the others, he realized that there was something different about the way Umber talked, an accent that the others did not share.

Round, thick-glassed windows lined the wall of the central cabin. Through them, Hap saw the sky turn from red to deep blue to pure black.

Umber finally inverted his goblet over his mouth, let the last drop of wine fall, and leaned back from the table and rubbed his belly. "Glorious!" he said, followed by a sigh. "All I need now is some fresh salty air. Come, Hap, let's see what's become of our pursuer."

Hap followed Umber out of the hatch. It was a warm evening, and a stronger headwind had sprung up. Now that he wasn't looking through the gauzy glass of portholes, he could see the numberless stars that bobbed in the black firmament.

Nima was at the back rail with her long hair streaming toward the wake like a pennant.

"Have we made our turn yet?" Umber asked.

Nima nodded. "It's been dark for a while. She should be well off our trail by now."

"She isn't," said Hap. Nima and Umber turned toward him. Hap shrugged. "The ship is there. Just like before." He looked again, to be certain. By starlight, he couldn't see it as clearly as before, but the ship was still in pursuit. No closer, no farther.

Umber answered the question that was likely on Nima's mind. "Hap can see in the dark. If he says it's there, you can believe him." He looked at Hap and smiled. Hap felt a small rush of pride to have this strange but significant man, who seemed to have a world of resources at his disposal, speak for him that way.

Nima frowned into the dark. "She follows us across a pitch-black sea. And into a headwind, no less, when any other craft would fall away. There is only one way to lose her now. Lord Umber, have Balfour put out the galley fires."

Umber bounced on his heels and nodded. "Of course, Captain! Come, Hap—it won't do to be standing on deck soon."

Hap felt the hairs on the back of his neck stand straight.

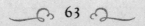

He followed close behind as Umber ducked into the hatch. "Why? Why won't it do to stand on deck?"

Umber raised a finger, telling Hap to wait. "Balfour! Out with the fires! Everyone, we're going to submerge. Now, Hap, what were you asking? Oh, you wanted to know—"

"*Submerge?*" cried Hap. "Under the water?"

Umber scratched his chin. "Does the word *submerge* have another meaning? Not in this context. Yes, Hap, under the water. But it's nothing to fear." On the other side of the galley doors there was a hiss of steam as water was poured over hot coals. "The leviathan barge is made for this. She was submerged when you met her, don't you recall? And wasn't Balfour downstairs the whole time, dry as a bone?"

"Fire's out!" called Balfour.

"Sophie, tell Nima we're ready," Umber said. Sophie ran up through the hatch. "Now, Hap, I know you're not fond of the water, but . . . Hap?"

Hap was sure the bones in his legs were dissolving. He staggered to the table and slumped onto a chair. Sophie came down the stairs again. Behind her, the hatch slammed shut.

Umber put a hand on Hap's shoulder. "We'll be fine. Boroon will make a sharp turn underwater, where this pursuer can't see us. He'll swim seven miles or so—that's farther than that stranger can see in the open water."

Hap shuddered. *Underwater for seven miles!* He seized the edge of the table as the barge lurched forward. The room tilted, and the lanterns swayed diagonally on their chains. An apple that had been left on the table rolled off and tumbled to the front of the cabin. Hap opened his mouth, forcing himself to breathe.

The others had taken seats elsewhere in the cabin. Umber sat next to Hap and clasped his arm. "We won't dive too deep. It wouldn't be healthy for us," Umber said. The words failed to reassure. The foaming sea rose over the portholes, and a roar enveloped the cabin from every direction. Hap sensed the weight of the water pushing down on the barge and felt a ringing pressure in his ears. When he worked his jaw up and down, the ringing ended with a hollow *pop*.

"Almost forgot," Umber said. "Watch this, Hap. You'll find it interesting." As the floor leveled off again, he stood and went to the side wall where nine hourglasses were mounted in a row. Each glass was smaller than the one on its left. Umber spun the fifth glass, and its sands poured into the empty half below. "I turn the fifth because we have five passengers," he said. "It tells how long we can stay under before the air is used up. But it really isn't necessary in this case. Nima will bring us up long before the sand runs out."

"Nima?" cried Hap, leaping up. "Nima never came down!"

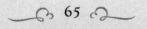

"No, she didn't," Umber said. "But, Hap—"

"We have to help her!" Hap shouted, pointing at the hatch.

"She's fine, Hap. Nima is . . . different from most people."

"Part fish," said Oates.

"Now, Oates," Umber said sharply, "I've warned you about interjecting your blunt self into conversations. The point, Hap," Umber said, turning back to Happenstance, "is that Nima is perfectly comfortable under the waves. You saw that yourself when she sewed up Boroon's fin. Nima is . . . well, she's . . ." Umber glared at Oates again, and then whispered in Hap's ear. "She's part fish. On her mother's side, to be precise."

The barge heaved to the left as Boroon made his turn. Hap heard a rhythmic *whoosh* amid the roar of water, certainly the sweep of the leviathan's great tail. He slumped onto the bench again and took the deepest breath he could manage. Water splashed his shoulder, and he looked up and saw drops raining down from at least a dozen places, and squirting in a fine spray at the edge of the hatch. His heart tried to climb into his mouth.

"Oh, never mind the few tiny leaks, Hap," Umber said, sliding a goblet under one of the falling streams that splattered the table. "That's to be expected. Although a better sealant would be a handy invention; yes, I think it's time for progress there. Oates, remind me to make a note of that."

"Doesn't anything frighten you?" Hap asked in a strangled voice.

"Of course, Hap. Hoyle, for one. The name alone freezes my spine. You'll meet Hoyle all too soon, I'm sure."

Hap couldn't take his mind off the notion of a finite amount of air trapped inside with them. He felt as if there were a belt squeezing his ribs and an invisible hand clapped across his mouth and nose.

Think about something else, he ordered himself. And he turned to another matter that preoccupied his mind. With his legs soft as jelly, he walked to where Umber stood, gazing at a chart on the wall. "Lord Umber," he said.

"Hmmm?" Umber replied, lost for a moment in his own thoughts.

"I would really like to know what that note said. Even if it was just for your eyes."

Umber turned to look at Hap. His face was a blank. "I don't think I ought to do that, Happenstance."

Hap's nerves were already on edge, and somehow that made his temper quick to rise. His fingers curled and squeezed. "But—did it say who I am? Did it say where I came from?"

Umber stiffened. "No. It doesn't say those things. I can tell you that much."

"But what *did* it say? Why won't you tell me?"

A harder, darker expression appeared on Umber's face. He shut his eyes for a moment. "In time, maybe. But no, not yet. You wouldn't understand."

Hap's voice rose, drawing the stares of the others. "But I don't know *anything!* Not who I am, or where I came from, or what I'm supposed to do!"

Umber put a hand on Hap's shoulder. "I'm sorry, Hap. I won't tell you."

Hap shrugged off the hand and stepped back. "It was in *my* pocket! It was about *me!*"

Umber shook his head. "It wasn't just about you, Hap. It was about me, too."

Hap stared at Umber, unsure what to say next. The floor shifted under his feet and he heard a thumping sound. The apple that had rolled to one end of the cabin was tumbling back the other way.

"Ah. We're surfacing," Umber said, relieved by the interruption.

The tilt of the barge increased, prow up, and then came the sound of water churning into air. With a groan of metal, the hatch was tugged open. Nima's head, dripping wet, appeared before a backdrop of stars. "Let the boy come on deck and see."

"Go on, Hap," Umber said.

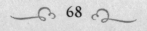

With his jaw clenched, Hap climbed the stairs and joined Nima at the stern rail. "I don't see that ship anymore," he muttered.

Nima's chest heaved as she gulped down deep drafts of air. Hap had observed this the last time she came out of the water. It seemed as if she was getting used to breathing air again. "Good," she said, panting. "Tell the others it is time to sleep now. Boroon will rest soon as well."

When Hap went back into the lower deck, he found the others settling down for the night. There were quarters in the rear, with a private berth for Umber, a small berth that Sophie took, and a larger room with cots and hammocks for more passengers. Hap chose a cot in the farthest corner of the big room. Balfour and a thunderously snoring Oates were asleep before a minute passed.

Umber's head angled into the threshold. "Tired, Hap?"

Hap answered without looking. "Not really."

Umber arched his back and yawned. "No? Well, it might be the excitement of the day. As for me, I could doze for a week. But I'll see you bright and early. We'll reach Kurahaven by noon, I believe. Try to sleep, all right?"

"I will," Hap mumbled. He watched Umber close the door. Then he put his head on the cot and shut his eyes. It was no use; he wasn't the least bit tired, nor could he imagine what the sensation felt like. He tried lying on his back like Oates, and curling up his side like Balfour, but no position brought sleep any closer. Finally, after what seemed like an hour, he stood quietly, careful not to waken the others, and opened the door to the central cabin.

The only light in the room was from a candle on the desk where Umber sat with his back to Hap. Umber's shoulders rose and fell slowly, and his head was down. Hap could hear his deep, tranquil breathing.

The hatch was still open. Hap wondered if Nima was on deck. He was about to mount the stairs to see if the pursuing craft was still out of sight, but froze in place when he took another look at Umber.

From this angle, he could see that Umber had fallen asleep on his arms. A pen and jar of ink were on the desktop, along with a few sheets of paper.

The note burned, Hap thought. *Was he writing down what it said, while he could still remember?* His mouth went dry at the thought. He crept toward the desk, stepping as softly as he could with his heels off the floor, praying that Umber's head wouldn't pop up. When he made it to the desk, he watched Umber's face. The man's eyes moved under their lids, and the corner of his mouth twitched, as if unpleasant thoughts were loose in Umber's mind. Hap wondered if that was what deep sleep looked like.

There were two pages that Hap could see. One was within easy reach, but blank. Another was pinned down by Umber's elbow. There was writing on that, but it was mostly obscured by Umber's arm.

Hap took another look at the blank page. Hints of dark lines bled through from the other side. He reached for it slowly, grabbed a corner between his thumb and finger, and turned it over. The candle, which had burned to an inch-long stub in its holder, flickered a little.

The parchment was covered with writing. Some of the lines had been crossed out and rewritten. Hap's hands began to shake as soon as he read the first words.

The original note from WN was consumed by some magical fire or chemical reaction. This is what it said, as well as I can recall:

Greetings to you, Umber. First things first: Now that you've begun to read this, don't put it back in anyone's pocket. You'll understand soon enough.

You know me not, but I know of you. And you must attend to this message carefully, because everything you once held dear depends upon it.

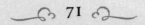

I leave this boy in your care. Call him Happenstance.
Keep him with you always, and bring him on all your
journeys. The boy needs to grow and learn; he must
adventure, or he will not become what he must. As he
is tested and challenged, you will observe certain skills
arising. And then you will know what to do with him.

Beware. Happenstance exists in violation of an
ancient law, and

The page ended. Hap's mind swirled with everything the note had already said. But what about the rest? What was the ancient law, and why did he have to *beware*? He eyed the second page, trapped below Umber's elbow. Part of him wanted to stop there and creep back to his bed. The thought of being caught in the act of spying horrified him. But he was desperate to know what the rest of the note said. He bit his lip. *How can I make sure he doesn't see me?*

Hap looked at the remaining stub of the candle, with its unsteady flame. Who would suspect that it didn't go out by itself? He leaned toward it, puckered his lips, and blew it out. The wick mourned its passing with a wisp of smoke.

Hap gave silent thanks that Umber hadn't used his jar of glimmer-worms for light. He reached for the edge of the paper and nearly gasped aloud as Umber groaned and shifted in his seat. Umber's arm lifted for a moment, and Hap slid the page out as far as he could before the elbow fell again, covering the last few inches. He read the visible words, poised to tug the rest out if the elbow lifted again.

there are those who will search for him in order to destroy him. There is also a particularly nasty and persistent creature named Occo that has been on my trail for a while. It would not surprise me if he picked up the boy's scent. That could cause you some grief, but you seem like a resourceful fellow. You'll manage.

By now you must be wondering: Why? Why do what this stranger asks? The reason is this: I know from where you came, Umber. I, too, know what happened to that world of yours. Quite a mess you folk made of that. I was there; I saw.

What if I told you

Umber's shoulders jerked, and a snort interrupted his slow rhythmic breathing. His head sprang up and his eyes turned toward Hap.

"Huh?" Umber said, squinting.

Hap's stomach lurched. He opened his mouth, ready to offer an excuse as soon as he could imagine one. Then he

realized that Umber was looking *through* him, not focusing on anything. *He can't see me*, Hap thought.

Umber rubbed his eyes and shook his head. "What?" he slurred. "You fell asleep, you fool . . . candle went out." A look of alarm crossed his face. He pushed his chair back and stood, and then patted his hands along the desktop, gathering up the pages as he found them. He turned and peered over Hap's shoulder, wide-eyed and fully awake. "Is someone there?"

Hap backed away, terrified to breathe, and still aching to know what the rest of the note said. Umber clutched the pages to his chest with one hand. As he fumbled his way toward his room he struck his hip on the corner of the desk and yelped.

Rather than open the door to his quarters and make a sound, Hap edged toward the hatch and mounted the steps.

CHAPTER
7

Hap was sure that Umber would dash upstairs soon, pointing and accusing, but he didn't hear a sound from below. *He must have gone to sleep*, he thought, feeling a flush of relief.

With his mind bewildered by what he'd read, it took a minute to notice that something was different about the craft. There was no rhythmic sensation of heaving forward with every sweep of Boroon's tail, and no sound of water frothing against the prow. He looked over the rail. The leviathan was lying still in the sea, an island of dark flesh. Hap wondered if their pursuer—the *nasty and persistent creature named Occo,* perhaps?—might have caught up while Boroon rested. But when he ran to the stern to look, he saw nothing but a sprawling expanse of water. Far to the right, however, a rough edge rose over the horizon. Land, perhaps, if it wasn't distant clouds.

He didn't see Nima anywhere. "Nima?" he called, to no reply. A lump formed in his throat. Had she fallen overboard and been left behind? He was about to wake the others when he heard a splash and saw the captain come to the surface of the inky sea, a stone's throw away.

Nima swept her arms and kicked her barefooted legs with grace as she swam toward Boroon. A rope hung from one of the leviathan's sides, and she grasped it and climbed up. She stood over the plate-size hole on Boroon's back and sang softly.

Hap didn't want her to think he was spying on her. Nor did he want to startle her. He cleared his throat, softly at first and then a little louder. She turned and squinted in the dim starlight.

"Is that you, Hap?"

"Yes, Captain."

"'Lo there. Would you like to come down?"

Hap bit his bottom lip. "Um. I guess," he said, but he didn't move. Boroon's back was bony and broad, but with no railings to hold, he would feel dreadfully exposed to the deadly ocean.

"It's all right," Nima said. "I will come to you." She climbed the stairs to the deck, sat on the top step, and patted the open space at her side.

Hap sat next to her. He felt safe enough there, with his elbow clamped on a baluster. His thoughts had already turned back to the strange contents of the letter when her question broke the silence.

"Why don't you sleep like the others, Hap?"

Hap shrugged. "I don't know. I just don't feel tired."

"All creatures must rest. Boroon is sleeping now."

Hap nodded. He wondered if the great leviathan dreamed.

"Why are you afraid of the water?" Nima asked.

Lord Umber must have told her, Hap thought. *Or she can just tell.* "I don't know. Maybe there's a reason. But I don't remember . . . what happened before."

Nima ran her fingers through her hair, squeezing more drops onto the stairs. "We are an interesting pair, you and I. You fear the water. It is the land that frightens me." She stared at what might be the distant shore.

"Why are you afraid of the land?" Hap asked.

"I don't belong there," was all she said. Hap glanced at her sideways. She fascinated him. There were things he wanted to know but was too shy to ask. Who was her mother? Were there others like her? Did she need the sea to live? Did her webbed fingers draw the same stares as his green eyes, and was that why she was not at ease on firm ground?

There was a long silence, broken again by her. "So the thing Lord Umber sought in Alzumar turned out to be you."

"I guess. I don't know."

"Consider yourself fortunate to be in his company. Lord Umber is an exceptional man."

Hap looked back at the open hatch, thankful again that he hadn't been caught stealing a glance at the note. "I don't know anything about him. Who is he?"

She leaned back and held one of her knees between clasped hands. "Who is Umber? I suppose he won't mind me telling you. Umber is the first citizen of Kurahaven, the Lord of the Aerie, and perhaps the most powerful man in his kingdom after the king and the three princes. He is a merchant, wealthy beyond imagination. An architect. Inventor. Explorer. Patron of the arts. Enemy of the wicked and the greatest friend the common man ever knew. But his greatest joy is to explore the world and chronicle all things strange and magical. He writes about them in his books: *The Books of Umber*."

Hap wondered if that was how Umber saw him: one of his strange and magical discoveries. "How do you know Lord Umber, Captain?"

"Umber has been a faithful friend to the Merinots—

shipbuilders and sailors, every one of us. Years ago, the improvements he suggested to the sails and rudders of my family's ships made them the fastest and finest in the world. And so we Merinots are sworn to serve him." Nima stretched and yawned. "Are you tired now, Hap?"

"Not really," Hap said. He wondered how that could be. The others were exhausted at the day's end. Shouldn't his limbs ache like theirs? Shouldn't his head nod, and his eyelids droop?

"I have kept watch so far, but now I need sleep," Nima said. "That brute Oates has the next turn. Would you wake him for me? He says things that make me want to strike him when I speak to him."

"I'm not tired. I can watch," Hap said.

Nima smiled. "You seem like a fine boy, Happenstance. But you are still a stranger to me, and new to Umber's company. You have not yet earned the right to stand guard by yourself. No matter how gifted your eyes may be."

After he prodded Oates out of sleep and the enormous man went grumbling to the top deck, Hap stayed behind on his cot, wondering about all the ominous things the note had said. He could recall nearly all of it, word for word, as if it had been seared into his brain. *I just wish I'd seen the rest.*

He was still awake when Oates returned a few hours later and sent Balfour to take a shift. He was still awake when Balfour rapped on the door to Nima's cabin and she went topside, and Boroon started to swim again. And he was still awake when the sun came up, and the door to Umber's cabin burst open, and Umber bounded out with a wide smile on his face, crying, "Omelets! I have a craving for omelets, and toasted cheese!"

"You didn't sleep at all? Not even a minute?" Umber asked through a mouth full of egg. "And you don't feel tired. No aching muscles, no sand in your eyes, no urge to yawn?"

Again and again, Hap shook his head. Umber tapped his plate with his spoon. "You're probably overexcited after yesterday's adventures. Well, we still have some hours before we reach Kurahaven. Take a nap if the mood strikes."

"I will," Hap said, though he doubted it would happen.

"Have any memories come back to you?"

"No," Hap said, under a wrinkled brow. "Nothing before I woke up in that room. When I try to remember more, it just . . . stops. As if there's a wall there."

"Interesting," Umber said, narrowing his eyes. "I'd like to try something that might help you break through. When we get to the Aerie, that is." When he saw Hap's questioning look, he added, "The Aerie is my home in Kurahaven. Sort of a tower . . . sort of a cave . . . you'll see when we get there. I'm sure you'll—" Umber tipped his head back and sniffed the air like a hound. A broad, toothy smile split his face. "Is that what I think it is?"

Balfour pushed the galley door open with his back. When he turned, he revealed a tray with another omelet and a mug of steaming dark liquid with a sharp, pleasant smell. "More food for the hungry boy," he said. "And, Lord Umber, I'd stored away a little—"

"Coffee!" Umber cried, leaping up from his chair and holding his hands out. "Sweet, bitter, aromatic coffee! I thought the last was gone!" He seized the mug with two hands, brought it to his face, filled his lungs with the steam, and took a lusty slurp. He shivered, and his eyes closed in ecstasy. "This cries out to be drunk in fresh air," he said. "Hap, meet me on deck when you've eaten your fill."

When Hap emerged from the hatch his eyes turned by habit toward their wake. But there was no craft in pursuit. The suggestion of land on the southern horizon had become a certainty: Swollen hills rose to craggy peaks that pierced a cloudless sky.

Umber was in the center of the deck, engaged in the

oddest behavior. He leaped up and down in place, with his legs alternately spreading and closing, while his arms rose over his head and clapped against his thighs in turn. Nima leaned against the forward rail, fighting a smirk at the corner of her mouth.

"What the devil are you doing now, Umber?" cried Oates, who'd followed Hap out of the hatch.

"These are called *jumping jacks*," huffed Umber. He timed his words to the rhythm of his leaps. "When we were on the run from the tyrant worm, I found myself a little short of breath. And I vowed to whip myself into better shape. You might try them yourself, Oates."

"I wasn't the one out of breath," the enormous man replied, yawning and scratching his hindquarters. "You were. And if you'd slowed down any more, I would've carried you like a sack of flour."

"Ha! No need for that, Oates. Soon I'll be capable of epic feats of endurance. Hello again, young man!" Umber came to a stop, shook his arms, and beckoned Hap. "Speaking of jumping, there's something I'd like to see." There was a long pole with a hook on one end hanging from the rail. Umber lifted it from its bracket and held it horizontally. "Now, my boy, forgive me for treating you like a circus animal, but could I persuade you to jump over this?"

Hap stared at the pole. It wobbled in the air at the level of his chin. "It's awfully high."

Umber narrowed one eye. "I saw that leap that you made to escape the worm, Hap. Just give it a try! My curiosity has been aroused."

"All right," Hap said, though his jaw tensed at the request. Was this the first of the tests and challenges that the note mentioned? He crouched, swung his elbows back, and leaped. Then his eyes widened as he found himself springing into the air. The force that bound him to the earth seemed to weaken for a moment; he soared and crested, with his heels well above the pole and even Umber's head. He saw Oates gape and heard Nima draw a sharp breath. Something like a laugh and a cry escaped from his own mouth. He came down on the deck, landing on his toes and the splayed fingers of one hand.

There was a clatter of wood. The pole had slipped out of Umber's hands. He clasped his hands near his chin and beamed at Hap like a man who'd just discovered a chest of gold. "Well. That was something."

"Boy's not normal," mumbled Oates.

"Who among us is?" replied Umber.

Hap straightened up. *How did I do that?* he wondered. A tingle plowed down his arms, seeding goose bumps. The others stared; Umber with that delirious smile, Oates with a frown, and Nima with a solemn and curious look. It was an awkward pause, broken suddenly by a low, trumpeting blast that came from under their feet. Hap felt the sound pass through his bones.

Nima leaned over the rail, with one ear lowered. "Boroon says the *Swift* is signaling us. Should we rendezvous?"

Signaling us how? thought Hap. He saw no ship on the horizon. And then he remembered the metal device that Umber had lowered into the water to summon the leviathan barge.

"Without question," Umber replied. He put a hand on Hap's shoulder. "The *Swift* will bring us into port. She's been waiting here, expecting our return, and signaling every half hour. We keep Boroon in the open sea; you can imagine the uproar if this magnificent beast swam into a crowded seaport." Umber cupped his hands around his mouth and shouted downward, *"And I do mean magnificent!"* He turned back to Hap. "There are times when more conventional transport is the ticket, and the *Swift* is a dandy ship, the fastest afloat. Thanks to me, I should add; her design was my contribution."

Hap felt himself leaning to one side. Boroon had changed course, veering toward the coast. Before long, they saw the *Swift* at the horizon. She was a sleek ship with a pair of tall masts. For the moment, her sails were furled, and anchor lines angled into the sea from her narrow prow and raised stern.

A dozen sailors lined the near rail and watched the leviathan approach. Boroon used his great fin to paddle his vast bulk sideways, closer to the smaller boat, which bobbed below where Hap and the others stood. Nima hurled ropes across the gap, which the sailors tied fast to the cleats of the *Swift*. The men nudged and whispered to one another while gaping in Nima's direction, but she acknowledged none of it. Once the ropes were secured, she unrolled the ladder. Its wooden rungs clattered on the smaller boat's deck.

A tall, graceful man with sun-bleached hair tied back in a ribbon stepped forward with his hands clasped behind his back. "You are welcome to board, Lord Umber. It is good to see you." He smiled at Nima. "And greetings to you, sister."

Nima nodded. "'Lo, brother."

Umber leaned over to whisper to Hap. "Same father, different mothers. That's Captain Sandar of the Merinots."

Hap took a closer look at the handsome man below. Sandar's fingers were splayed on the railing, and Hap saw no webbing between them. The chief resemblance between the siblings was the heart-shaped faces and high cheekbones.

"Nima, are you sure you don't want to add a crew member? I'm certain I could find a volunteer," Sandar called up. A smile teased the corner of his mouth. Around him, the young sailors coughed and yanked on the bottoms of their shirts to smooth the wrinkles.

"Boroon is all I need," Nima said. She crossed her arms and turned to Umber with a flush of red on her face. "Your party may disembark now."

Umber bowed. "We thank you, Captain, for your service. I'm sure we'll see you again soon. Ready, everyone?" He gestured for the others to climb down to the *Swift*. Sophie, Oates, and Balfour descended, each tossing a pack of belongings to the sailors below. *And I have nothing,* Hap thought. The notion gnawed his heart. *No stuff. No memory. No life.*

While Umber said a few quiet parting words to Nima, Hap went down the ladder with his back to the crew members below. When he reached the deck of the *Swift*, he turned around. The air filled with gasps, and Hap winced. He'd forgotten how people reacted to the first sight of his luminous eyes.

The moment seemed eternal, and was only broken when Umber hurried down the ladder and glared at the crew. "Paint a picture, it'll last longer," he snapped, stepping in front of Hap.

Sandar took note and raised his voice like a trumpet. "That's right, you pack of dogs! Make yourselves busy. Anchors and sails, anchors and sails!"

Umber put a hand on Hap's shoulder. "Thank you, Captain Sandar. Now I want you to meet a new friend. His name is Happenstance."

Sandar bowed, transforming instantly from stern captain to gracious host. "A pleasure, Happenstance. As a friend of Lord Umber, you can count on my loyalty and service." He seemed to mean it, and so Hap found himself liking the man immediately.

"Excellent," Umber said. "Now, good Captain, I wish to quietly put in at the outer dock of the Aerie. I don't care to deal with Hoyle just now; she's probably in a snit."

Sandar's handsome face went pale. He coughed into his hand. "Lord Umber, about Hoyle . . ."

Umber blanched. Not far from where they stood was a door to a cabin on the *Swift*'s main deck. That door exploded open, hitting the wall with a thunderous crack. A short, squat woman with a doleful expression on her chunky face filled the shadowy threshold. She raised a finger and pointed. "You!"

Umber drew his head between his knobby shoulders, much like a turtle. "N–now, Hoyle," he stammered, raising his palms. "You know perfectly well that I need to take the occasional jaunt . . ."

Hoyle advanced and Umber retreated until his back was pressed against the railing and she was an inch away. She mashed her fists into her plump hips and glared up into Umber's face. "A *jaunt*? Is that what you call these silly expeditions? Do you have any idea how much you've cost us? Of course you do! That's why you were going to sneak into the outer dock like a common smuggler. You wanted to avoid me! Well, that's exactly why I came on board to intercept you! You're an impulsive pudding-head, that's what you are, and a ridiculous businessman. The leviathan barge is the most valuable asset in our fleet, you dolt. While you were gone, word came of a wondrous opportunity: rare perfume out of Andobar! And where is our best cargo ship, the one that's impervious to headwind and doldrums and buccaneers? Off on a lark, a fool's errand, a goose chase, in search of some pointless and probably mythical treasure. And you didn't even *tell* me you were commandeering Boroon! You snuck away, and I'll wager you came home empty-handed! Well, what do you have to say about it, Lord Umber?"

There was a grim silence. The sailors edged away as if their eyebrows might be singed if they stood too close. Sandar leaned back, massaging his throat. Nima observed with interest from the barge. From under the sea came a comment from Boroon: a long, deep *hmmmmmmmmm*.

Umber coughed and tugged at his collar. His head slowly emerged from between his shoulders. His voice squeaked at first, and then gathered strength as he spoke. "I do have something to say, in fact. Firstly, at a time like this, Hoyle, I almost forget that you work for me and not the other way around. Secondly, much of our mutual success has sprung from these *jaunts*, and I trust you'll bear that in mind. Thirdly, I was presented with information about something important that might be retrieved, and I had reason to believe that haste was crucial. That is why I asked Captain Nima to take me. Fourthly, I am not a pudding-head. And fifthly, I did not come home empty-handed."

"Oh, really?" Hoyle said. Her glare had lost a fraction of its heat. "And what did you find?"

Umber raised a finger toward the sky, twirled it in the air, and brought it down over Hap's head. Hoyle looked at Hap for the first time, and she took in a sharp breath when her eyes met his.

"A *boy*?" She turned to Umber with one eyebrow arched high. "Lord Umber, you can't just run out to a distant shore and collect a *boy*."

"Normally I'd concur," Umber said, "but this particular boy—who has a name, incidentally, which is Happenstance—needed to be collected. *Rescued,* in fact, from a cruel fate. Happenstance has no memory, you see, and no one to take care of him."

Hoyle took a second look at Hap. Her jaw slid from side to side. "So you've fallen into Umber's company, young man? One piece of advice: Don't let him take you on any more of his adventures, or something horrible might happen to you."

Hap nodded vigorously. He was eager to agree with this formidable person.

"Madam Hoyle!" It was Nima, calling down from the barge.

Hoyle looked up, and somehow her harsh features formed a genuine smile. "Nima, darling! How are you, my dear?"

"Quite well, thank you. You spoke of perfume: Is it the usual port in Andobar?"

"Why, yes it is."

"And how much head start did our rivals get?"

"Nearly two days, I fear."

Nima raised her face to the sky. "There is not much wind, and it is against them. Also, they will have to sail around the Straits of Maur, for fear of pirates, while Boroon can swim straight through. So I can still arrive before them."

"Can you really?" Hoyle said. She stroked her palm with her fingers, counting coins in mime.

"I should leave at once," Nima said.

"Aren't you a delight! Meet our agent at the usual rendezvous, and he'll arrange for the cargo to be loaded. Captain Sandar, please have your men bring the chest of gold to Nima." Hoyle whipped back toward Umber, and her ferocity returned for an encore. "And *you*, Lord Umber, will meet me in the cabin, where we shall discuss our mutual responsibilities at length."

Umber trudged into the cabin like a man approaching the gallows, while a small but weighty wooden chest was carried up to the leviathan barge. The sailors swarmed over the deck of the *Swift* and crawled aloft like spiders to drop the sails. Furls of canvas snapped into taut expanses. Lines were heaved back to the leviathan barge, and the crafts drifted apart. Nima waved, and Boroon's sweeping tail propelled them away.

"Are we going to Kurahaven now, Captain Sandar?" asked Hap.

Sandar took a deep breath of salty air. "Yes, Master Happenstance. And that is a sight you will never forget, I promise you."

CHAPTER
8

The notion of cold, dark water below still jangled Hap's nerves, but curiosity drove him to crouch near the prow, where he hugged the rail tight. There was another reason to stand there with his back to the crew: Nobody could stare at his eyes. After a while, Sophie came forward as well, without a word, and stood several paces away.

The mountains on the horizon grew wider and taller as the *Swift* approached land. They bounded past rocky isles, and then ships of all sizes and shapes appeared as they plunged into a busy shipping lane. Suddenly there were gray-white sails all around and gray-white gulls overhead, filling the air with haunting cries. All the vessels came and went through a gap in the mountainous terrain, directly ahead. The wind gusted, Sandar barked out orders, and Hap felt the *Swift* earn her name. She swept past every boat on the same course while other captains frowned with envy.

As they approached, Hap saw that the gap was easily a half mile across. When they reached the opening and passed the peaks that blocked the interior from sight, he saw the harbor of Kurahaven for the first time, a calm circle of water inside the mountains' embracing arms. For a moment he neglected to breathe.

The first wonder stood just inside the gap, near the shore to his left. It was an ancient castle, built on an island so low that its walls seemed to erupt straight from the sea. Surely, it was no longer inhabited, because what was left was in a precarious state. There had once been four towers around a domed keep. Now two were collapsed with their remains jutting from the sea, one was broken in half, and one sagged at such an angle that it was hard to conceive why it hadn't already tumbled.

"What is that place?" Hap said.

Sophie looked around and saw that no one else was there to reply. She answered in a whisper while looking at her feet. "Those are the ruins of Petraportus. It's very old. That's where the kings lived long ago."

"Oh. Thank you," said Hap. He could have stared at the

broken castle for hours, but there was more to see. At the far end of the harbor, in stark contrast to the ruins, stood the dazzling, flourishing city of Kurahaven. He had no memory of the world of his past, but he was sure there couldn't be a more remarkable place anywhere.

He let his eyes wander across the great vista, starting with the ruined castle on his left. Behind that, a lofty pillar of rock stood out from the cliffs. Through some unimaginable act of carving, the rock had been transformed into a tower fortress. Columns, stairs, arches, balconies, and windows had been sculpted into its surface. Near the top, part of the rock jutted from a corner, and this outcropping had been carved in the likeness of a head with a craggy face, a flowing beard, and windows for eyes.

Near the bottom of the pillar a thick jet of water shot from a crack in the rock. A boat was floating where the stream splashed into the sea. The craft was so tiny that there was barely room for the gray-haired man and woman who occupied it, and the barrels they were filling.

"They call that the Spout," Sophie offered. "See that little boat? That's the old fisherman and his wife, who live in the ruins of Petraportus. They keep to themselves mostly. We don't even know their names. Nobody else is crazy enough to go in there, because the rest of it could collapse any minute."

"And what is that place?" asked Hap, looking toward the carved pillar.

"Why, that is the Aerie," Sophie replied. Her voice had gained strength, and he was glad to see that she'd moved a little closer.

The Aerie. Of course, Hap thought. Umber could not live in an ordinary home; it had to be something remarkable. He took a closer look. At the top a short, narrow tower stood at one corner. At the bottom was a boxy gatehouse, dwarfed by the pillar that loomed over it. Descending from there, a stone causeway spanned a frothing white river that spilled from the mountains to the harbor. The causeway flattened into a road that led to the magnificent city.

To behold the city from the harbor was to look up a series of steps. First, all around them were the watercraft—too many to count, from tiny rowboats to great cargo ships, cluttering the docks and moored offshore. Sophie followed his gaze. "Have you ever seen so many ships?" she said. "The merchant vessels are there . . . the king's navy is in the middle . . . and the fishing boats are there. And look—there's the shipyard." Hap followed where her finger pointed and saw, on the far side of the harbor, a dozen ships in every stage of construction. Some were just skeletal rows of ribs, others were partially clad with curving planks, and some needed only a mast and sails before they could swim.

Behind the docks was a high stone wall, daunting to any invader. Past that, the city sprawled on a gently sloping hill. There were buildings with magnificent columns, arches and domes, and neighborhoods packed tight with tall, brightly colored houses.

In the center of it all was a palace. The great building looked like something sculpted from sand. Its elegant towers, clustered tight and rising ever higher near the center, were topped by swallow-tail banners that snapped in the ocean breeze. The tallest tower was adorned by a clock with a face as big as the moon. Gardens surrounded the castle, and even from this distance Hap could see the riot of hues in bloom.

Behind them, Hap heard the door to the cabin open. Umber stepped out. When he saw Hap he wiped the back of his hand across his forehead in exaggerated fashion, and then broke into a wide grin. "Well, I suppose I deserved that tongue-lashing. Don't get the wrong idea about Hoyle, though. She's a fine person, though mortally addicted to profit." Umber swept his arm across the panorama before them. "So, what do you think of Kurahaven? Does it tickle your memory?"

"If I saw this before, I hope I'd remember," Hap said.

"Trust me, it's just as beautiful up close. I have so much to show you, Hap. So much to explore!"

Sandar shouted orders. Sails were furled until only one remained to nudge the *Swift* forward, and the crew skillfully guided her to her berth. Hap sighed with relief as the ship squeaked against the dock. He was eager to leave the menacing sea behind at last and set foot on sturdy land.

Hoyle scowled at Umber one last time, and then stomped down the plank, across the dock, and up the wide stairs of a tall, white building with a sign that made Hap look twice. Under a large decorative letter U it said THE UMBER SHIPPING COMPANY.

Hap followed the others down the plank. The dock was busy as an anthill. Grunting, laughing, sweating, singing men loaded and unloaded the ships. Barrels were rolled up and down ramps, chests were balanced on shoulders, and crates dangled high from ropes and pulleys.

Word somehow spread that Umber had arrived, because a stream of men ran up to greet him, ask whispered questions, and hand over documents for him to peruse. Odd things happened between those mundane pieces of business. Someone handed Umber a nasty-looking rat in a cage. Umber accepted it happily, thanking the fellow for his thoughtfulness. Another man approached with a small wooden box. Umber was delighted to receive it. He swung the hinged lid open, revealing a mass of packing straw inside. Umber dug in and pulled out a bottle, not so different from the one he'd thrown at the tyrant worm. It was made of orange glass with a fat bottom and narrow neck, sealed with cork and wax.

"What exactly is the effect?" he asked the man who'd brought it.

"Not *precisely* sure, my lord," said the man. "Serpents, I believe. But the wizard said it ought not to be used in a crowd."

"Well done, Flugel. Worth whatever we paid, I'm sure. The prince will be delighted."

A carriage drawn by a pair of sturdy horses appeared. Umber waved to its driver and looked back for his companions. "Hap, Sophie, Balfour, our ride is here. Where is Oates? Where'd that bruiser get to now?"

Hap looked to his left for the big man. A sound from the other direction caught his attention: the unmistakable slap of a hand on flesh. He saw Oates a few paces away with a bright red mark on one cheek. A young woman stood before him, flexing her fingers. She darted Oates a poisonous stare and muttered something dreadful before stomping away with her dress swishing violently from side to side.

"Not again," said Umber. "Poor Oates. I've told him not to talk to women. Honesty gets him nowhere."

The carriage rocked as Oates clambered in. "Nobody talk to me," he said, holding his cheek with one hand.

"I wouldn't dream of asking. Stow this, will you?" Umber replied, handing Oates the caged rat. Oates sighed and put the cage under his seat.

Hap leaned out the window, absorbing the scene that rolled by. The carriage clattered over cobblestones and through one of the open gates in the harbor wall. Every gate had heavy doors that could be shut fast—in case of some enemy's assault, Hap figured. But this was clearly a time of peace, because the doors were open wide, and only a few soldiers occupied the watchtowers that topped the wall a hundred yards apart.

The carriage reached a crossroads and turned sharply left, heading for the Aerie. They were on the sloping road that Hap had seen from the harbor, and soon the carriage rattled across the causeway. Hap saw the foaming river that tumbled through a gap in the mountains, thundered over rocky steps, and churned the sea.

"The river Kura," Umber called over the roaring cascades.

The causeway angled higher, and Hap had to lean forward

to keep his face at the window. Ahead was a stone gatehouse at the foot of the Aerie. The clopping of hooves slowed and the carriage stopped in a small courtyard.

"Here we are, Hap," said Umber. "I hope you'll call this home."

There were two doors that led into the Aerie. One was made of dark wood covered with plates of iron; it was just wide enough to let a single person pass. The second door was twice as high and five times as wide. It was crafted from some glossy black material, seamless and unblemished, like a pool of ink standing on edge.

"We could use the little door, but the big one's more fun," Umber said. He rubbed his hands together and grinned. "Ready for some magic?"

"Um. I guess," Hap replied.

"Hurkhor!" Umber called aloud, facing the door, with one hand raised high.

That means open, Hap thought, deciphering the strange word. *But it's not the same tongue we've been speaking.* He was going to ask Umber about it when something remarkable happened. A thin vertical line appeared in the center of the shiny black door. The crack widened, and the door split in two and swung inward. Its only sound was a soft whisper.

"You made it open by saying that word?" asked Hap.

Umber nodded and laughed.

"But that doesn't make any sense," said Hap.

"If it made *sense*, it wouldn't be *magic*." Umber showed Hap the back of his right hand. There were several rings on Umber's fingers, but he wiggled the third digit. That ring had an oval stone made of the same black material.

at least seven hundred years. An army of Dwergh (also known as Dwarves, a term they find disagreeable) chiseled their way into the great cliff overlooking what is presently the site of Kurahaven. Taking full advantage of the wondrous natural caverns inside the rock, they built a lavish dwelling that centuries later would one day be given to King Nodd the Second as part of the n[...] ancient truce. The Aerie is a fortress of surprising

CHAPTER
9

"Welcome home, Lord Umber," said a tall woman with short white hair. Her silver gown brushed the floor. She stood on the other side of the black door, alone in a lofty room. Her voice was raised because there was another sound inside, thunderous and constant.

"Always good to return, Tru." Umber waved the rest of them inside.

Hap stepped into the room to find another stunning scene. The walls of the room were chiseled out of solid stone, hollowed completely except for two pillars that were carved to look like a great pair of legs, with boots at the bottom and the knees blending into the stone ceiling above.

A staircase zigged and zagged up the opposite wall to the

upper levels of the Aerie. To his right, Hap saw the source of the thunderous sound: A waterfall emerged from a cavity above and dropped into a dark channel at their feet. The rushing water turned a paddle wheel, which was connected to a complex contraption: gears, ropes, and wooden platforms that could rise, disappear through a hole in the ceiling, and return again, completing an oval journey. For the moment, however, only the paddle wheel was moving.

Umber had paused, giving Hap a moment to take in his surroundings. "Lady Truden, this is Happenstance. I'll explain him later. For now, I'm sure young Hap could use a soft bed and a few hours' sleep. Am I right in that, Hap?"

Hap bit his bottom lip. "I . . . I still don't feel tired." He didn't look up at Lady Truden, because he was sure she was staring at his eyes.

"There's something strange about this boy, Tru," said Oates. "Sorry," he added quickly toward Umber, who'd shot another lethal glare in his direction.

"It's fine if you're not tired, Hap," Umber said. "In fact, it's wonderful. You can get to know the place right away. Tru, Hap will need a room of his own. Something with a view of the city would be nice."

"Of course, Lord Umber," Lady Truden said. "Shall we use the stairs or the lift?"

"Oh, the lift is much more fun," Umber said.

"I hate the lift," muttered Oates. He plodded toward the stairs, carrying the boxes that Umber had been given, with the rat in its cage on top of the stack.

Lady Truden led the rest over the deck that surrounded the paddle wheel. She pulled a wooden lever, and Hap heard a ratcheting sound as cogs and wheels meshed and the ropes turned. There was room for two or three on each wooden platform. Sophie and Balfour stepped onto one and were lifted toward the higher levels of the Aerie.

Umber took Hap's elbow as the next platform arrived. "Carefully now, Hap . . . here we go." He stepped on, taking Hap with him, and Lady Truden joined them.

"Did you find what you sought?" she said quietly to Umber.

"Um . . . hard to say," Umber replied. Hap stood between them, so the conversation took place over his head. He heard every word, but understood none of it.

"And how did you feel? Was there any . . ." Lady Truden had dropped her voice even lower, and it faded to nothing.

"None of that, all was well," Umber said, waving his hand. "And how is everything here? How is our guest?"

"There is no change."

"Still, eh? Don't know what to do about that." Umber

tapped Hap on the shoulder. "The grand hall is up ahead. Let's get off here." They passed through the opening in the ceiling, and Hap saw another handsome room, much larger than the one below. As the platform reached the level of the floor, they stepped off. Overhead, Hap saw Balfour and Sophie still rising toward a third story.

The grand hall had a wooden table in the middle, surrounded by chairs. Shelves and bureaus were cluttered with fascinating objects that would take days to explore. Paintings depicted all manner of subjects: portraits of people in odd clothes, fantastical creatures, maps of kingdoms and wild lands, and things that Hap could not decipher at a glance.

Corridors on either side of the hearth plunged deeper into the rock. The smell of bread and other foodstuffs drifted out from one, and Hap glimpsed a kitchen beyond swinging doors. Another archway framed a staircase, and Oates climbed into view, carrying the boxes.

"Oh yes, the rat!" Umber said. He took the cage from the top of the stack and, to Hap's surprise, unlatched the lid and turned it sideways. The rat spilled onto the ground, twitched its nose, and scurried under the nearest cabinet.

"Oh, dear," Umber called out, in a voice too loud to be intended for anyone in the room. "Did you see that? A rat's gotten loose in the grand hall!"

Hap looked at the others. None of them seemed to find this behavior odd. He added it to the growing list of things for which he hoped to find an explanation. Umber put the empty cage on the table and wiped his hands on his pants. "Tru, will you give Hap a quick tour? I'll show him the caverns another time—no need to boggle his mind more than we've done already. Let him choose any vacant room for his own. By the way, Hap will join me for that party tonight. I suppose we should stop at the market to get him some decent clothes. But first I need to pop into my tower, and I shouldn't be disturbed. Shall we meet back here in two hours?"

Umber bounded up the stairs, and Lady Truden led Hap around the Aerie. From the grand hall, they ventured past the kitchen, which smelled wonderfully of spice and bread and roasted meat. She took Hap down another corridor, pointing out a privy first, storage rooms, and then a door with a barred window at eye level. "Umber's archives," she said. "You might see a strange fellow inside. It's only Smudge. I'll leave it up to Lord Umber if you ever meet him. Don't wander in there alone, if you don't want to get bitten."

Bitten? Hap peered inside the window. The room was bigger than he'd expected. Exactly how deep it plunged into the pillar of rock he couldn't tell, because the space was cluttered with tall shelves that were stuffed with books and crates. An ink-stained desk stood near the door, where scrolls were unrolled and a half loaf of bread sprouted a garden of mold.

A flicker of motion attracted Hap's eye, and he jerked his head to one side to avoid the thing flying their way. It struck the bars in the window and dissolved into pieces, splattering him and Lady Tru with something orange, moist, and sticky.

"Ew!" Hap said, wrinkling his nose. He looked at the floor, where the slimy remains of a rotten peach had fallen. A snort and a giggle came from somewhere in the archives, then footsteps padded away into silence.

"He's thrown worse," Lady Tru said with her lip curled. She flicked a splotch off her shoulder with the long nail of one finger. "Let's move on."

There was more beyond the archives, but Lady Tru said she would leave that for Umber to show. "If he thinks you ought to see it," she added with a sniff. They returned to the grand hall, stepped back on the lift, and rode to the third story of the Aerie. "The residences," she said when they arrived.

She opened the doors to unoccupied rooms and told Hap to select one for his own. Each was unique, as if a craftsman from a different corner of the world had created each bed, desk, table, chair, or ornament on the wall. Hap was reluctant to choose; he hardly felt like he'd done anything to deserve such a splendid place to stay.

"You won't want this one," Lady Tru said, opening the last door in the corridor. But as soon as Hap peered inside, he knew it was for him.

Somebody else might have claimed it, if not for its tiny dimensions. There was barely room for the bed, desk, and chairs. A pair of tall, oval windows dominated the walls that angled together. Between them was a golden spyglass, on a stand that could swivel in any direction. The space was modest and curious, and yet it simply felt right.

"I think I'd like to stay here," Hap said.

"Surely it's too small. We only use this when there are too many guests."

"It's not too small for me." The windows were barred, like the others in the Aerie. But outside the bars was mullioned glass of wonderful clarity. He turned the latches and pushed on the iron frames. Fresh air gusted in as the glass panels swung wide.

Ever since they left the harbor, they had climbed—up the steep causeway and up again through the three stories of the Aerie. And so from the left window he could behold, from a height normally reserved for birds, the glory of Kurahaven, and even the farmlands beyond the city. Through the right window he could watch the Rulian Sea and the busy harbor below.

Hap stuck his head between the bars and looked down. He realized precisely where this room was: inside the carved head he'd seen from the *Swift*. The oval windows were its eyes. He gazed at the harbor. And then a sight struck him like an arrow between the eyes. He staggered and gripped the bars.

"Young man—what's the matter with you?" asked Lady Truden.

"The ship," Hap said between gasps.

The ship that had pursued Boroon all those miles was anchored in the middle of the harbor. He was sure of it—and surer than ever that the creature named Occo had indeed picked up his scent, as the note that he wasn't supposed to read had warned.

CHAPTER
10

Hap bounded up the stairs, heading for the roof of the Aerie, where he might find Umber. Lady Truden called after him: "Young man! You're not to be running off by yourself!"

Hap waited for her to catch up. His heart thumped hard and fast against his chest, as if hammering out of its cage. "I have to tell Lord Umber about the ship!" Back in the little room he'd trained the spyglass on the craft. Every detail matched his memory: pale wood and a curving prow carved like a serpent's head. The only difference was that the tall figure no longer stood on the deck. As far as he could see there was nobody on the ship at all.

The landing opened onto a garden terrace that was lush

with a staggering diversity of shrubs, trees, and flowers; even in his frantic state, Hap was struck by its beauty. But he would have to appreciate it later—Umber needed to know about the ominous ship *now*. And Umber was certainly inside the structure at the corner, a tower erected on the flat top of the natural stone. The only entry was a barred door. "That is Lord Umber's study and his quarters," Lady Truden said, huffing. "Nobody is allowed there without his permission. And he told me quite plainly he wanted time to himself."

"You don't understand," Hap said, with his voice rising to a shout. "That ship was following us. And now it's *here*. Lord Umber has to know!" He saw a window at least ten feet overhead, and called out: "Lord Umber! *Lord Umber!*"

"Master Happenstance, I must ask you to—"

Hap didn't mean for the next thing to happen. In his frantic state, he jumped. He only wanted to be heard more clearly through the window, but he'd forgotten how high his legs could propel him. The curved blocks of stone flew past, and his chin rose past the windowsill. He heard Lady Truden gasp. Before he dropped earthward again, in that instant between rise and fall, he glimpsed something he wasn't meant to see.

Umber sat at a desk inside. He'd turned halfway around, probably wondering about the shouting, and so he saw Hap's face appear. Umber raised his hand, palm out, and leaned sideways to hide whatever was on the desk. Hap saw the corner of something smooth, bright, and silver. From behind Umber's shoulder came an alien glow with a cold, blue quality that Hap had never seen before.

A terrible expression transformed Umber's face. His eyes widened at first, and his jaw fell, but then fury ignited in his eyes and his lips pulled back in a snarl. "Hap—*never*!" came his shout, even before Hap's feet touched the ground again.

Lady Truden's fingers dug into Hap's shoulder like an eagle's talons.

"I'm sorry! I didn't mean to!" Hap cried.

"Lady Truden!" shouted Umber. He was at the window now, with his fists around the bars.

Lady Truden's teeth were clenched, and her ashen face trembled. "My apologies, Lord Umber, the boy ran ahead, and I had no idea he could leap so high."

Umber rubbed his face up and down and took an enormous breath, holding it before exhaling. When he lowered his hands, his face had returned to a more normal state. It wasn't the happy countenance that Hap had gotten used to, but at least Umber didn't look ready to commit an act of violence anymore.

"I'll be right down," Umber said. He reached out and closed the window's shutters.

"That was unforgivable, young man," Lady Truden said,

tightening her grip. "Above all things, Lord Umber's privacy must be respected. No one who breaks that rule is allowed to stay."

A lump swelled in the middle of Hap's throat, making it hard to breathe. His eyes felt warm, and moisture blurred his vision. *Where will I go now?* he wondered. He knew no family, no friends; only the people he'd met since he awoke underground.

The door to Umber's tower opened, and Umber stepped out. His face was red, and his mouth was a thin, straight line. "Tru, why don't you head downstairs? I'd like to talk to the boy."

Lady Truden released Hap's shoulder and clasped her hands in front of her waist. "Shall I pack his things?"

"Hap doesn't *have* any things. And he isn't going anywhere. We can hardly banish him for breaking rules that were never explained. Don't you agree?"

Lady Truden's shoulders twitched. "Of course, Lord Umber. I will be in the grand hall if you need me."

Umber nodded. He watched her descend the steps. Then he turned to Hap just as Hap dabbed the corner of his eye, smearing a tear before it trickled down.

The corner of Umber's mouth turned up. "Don't worry, Hap. You won't be evicted." The half smile vanished. "But you have to tell me something. What did you see, when you were at the window? I want to know exactly what you saw."

Hap's hands shook, so he stuffed them in his pockets. "N-nothing, really. I saw you, at a desk. And behind you . . . there was a glow. I saw the corner of something . . . just a corner. It looked like silver. Shiny silver."

"That's all you saw? Are you certain?"

Hap nodded. Umber scratched his chin and took another deep breath. "I have a few . . . *magical* objects, Hap. Some I keep to myself, that's all. But nothing like that will happen again, will it?"

Hap swept his head vigorously from side to side. "No. Not ever."

Umber rubbed his hands together, and the sparkle returned to his eyes. "Well, as I recall, you were shouting for me. What was that all about?"

Hap's eyes widened. For a moment, he'd forgotten. "The ship that followed us—it's here!"

Umber hurried to the terrace wall and squinted at the distant vessel. There were more ships in the harbor than the docks could accommodate, and many were anchored offshore. The ship with the serpent prow was moored farther out than the rest.

"Could be the same vessel," Umber said. He gnawed his bottom lip for a moment. "I'll send word ahead, and my men can investigate. You and I will head to the market soon, and then we'll stop at the docks to learn what we can."

The market was colorful, noisy, and crowded with jostling bodies. Musicians, jugglers, and acrobats performed, and shoppers haggled over food, furniture, clothes, jewelry, perfumes, and other wares. Hap would have been enthralled if he weren't so busy watching for his stalker. Was Occo closing in even now, sniffing the air for his green-eyed prey? He was glad Oates was with them, leading the way through the crowd.

Perhaps sensing Hap's nervous state, Umber pointed out the Kurahaven Guard: soldiers of the king who patrolled the streets and the top of the harbor wall. They were easy to spot with their feathered hats, sleeveless purple surcoats and capes, and the sabers at their hips. "See the four symbols on the royal coat of arms?" Umber asked, pointing at the shield-shaped emblem on their chests. "The crown, the sun, the mountains, and a shell for the sea. Those are the king's guard, sworn to protect the people. But if you see silver or green capes, those are the private guards of the princes—Argent the eldest, and Loden the youngest."

Hap thought that a distasteful expression had flickered on Umber's face when he spoke that last name. Then he remembered something else he'd been told. "Aren't there three princes? Doesn't the middle prince have his own guard?"

Umber laughed. "Galbus? Oh no, his interests lie elsewhere. You'll see when we go to the palace. It's his birthday celebration tonight, you know."

Wherever they walked, Umber drew attention. He had his hand shaken so often and so vigorously that Hap thought it might snap off. Women smiled and children waved. Nearly as often, Hap's eyes captured less flattering attention. The adults nudged and whispered while children pointed and stared. Hap took to walking about with his lids squeezed nearly shut, peering through the narrowest of slits.

"Finally," Umber said as they arrived at a green- and white-striped tent. "The clothier. Do you know what a clothier is, Hap?"

Hap thought about it. It was like pumping the handle of a well; the answer gushed out a heartbeat later. "Someone who makes or sells garments."

Umber gave Hap the usual curious, delighted stare. "That might have been an obvious one. But still, for a boy with no memory, you have an astounding vocabulary, Hap."

Before Hap could think of a reply, the flap of canvas that served as the door flew open and a plump, well-dressed man burst out of the tent. A gap-toothed grin erupted between the fellow's curling mustache and sculpted beard. All the hair on his face was shiny with wax and never moved, even when he turned his head from side to side.

"Lord Umber, my valued friend and customer!" the fellow cried.

"Poncius! May we enter?"

"Of course, of course!" Poncius bellowed, holding back the canvas door. Umber and Hap went in while Oates stood at the entrance with his burly arms crossed, facing the crowd.

"Let me get directly to the point, Poncius," Umber said. "This boy Happenstance has only the clothes on his back."

Poncius wrinkled his nose at the sight of Hap's bedraggled tunic. "An insufferable tragedy."

"Hap will meet the royals this evening and must be suitably dressed," Umber said.

"Unconditionally!" the clothier exclaimed. His eyebrows contorted as he inspected Hap from head to toe.

"A full wardrobe from the shoes up."

"Wonderful," Poncius said, tapping his fingertips together.

"He should also have a hat. One he can pull down to shade

his eyes when he likes. Perhaps you've noticed his striking eyes."

"Not until you just mentioned them," Poncius said, stealing perhaps his seventh glance at Hap's eyes. "But a hat he shall have."

Hap felt his heart warm. He would like very much to be able to tug the brim of a hat over his brow.

Hap stood on a box in front of a tall mirror as Poncius buttoned him into yet another silk shirt. His old tunic, trousers, and undergarments were heaped on the floor. The clothier had dropped them there, unwilling to touch them for a second more than necessary.

"Look at that mirror, Hap," Poncius said. "Have you ever seen a glass like that? What a reflection! It was a gift from Lord Umber. Another one of his miracles."

"A minor innovation," Umber said, waving his hand. He stood by a rack of clothes, pawing through them.

"Minor, my eye!" Poncius cried. "The wonders never cease with your master, Hap!"

"I'm nobody's master," Umber said.

Poncius prattled on. "The master of progress, that's what you are. Lord Umber brings us music, plays, medicine. He tells us how to properly design our buildings and ships. We are

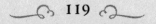

a nation transformed, in a matter of years. He even creates cuisine! That wonderful dish, Lord Umber, the one that's round and flat, with the toppings. What do you call that? Pete-something?"

"Pizza," Umber replied absently, examining a shirt he'd pulled from the rack.

"Pete-suh! A glorious concoction." Poncius yanked on the hem of Hap's shirt, smoothing the material. "Look at you now, Hap! Quite an improvement over that ancient, back-country tunic."

Umber's head snapped toward them. "Back-country? Of course, I should have thought to ask! Poncius, what do those old clothes tell you about the wearer? You of all people would know."

The clothier's lip curled as he lifted the tunic to inspect it. "Well. No offense, young man, but these belong to a country lad of modest means. Made of a coarse and cheap grade of wool, when linen would certainly be more comfortable." He thought for another moment. "It's quite out of style. Ancient is an exaggeration, but look at those boots: square-toed. Ugh! And I haven't seen toggles like that for years. Hand-me-downs, I suppose. Yet they're not so worn, are they?"

Umber stepped closer, staring with his head tilted to

one side. This was a customary gesture of his, Hap realized, whenever Umber's attention was keenly focused. "Old, you say. But could you guess where they came from?" Umber asked. "What land?"

Poncius brought the fabric to his face for a closer look. "The red dye doesn't tell me much—probably from madder root, and that's common everywhere. Still, from the cut and the stitching, I'd say these are not from so far away. Not Kurahaven, certainly, but maybe the hinterlands of Celador."

Poncius would have continued, but the tent brightened as someone pushed the door aside and entered.

"Hello, Sandar," Umber said. Captain Sandar bowed to Umber and nodded to Hap, who raised a hand in greeting.

"Pardon the intrusion, Lord Umber," Sandar said. "I have news about that ship, and I heard you'd come this way."

"Tell me," Umber said, clasping his hands behind his back.

Sandar cleared his throat as if his mouth had gone dry. "The ship is deserted. I had a pair of my crew row out and hail her. Nobody answered. The boys drew closer, meaning to board, but . . . a strange thing happened."

Hap felt like he couldn't breathe. Umber's head listed even farther to the side. "Yes?"

"They . . . got spooked. Something large bumped them from below and nearly tipped them over. Nothing happened after that; it was like a warning. But they rowed back as fast as they could."

Umber bounced on the balls of his feet. His eyes gleamed. "Really now?"

"That's not all, Lord Umber. Others in my crew were in the market this afternoon. They say a stranger is wandering around asking questions. I think he's looking for Hap."

"What!" cried Hap. He nearly fell off the box, but Poncius steadied him.

"It's true," Sandar continued. "My first mate Jonas saw the stranger himself. He said it was a tall fellow in a weird sort of cloak. And his whole face was covered by a sack of gauze, with a single eyehole on one side. Jonas said the stranger had an odd manner of walking as well, like a long-legged bird. He just calls him the Creep now, he frightened him so."

"The Creep," Umber repeated, smiling.

Sandar shook his head. "The Creep asked Jonas, in a whispery sort of voice, 'Have you seen anyone with eyes like these?' He held out his hand—hands with gloves on them, even on this warm day—and showed Jonas a pair of sparkly green marbles. Jonas said they looked just like Hap's eyes."

Hap put his fingertips to the corner of his eyes. His legs felt numb. He heard Poncius gulp beside him.

"What did Jonas do?" asked Umber.

"Jonas is no fool. He told the Creep he knew nothing," Sandar said. "The Creep said Jonas should come to the docks at midnight if he learned the whereabouts of this green-eyed person, and he would be rewarded. Then he showed Jonas a bag filled with gems."

"Perfect," Umber said, clapping his hands.

"Perfect?" Hap cried, as his voice cracked. "How is that perfect?"

"Perfect because we know where and when to find this Creep. At midnight, we'll set a trap for our pursuer, and find out what he wants. Don't look so down, Hap! Let's not presume he's evil. Perhaps he's a friend, with information. Maybe this will help us solve the mystery of you."

Hap's shoulders slumped. "I suppose." But he'd read the note. He knew better.

Umber rubbed his hands together. "For now, while this Creep is lurking about, we should get you back to the Aerie. Poncius, we'll take all that stuff, and what Hap is wearing now. Throw in some everyday garments as well. And quick, find us a hat."

The hat looked like an enormous blue acorn, but Hap was pleased to put it on and pull its brim down. They walked briskly through the crowd, with Oates in front and Umber and Sandar at his sides, heading for Umber's carriage.

"Hap, let's try to keep your abilities a secret for the time being," Umber said. "I wouldn't go leaping about, for example. And wear that hat just like you're doing. Just to be safe."

"Lord Umber?" Hap said quietly.

"Hmm?" Umber's eyes darted left and right across the market.

"About that note . . ." Hap's voice faltered. He wanted to tell Umber that he'd read at least part of the message from WN. It would be a relief to talk openly about this "Creep" who might be the creature named in the message. And he ached to know what the rest of the strange contents of the note might mean: What sort of skills were supposed to arise in him? What was the ancient law that he violated merely by existing? What did WN mean when he wrote to Umber about "that world of yours"? And, most of all, what did the rest of the message say?

But the guilt of spying and the fear of how Umber might react overwhelmed him, and he couldn't squeeze out the confession. Before he gathered his strength to try again, Umber spoke.

"Now, Hap. I know you're curious about the note. But I already told you. I'm not going to—"

Umber ended the sentence abruptly as the crowd before them shifted. A tall figure in a pale cloak stood a few strides away. His head was covered by a sack of gauzy material, with a single ragged hole for one eye. He was leaning on a staff and towering over a merchant whose table was covered with candles. Hap saw a large gloved hand come out of the long-sleeved cloak, cupping a pair of glittering green spheres. And he heard, quite clearly, the hoarse, whispering voice: *". . . with eyes like these?"*

CHAPTER
II

"The Creep," whispered Sandar.

Hap didn't mean for his head to jerk up and lift the brim of his hat. It happened instinctively as he tried to get a better look at the stranger. At the same moment, the candle seller, looking for help, glanced in Hap's direction. The man's mouth dropped open, and the gesture caught the Creep's attention.

Hap lowered his face to shield his eyes as the Creep's gauze-covered head snapped around. The Creep came toward them, putting himself in the middle of the lane with one enormous stride. There was a disturbing, unnatural quality to the way his legs shifted inside his long cloak.

"Step away from the little one," he said. He sounded like a man who'd shouted all day and lost his voice. The sun shined into the ragged hole in the sack that masked his face, and Hap glimpsed a blue eye inside. It was nested in a raw, wounded-looking socket. The Creep blinked, and a wrinkled lid flapped across the eye.

Oates widened his stance and crossed his arms, and Sandar put a hand on the hilt of his sword. Umber cleared his throat and spoke. "Hello, stranger. Perhaps we should introduce ourselves?"

Hap gritted his teeth. He'd had enough of keeping his face down and stealing glances; he wanted to see what was happening. When he looked up, and his green eyes were revealed, the Creep shuddered, and a foul slurping sound came from behind the gauzy mask.

"Leave him for me," the Creep said. He took another long stride forward, halving the distance between them. For just a moment, the tip of the Creep's bare foot poked from the bottom of the cloak. His toes were long as fingers, splayed wide, and each ended in a hooked yellow nail.

"I don't think he's a friend," Hap said, stepping back.

Beside him, Sandar quietly drew his sword. "Steady, Happenstance."

The crowd sensed something was about to happen. The people drew back, creating an arena in the center with spectators at either end. Behind the Creep, two of the

Kurahaven Guard pushed their way into the open space and drew their sabers. They jutted their jaws, eager for a fight. One of them took a hunter's horn from his belt and blew a piercing note. The Creep's head listed at the sound, but he didn't turn to look.

Umber stepped up beside Oates and spoke to the Creep. "Tell me your name, and what you want. And why don't you take that cheesecloth off your head so we can know you better?"

The Creep responded with a hiss. He pulled off one glove, and then the other, revealing bony hands with elongated fingers. He raised the staff over his head.

"Hold! Don't move!" called one of the guardsmen. They strode toward the Creep with the points of their sabers outstretched.

The Creep tugged on the head of his staff, sliding out a long blade that was concealed inside. He flung the empty wooden sheath at the soldiers. It struck one of the young men at the waist, crumpling him. The Creep arched back as the other soldier charged. His long leg shot out and his clawed foot struck the second guardsman in the chest, flinging him backward into the crowd. People screamed and ran.

"Oates," Umber said coolly. Oates seized one end of the candle merchant's wooden table and flung it. A hundred candles of every color and shape scattered in the air. The Creep turned too late; the table walloped him across the stomach. He was batted across the street, bowling through benches and tables as he flew, and hit the side of another small tent. The canvas swallowed him whole, and the tent collapsed in a heap.

A silent pause followed. The crowd gawked, Oates picked a splinter out of his palm, and dozens of spilled candles rolled to a stop.

Umber rubbed the side of his face. "Overkill, Oates? I hope you left something alive for us to talk to."

The guardsman who'd been hit by the staff limped toward the crumpled tent. The saber trembled in his fist. "What was that thing?" he asked, coughing. He prodded the canvas with the saber.

"You ought to be careful," Umber called, raising his hand. But he'd hardly gotten the words out when the guardsman screamed, stumbled back, and clamped a hand on his thigh. A blade had pierced the canvas of the fallen tent, and the silver tip was stained red. The blade cut a wide slit and the Creep bounded out, landing in a crouch. His head swiveled until the eyehole found Hap.

Umber spoke with his hand covering his mouth. "Hap, remember what I said about not jumping or drawing attention? Disregard that. We'll try to stop him, but run if you have to."

The remaining spectators had seen enough. They stampeded out of the market. Parents slung the youngest ones over their shoulders and dragged older children by the hand.

Oates heaved a bench at the Creep, but this time the stranger was ready, and he ducked low. The bench shattered in the lane a hundred feet away. Before Oates could find another piece of furniture to throw, the Creep rushed at Hap. Sandar stepped in his path. Their blades clashed. The Creep's clawed foot darted up again, and Sandar tumbled through the air. Umber made a vain attempt to trip the Creep by sticking out his foot. The Creep could easily have run Umber through with his sword, but his attention had locked onto his green-eyed prey.

Hap whirled and ran, into a new group of five guardsmen who'd responded to the call of the horn. They let Hap through and spread out shoulder to shoulder. Hap stopped on the other side of the blockade and turned to watch.

The Creep skidded to a halt in front of the guardsmen. He flashed his sword back and forth, whipping the air. Hap heard the terrible slurping sound again.

"Drop that blade!" shouted the leader of the five. The Creep coiled and sprang. His tall, arcing leap cleared the heads of the five startled men. *I'm not the only one who can jump,* Hap thought. The middle guardsmen slashed upward with his sword, splitting open the bottom of the cloak but missing the Creep's limbs.

The Creep would have landed on Hap, but Hap responded with a leap of his own, his highest yet. Twin jolts of fear and exhilaration surged from his heart as he soared to the top of the nearest tent, his new hat flying off his head. If the Creep was surprised, he didn't let it stop him. He gathered himself and bounded toward Hap's perch. Hap left before the Creep arrived and touched down in the lane. Before he bolted, he heard one of the guardsmen call out: "It's like a frog chasing a grasshopper!"

Hap ran to where Umber knelt beside the wounded, groaning Sandar. Oates had pulled the long, thick support pole out of the fallen tent, and he stood ready to wield it as a club. "There—he disappeared between two tents," Oates said, pointing.

As Hap turned to look, he saw a flash of motion in the other direction. The Creep had shot down an alley, circled the tents with alarming speed, and emerged on the other side of them. A terrible realization dawned on Hap: He was putting his new friends in danger by staying near them.

Hap leaped again, to the top of the candle seller's tent. His feet slipped when he landed and he sprawled on the canvas, seizing the tent pole so he wouldn't slide off.

Hap looked back with his breath caught in his throat, expecting to see the Creep swooping down upon him. But Oates had swung the club, splintering it on the ground as the Creep stepped back. The Creep's foot came down on a candle, which rolled underneath him, and he stumbled wildly before catching his balance. One of his feet kicked high in the air, and Hap saw most of the Creep's legs through the tear in his long cloak. Hap nearly lost his grip when he realized why the Creep's gait was so strange. His knees bent the wrong way: backward, like a long-legged bird's. "He's not human!" cried Hap.

"I know! I saw it too!" shouted Umber, grinning widely. Sandar looked at Umber as if he'd lost his mind.

"Stand still so I can hurt you," Oates said to the Creep, waggling what was left of his club. The Creep sprang again. Hap's feet slipped as he tried to find purchase on the slick canvas. When he glanced over his shoulder he saw the pale figure soaring up toward him with the torn cloak flapping in the wind.

The roof of the tent bounced underneath him. Hap looked down and saw the Creep clinging to the tent with one hand, just below his feet. The Creep's sharp fingernails punctured the canvas, holding him in place. In the other hand, the Creep still had the long blade, which cut the air with a *whoosh,* right at Hap's legs.

Hap drew his legs up. He felt the tip of the blade strike the heel of his shoe and sting his flesh. The Creep dug into the tent with his sharp toenails, and lunged closer. The hand groped for Hap's leg. Hap opened his mouth to scream.

The Creep suddenly bent sharply at the waist and flew off the roof of the tent, letting out a loud, hoarse *OOF!* A huge fist had punched through from inside the tent.

Hap heard Oates shout from below. "Got you! Wait, that wasn't Hap, was it?"

"No, it was him," Hap said in a quivering voice. A small, glittering sphere fell out of the sky, hit the roof of the tent, and rolled toward Hap. It was one of the Creep's green marbles. *How strange,* Hap thought as he watched something that resembled one of his own eyes roll by.

The Creep crashed to the ground in the lane. He shook his masked head and pushed himself to his feet. He wobbled and nearly fell, as if one of his strangely jointed legs had been broken.

Three more guardsmen arrived, armed with bows. They kneeled and fired, and a trio of arrows whistled through the air. One missed, one snagged in a loose fold of the Creep's robe, and one lodged in his shoulder. He grunted, plucked the arrow out, and flung it to the ground. As the archers prepared to fire, the Creep threw his head back and let out a harsh, piercing cry. Hap would have clapped his hands over his ears if he hadn't needed to hang on to the tent pole.

The Creep was trapped between the archers and the swordsmen, and Hap heard the stomp of more boots approaching.

Umber stepped into the street and raised both hands, palms out. "Wait! Don't fire!" He pressed his hands together and turned to the Creep. "Your name is Occo, isn't it?"

The Creep had been staring up at Hap with his shoulders heaving, but his head snapped toward Umber when the name was spoken. *It's him,* Hap thought.

Umber spread his arms wide. "Look, Occo—you're surrounded. And you're wounded. Surrender and let us talk! Before more blood is spilled!"

Occo replied with a hiss. The archers drew back their bowstrings, but turned to look over their shoulders as a dark swift shape approached from behind. It was a horse of some kind, but with a ridged, hairless hide. There was a bit in its mouth and reins, but no saddle. The archers leaped aside to keep from being trampled.

The strange horse barely slowed as Occo grabbed its reins, swung awkwardly onto its back, and rode away. An instant later, a band of mounted guardsmen thundered down the lane in pursuit.

"Stay up there, Hap!" cried Umber. "You have eyes like an eagle—tell me what's happening!"

Hap pulled himself to the peak of the tent and watched the chase with one hand shading his eyes. "I don't—wait, now I see them again! They're right behind him—he's heading for the harbor."

Occo hurtled toward one of the gateways in the harbor wall. The guardsmen stationed there scrambled, but couldn't shut the doors in time to stop the horse.

Hap lost sight of the Creep for a moment as the wall blocked his view. "I can't see—hold on, there he is!" Occo steered his horse onto a narrow pier that jutted into the harbor. The horsemen in pursuit cut off any hope of escape. "He's trapped!" Hap shouted. Then he squinted, trying to see better, because something was happening to Occo's horse. He wasn't sure what to tell Umber next. What he saw didn't seem possible.

The horse was *transforming* as it raced to the end of the dock. The neck stretched and stiffened. The ridges on its hide grew more pronounced. At the end of the planks, the horse took a great leap over the water. The transformation continued as it soared. The front legs folded against the body and vanished. The hind legs clapped together and fused, and the hooves broadened into something like a fish's tail.

The creature hit the harbor and threw up a foaming wave on either side. It churned forward and submerged a moment later. The mounted guardsmen pulled back on their reins at the edge of the dock, and their horses pranced nervously on the planks.

Hap looked down at Umber with his mouth hanging open. "He got away."

"Got away? But how?" asked Umber.

"The . . . the horse . . . it turned into a . . . a . . . *sea horse.*"

"Turned into a sea horse? You mean, by magic?" Umber stamped the ground with his boot. "Bloody bells, I can't believe I missed it!"

CHAPTER
12

"How did the Creep follow us, anyway?"
Oates asked as the carriage clattered over the causeway. "You
said we lost him at sea when Boroon dove."

"So I thought," said Umber. "Perhaps he guessed our
destination."

"Humph," said Oates. He turned to Hap. "Well. At least
you bleed like a normal person."

Hap sat with his bare foot propped on the bench, pressing
a cloth against his heel. The fabric was dark with blood, but
the flow had slowed to a trickle. His hands still trembled
from the encounter. "Will those guardsmen be all right?" he
said to Umber.

"I suppose," Umber said, shrugging. Hap wished that

Umber would show more concern. While Sandar seemed all right, the fellow who'd been kicked by Occo was in a terrible state and had been carried away on a litter. But Umber was preoccupied; he hummed to himself as he pulled his notebook out of a vest pocket and scratched out words.

"How did you know his name, Lord Umber?" asked Hap.

Umber stopped writing and turned his gaze slowly toward Hap.

"That's right," said Oates. "You called him Occo. How did you know that?"

"Lucky guess," Umber said without a hint of humor. He went back to scribbling.

Hap wanted to shout, *It was in that note!* But he just leaned back and sighed. *Won't I be allowed to know anything?* Then he recalled a promise Umber had made a while ago, that might offer some answers. When the tension of the moment had passed, he spoke again. "Lord Umber, you told me you might be able to help me remember. You said you'd try something when we got to the Aerie."

Umber smiled and put the notebook away. His moods were like the weather, Hap observed. There might be a momentary darkness, but soon the clouds would pass and the sun would shine again. "That's right," Umber said. "I was working on that when you suddenly popped up outside my window. We'll give it a whirl after the party, if you're willing. It's called *hypnosis*. Do you know the word?"

Hypnosis, Hap repeated to himself. There was nothing familiar about the term. "No, sir," he said.

"You don't know *that* word? Interesting—I wonder . . . Hap, tell me if these mean anything to you: *microwave. Baseball. Thermonuclear.*"

Hap shook his head at each strange word.

"You made those up," said Oates.

"I did not." Umber sniffed. "But now I understand the boundaries of your vocabulary, Hap." Umber interlaced his fingers and cracked his knuckles. "Now, what were we talking about? Oh, yes—hypnosis. That means I will relax your mind and induce an altered state of consciousness. Something like sleep, but not exactly. If I succeed, you might recall what happened before Alzumar. It's not as scary as it sounds, Hap. You might even enjoy it. Would you like me to try?"

Hap nodded. He was starving for answers. "Yes. I would. But . . . do I really have to go to the palace tonight? I'd rather stay in the Aerie, if that's all right."

Umber patted Hap's knee. "I know you've had a scare. But I want you to join me. Don't worry, you'll be well guarded. Besides, a prince's birthday is a grand event!"

Hap tucked his head between his shoulders. He tried to put his unease into words. "Ever since I . . . woke up . . . I've rushed from one place to another. I feel as if I don't belong anywhere. It would be nice to stay in one spot for a while. And besides, didn't the clothier say I had the clothes of a country boy? Maybe I don't belong with all the royal folk."

"Umber just wants to show you off," Oates said out the window.

"Oates! Another word and it's the muzzle for you!" snapped Umber. His face reddened with anger. "Hap, you know that Oates only says what he *thinks* is true. That doesn't mean it *is* true. Or in good taste."

Oates stuck out his tongue and made an uncouth sound. Umber waved him off.

"You don't believe that, do you, Hap?" Umber asked. Hap shrugged. Umber leaned close. "Happenstance. Listen to me. I am not bringing you to the palace to display you like some exotic creature that I've acquired."

Hap wiped his cheek with his sleeve. "There will be more strangers, Lord Umber. They'll stare at me and my eyes. Now more than ever, after what happened in the market."

"Let them stare!" Umber said, slapping the bench. "Be proud of those eyes! People gaze at me constantly, Hap—

particularly the women—because of my unusual good looks. I've learned to deal with it."

Oates turned away and snorted.

"I promise you, Hap, I'm not bringing you to show you off. You believe me, don't you?"

Hap sniffed and nodded. "But why do I have to go?"

"Trust me, there's a reason."

Hap covered his face with his hands. He knew exactly what the reason was. It was part of the note: *Keep him with you always, and bring him on all your journeys. The boy needs to grow and learn; he must adventure, or he will not become what he must.* "But why does the reason have to be a secret?" he asked, trying to draw out the truth.

Umber took in a deep breath and held it for a long time. The carriage passed into the gatehouse and rolled to a stop, and he finally exhaled. "Oates. Out you go."

"So you can tell him something I'm not supposed to hear," grumbled Oates. The carriage rocked as he stepped out.

Umber waited until the big fellow stepped away, and then spoke quietly. "Hap. I don't mean to be unkind, but I simply can't answer all your questions yet. There are things going on that I don't understand: events being set into motion and possibilities about to unfold like flowers. My instincts tell me to proceed cautiously. And the note advised me to follow my instincts. So I will keep my secrets, and I won't apologize for that. When the time is right, I'll tell what I can. And that's that. Now, let's get you changed for the prince's party. I'm afraid what you're wearing got roughed up by our adventure with the Creep."

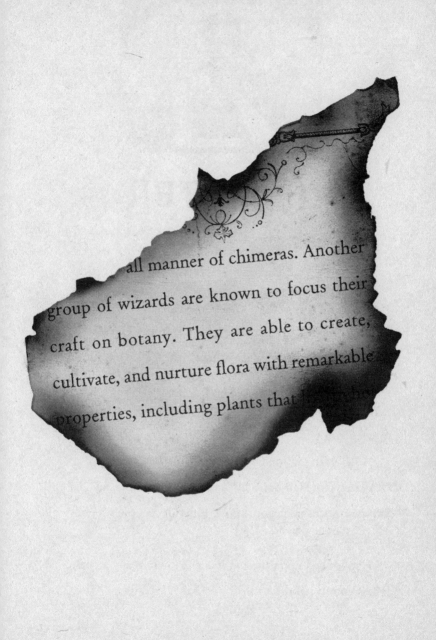

all manner of chimeras. Another group of wizards are known to focus their craft on botany. They are able to create, cultivate, and nurture flora with remarkable properties, including plants that

CHAPTER
13

Hap followed Oates up the stairs, toward the terrace, where they were to meet Umber. "Mister Oates, I've been meaning to thank you for saving me in the market," Hap said.

"It's just Oates. And I only did it because Umber told me to keep you safe."

"Oh," Hap said quietly. "Well, thank you, anyway."

Oates saw Hap hang his head, and he grimaced. "I don't like being this way, you know. Hurting people's feelings all the time."

Hap looked up at the big man. "Is there really a curse that forces you to tell the truth?"

"Yes," Oates grumbled. "Umber has been looking for a cure for years."

"Who did it to you?"

"I have no idea. I made the wrong person angry, I suppose. Some witch or wizard."

"But if you don't want to say the truth, why don't you just keep quiet?"

Oates rolled his eyes upward and shook his head. "You don't understand. I can't help saying it out loud. It just blows out of me, like a sneeze."

How strange, Hap thought. "Do you really think Lord Umber can fix it someday?"

"I don't know," Oates said. "I don't want to go on like this forever. But I'm worried about what would happen if he does."

"Worried? Why?"

Oates groaned and slumped, as if he had dreaded the question. "I don't think he'll let me serve him anymore. He'll send me away."

Hap's eyebrows rose. Oates's strength had saved Umber more than once. He couldn't imagine why Umber would make him go. "What? Why do you think that?"

Only then did Hap realize that Oates was growing angry.

His enormous hands curled up into great fists, and he growled his answer. "I wasn't a good man before this curse, all right? I was a thief. A bully. A liar. Umber trusts me only because I *have* to tell the truth. If I'm cured, I'll be the man I was again, and I don't know if he'll let me stay. *Does that answer your stupid question?*" He bashed the wall with his bare hand. Bits of stone clattered on the stairs. "What's the matter with you, boy?" he snarled. "Why do you ask these things when you know I have to answer?"

Hap took one step backward, suddenly aware of how vulnerable Oates was because of the spell. "I'm sorry! I didn't mean to pry! But . . ." He hesitated, then went on, anxious to make amends but careful not to pose another question. "Maybe you've learned how to be truthful while you've had this curse. You could be a different man, even if you're cured."

Oates sniffed, and looked at Hap with reddened eyes. "Do you really believe that?"

Hap was glad he wasn't the one with the curse, because the truth was that he had no idea. "Yes, Oates, I really do," he said.

Lying is a funny thing, Hap thought. Telling a lie made him feel worse. But the trace of a hopeful smile on Oates's face made him feel better.

Hap stepped onto the terrace behind Oates. He heard the hush of the evening breeze and the cry of gulls skimming the waves. Across the harbor, the falling sun roasted the bellies of the clouds.

Umber was in the garden, sitting on a bench below a tree that grew from an enormous stone planter. With a broad smile, he waved Hap over. Oates stayed back and leaned against the wall. He pulled a tiny flute from his pocket and played a sad, lovely tune with a skill that surprised Hap.

"I hope you don't mind Oates hanging about," Umber said. "But I think you should be well guarded until we're certain Occo is gone." Umber had an apple in his hand. He cut it into pieces with his knife and popped them into his mouth. "Would you like some fruit, Hap? Take anything you like."

Hap looked up and his jaw dropped. "How . . . ?" he said. The tree was of moderate size, perhaps ten feet tall, but far wider. Its branches sagged under the weight of dozens of fruits. But they weren't just apples; the tree bore all manner of fruits and berries. Some should have been on bushes, and some on vines, and yet they were all together: apples, pears, peaches, plums, oranges, lemons, limes, strawberries, clusters of grapes, and others he did not recognize. An intoxicating odor met his

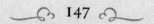

nose because the tree was also bursting with blossoms.

"Something, isn't it?" Umber said, spitting an apple seed. "It's my tree of many fruits. A gift from a wizard I know. He's devoted all his magical craft to botany. Perhaps you'll meet him someday; he's on one of the thousand isles out there in the Rulian Sea."

A fist-size strawberry dangled over Hap's head. He plucked it and took a bite. The sweet taste was so intense that his eyes closed on their own. "Wonderful," he said when he'd swallowed.

"Don't get juice on your shirt. You've gone through enough clothes for one day." Umber leaned back on the bench and took a deep whiff. "I've got some other magical plants up here. There's one that purrs when you touch it, one that grabs flies out of the air with a tongue like a frog's, and one that crawls from pot to pot when nobody's looking. This tree is my favorite, though. I sit on this bench many nights just to savor the fruit and watch the stars. It relaxes me when my mind buzzes like a beehive, as it's prone to do." Umber tossed what was left of the apple into another planter nearby. The vines of that plant slithered and wrapped around the core. "I could walk you around, but it's getting dark and we're off to the palace soon. Tell me, are you tired at all?"

Hap shut his eyes and took a silent inventory of his condition. He was bruised and scraped. The nick on his heel was still tender. His jaw hurt; he suspected he'd been clenching it since the encounter with Occo. But while his muscles could certainly wear down after a while, so far it didn't seem like his mind needed rest. "No. I'm not tired."

Umber's eyes twinkled. "It's been days now. I think it's safe to assume that you simply don't need sleep."

Hap lowered his head. He couldn't even imagine how the urge to sleep would feel. "That isn't normal. Is it?"

"Well . . . no. It's extraordinary. I'm jealous, honestly. I like my sleep, but imagine how much more a person could accomplish if he didn't spend a third of his life in a stupor!" Umber shaded his eyes and looked to the western horizon. "Nearly sunset. Come on, Hap. This is worth a look."

Hap followed Umber to the edge of the terrace, where Oates had just finished playing the tune he'd begun.

"That was a nice song," said Hap.

"Umber gave me the music," said Oates.

"There's a thought, Hap—tell me, did that tune sound familiar?" asked Umber, tapping his fingertips together.

"No, sir," said Hap. "What's it called?"

"It's a movement from something called the *New World Symphony*. By a most excellent composer named Dvořák. Play

some of the other stuff I've given you, Oates. And Hap? Let me know if you hear anything you know."

Hap nodded. Oates shrugged and started a new song.

As Hap listened, he couldn't help but stare down at the water and look for the Creep's ship.

"It's not there, Hap," Umber said. He had a knack for guessing Hap's thoughts. "The guardsmen said the Creep got to his ship and took off in a hurry, without bothering to hoist a sail. The sea horse tows him, apparently. They said not even the *Swift* could have caught him. He was badly injured, you know. Perhaps he's scared off for good or crawled away to die."

Hap doubted that. But he relaxed a little, and tried to appreciate the beauty spread out below. His eyes were drawn to the ancient castle that Sophie had called Petraportus.

The once majestic form had fallen into ruins on the rocky island near the foot of the Aerie. Hap saw a crude breakwater of jumbled stone that spanned the watery gap between the two. A closer look told him what that formation really was: The nearest tower had toppled into the water, forming an accidental bridge. It looked like one could reach it by a narrow staircase that was carved into the Aerie's side.

The great dome of the old keep was half collapsed. Hap saw an old man and woman standing at the foot of the broken walls.

The wind blew the man's gray beard over his shoulder as he threw a weighted net into the bay. *The fisherman and his wife,* Hap recalled. *The only ones crazy enough to live in a crumbling castle.*

"Lord Umber, what happened to that place?" he asked, pointing.

"Petraportus! Where do I begin?" said Umber. "Two centuries ago, a different city stood by this harbor, as grand as Kurahaven is today. The power of that kingdom grew, and the ambitions of the kings swelled with it. They had been traders, but suddenly they decided their goals could be better met through aggression. Their ships of exploration became ships of war, and they sailed out to conquer lands far and wide and bring fortunes back. Eventually they built Petraportus, the wonder of its age, which seemed to rise right out of the sea. In fact, the sea flowed into the domed keep, through a gated arch so wide that ships could sail *inside.* Imagine the splendor! And around the keep stood four enormous towers, one for each point of the compass. Only the west tower remains."

A warm breeze kicked up, bringing with it the salted scent of the Rulian Sea. Umber paused to tilt his head back and sniff.

"What happened to Petraportus?" asked Hap.

"Torn to pieces," Umber replied. "There was an invasion of sea-giants—enormous beings that, legend says, awoke from their slumber in some hidden cavern and marched up from the depths of the sea. They fell upon the city and did what sea-giants do: eat people and steal treasures. Nearly all the buildings where the city now stands were flattened, and most of those who didn't flee were turned into supper. Except for Brinn the Bold, that is. He sat on the throne of Petraportus in those days. History says he was a stubborn man. He probably should have hopped on his fastest ship and sailed away, or taken refuge in the Aerie. But he thought Petraportus was strong enough to keep him and his court safe. Sadly, that was not the case. Brinn's army couldn't hold the monsters off. The sea-giants tore at the walls until the castle began to tumble. The keep caught fire, and Petraportus turned into an inferno. They say Brinn jumped from the west tower, swinging his battle-ax as he fell onto a giant hundreds of feet below."

"Did he die?" Hap asked.

"Not until he landed!" Umber chuckled. "After the fire went out, the giants plundered the castle's treasury. What was left of Petraportus has been in a state of slow collapse ever since. See the tower that's broken off halfway up? That was the south tower, and it fell only five years ago. I've been inside a few times, playing the archaeologist. You can hear the stones shifting when the wind blows hard. I don't go much these days—that old fisherman and his wife prefer to be left alone. But it's quite exhilarating, being in there."

Oates pulled the flute from his lips. "It's quite stupid, being in there. You could get killed."

Umber rolled his eyes. "Thank you as always for your candor, Oates. Play something else now. Have you learned the latest tune I gave you? 'Yesterday'?"

Oates frowned as he concentrated. "You last gave me a tune two weeks ago."

"No, you dolt! The song is called 'Yesterday'."

"Right. Another song from wherever it is you came from."

"Just play the tune, Oates."

Oates grunted, licked his lips, and began a slow, haunting tune. For a moment, Umber's eyes lost focus as his attention drifted to some inward place. Then he blinked and returned to the moment. "Where was I? Oh yes. So, the sea-giants lived in the ruins of the old city. Nobody dared come near the place. The Aerie itself was too strong for the giants to break in, but people were still afraid to stay. All of Kurahaven was deserted for a century or so until the invaders were driven out."

"By who?"

"A sorceress named Turiana. Her powers, and her knowledge of the magical creatures and monsters of the world, were amazing. She had a talisman that allowed her to command the minds of other beings, and she ordered the sea-giants to return to the sea. Just like that, those behemoths waded into the depths and disappeared, and they haven't been seen since. This was still a few centuries ago. Once the sea-giants were gone, Turiana took the Aerie for her home. After a while, people returned—this bay is irresistible to merchants—and the city rose again on top of the ruins. The old line of regents was gone, but a new king from the south of Celador came to rule. That royal line continues to this day."

Hap nodded, soaking up the history. "What happened to the sorceress?"

Umber put his elbows on the wall. "A sad tale. She was a friend to the kingdom for a long time, and even came to the palace once in a while to advise the king. It was always an event when she emerged, because Turiana was more beautiful than you could imagine. Men came to Kurahaven from all around just to get a glimpse of her. But while she would leave the Aerie occasionally, nobody was ever allowed to enter. Over the years she kept to herself more and more, until she was only glimpsed on the roof in the moonlight. Strange things started to happen. Terrible noises came from the Aerie: shrieks, moans, and animal cries. Sometimes a dark cloud hovered over this place when the rest of the sky was clear. And there were rumors of foul creatures that emerged at night and prowled the streets. The city was fine by day, but anyone who wandered outside after sunset was liable to disappear. Even the king's guard wouldn't venture out."

Hap looked down on the vibrant city, imagining a time when everyone bolted their doors at night. "But why? Why did things get so bad, after she did so much good?"

Umber propped his chin on one hand. "I suppose magic is a little bit like invention, Hap. One can dive in with the best intentions, but it's just as easy to get seduced by the sinister possibilities. Take fire, for example. You can harness it in a lantern, a kiln, an oven, or a furnace. Or you can use it to burn a village to the ground.

"Who knows exactly why Turiana went bad? I suppose she opened too many spell books, collected too many wicked talismans, and made contact with too many diabolical beings. I think her intent was to master dark magic and use it for good, the way she saved Kurahaven from the sea-giants. But finally the wicked side beckoned."

Umber took a moment to watch the top of the sun melt behind the craggy western horizon. Oates had finished his song—or let it simply die away—and stared at Umber.

"This is the way things go, Hap," Umber said. "When a weapon is created—whether it's a war machine, or a wicked spell, or some chemical monstrosity—it's bound to go off eventually.

Turiana went off in the worst way. She cast unspeakable spells and murdered anyone who stood in her way. She demanded an enormous tribute of gold and jewels, and threatened to bring greater harm if her demands weren't met. For a while, it looked like Kurahaven might become a ghost city all over again."

"But it didn't?" asked Hap.

"No. Someone showed up and defeated Turiana."

"Who?" asked Hap.

Umber stood up and grabbed the lapels of his vest. "You're looking at him. And as a reward, I was given the Aerie as my home."

"You?" said Hap. "You killed Turiana?"

"Do I strike you as a violent man, Hap? I didn't kill her. I just defanged her."

"But where did she go?"

Umber cleared his throat. "Nowhere, my boy. She's still here."

Hap wobbled where he stood.

"It's true," said Oates.

"Of course it's true," said Umber. "Perhaps you've heard me talk about our 'guest'? That's Turiana. She's in the caverns behind the Aerie. Locked up tight for the good of the kingdom, but treated well enough. But enough history, Hap! The night is here—time to head for the palace."

* * *

Hap followed Umber to the gatehouse. They could have used the smaller exit, but Umber opened the black door, delighted to show off the magic once again. One of the men who always guarded the entrance was holding the carriage door open. With his other arm, he held a squirming black cat with a splash of white on one paw.

"A cat, Dodd?" Umber asked with one eyebrow raised. "You know they aren't welcome here."

"Beg pardon, Lord Umber," Dodd said. The cat dug its back claws into his side, squirmed loose, and ran under the horse. "Ouch! She wandered up this afternoon."

Umber watched the cat slink from sight. "Let's go," he said to Hap, and climbed inside the carriage.

"Isn't Oates coming?" asked Hap. He wasn't sure Oates liked him, but he always felt safer with the big fellow near.

"Bringing Oates to the palace is dicey," replied Umber. "I never know what important person his brutal honesty will offend."

"Or what fine lady will slap him," said Dodd.

"True, true," Umber replied, laughing. "Hap, we'll make do with my private guard: Wilkin, Barkin, and Dodd. As long as they don't mind giving up their card game for a while. That's not a problem, is it, Dodd?"

"Certainly not," said Dodd, the guard holding the door.

"He would say that," said Barkin, who climbed to the driver's bench to take the reins. "Since he always loses."

"Though my sword has some repute, cards were never my strong suit," recited Dodd. A laugh came from the rear of the carriage, where the third guard—Wilkin, Hap deduced—mounted the back of the carriage. Wilkin had dark hair to his shoulders, Barkin's mane was wiry and the color of rust, and Dodd was hairless except for the rectangle on his chin. They bristled with athletic confidence and were well armed, so Hap's mind eased a bit. He heard Barkin call to the horses and snap the reins. The carriage lurched and rolled.

"Oh!" said Umber. As an afterthought, he flashed the black-stoned ring at the door, and uttered a word that Hap knew meant *close*. The black door swung shut and sealed itself tight.

They rattled onto the causeway at a greater speed than any previous trip. Hap clutched a strap that dangled from the ceiling. *They think Occo might attack,* he thought as he rocked from side to side.

"Hap, did I mention that Dodd is a poet?" Umber said. He shouted out the window. "Isn't that right, Dodd?"

Dodd clung to the side of the carriage. He put his face in the window and touched a hand to his forehead, saluting.

"Give him a topic and he'll compose a rhyme on the

spot," Umber said. "Come on, Dodd, what do you have for this occasion?"

Dodd scratched his chin for a moment. Then he began, raising his voice so the others could hear over the clattering wheels:

"Recently our good Lord Umber
Added to the Aerie's number
A fine young chap, a lad named Hap
The green-eyed boy who knows no slumber.

"Now they ride beside the sea
With presents perched on Umber's knee
Off to the palace to drink from the chalice
And meet the royal princes three.

"One prince loves to fill his glass
One we are sure is a snake in the grass
The other royal is steadfast and loyal
But frankly a pain in—"

The recital ended abruptly as they hit a bump in the causeway. Hap popped off of his seat. Umber thumped his head on the roof. "This is bracing!" Umber said, rubbing the top of his skull.

* * *

The road curved with the harbor wall for a while, and then they turned up the long slope that led to the palace. Hap leaned out to watch the great structure growing before his eyes. It was even more beautiful in the dark, with tiny lanterns burning like stars in the highest windows.

They rolled across the wide wooden bridge that spanned a ring of water surrounding the castle walls. "Moats are usually foul, but you could drink from this one," Umber said. "It's fed by the spring at the center of this palace: the Heartspring."

Hap nodded. But even a glimpse of deep water pinched his heart with cold fingers.

The carriage rumbled through a tunnel in the outer wall. They veered onto a paved circle of stone and jerked to a stop. Dodd opened the door. "After you, Hap," Umber said. He handed Hap a colorfully wrapped box. "Carry this for me, would you?"

Hap stepped outside. The hiss of falling water caught his ear, and he saw a fountain in the center of the courtyard. It was three tiers tall and populated with sculptures of sea-creatures that fired jets of water. "Does the Heartspring make that water go too?"

"Right you are," Umber replied.

Around them a parade of carriages disgorged their pas-

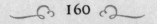

sengers and rumbled away. Hap watched the giddy guests walk toward a tall open door. The men puffed their chests and the women tugged long dresses an inch off the ground. Hap found his head tilting up, up, and up again as his eyes followed the lofty lines of the palace, all the way to the illuminated face of the enormous clock.

"Careful you don't fall over," Umber said, stepping up beside him. "I've seen it happen."

They went past a gauntlet of guards, up a wide set of stairs, and into a room that seemed as broad as the sea. Clusters of flowers hung on strings from the soaring ceiling, with petals fluttering down like snow. The chatter of hundreds of guests filled the air, and a pack of musicians in one corner added sprightly music. Servers buzzed among the crowd like bees with drinks and delicacies.

Umber attracted people the way lanterns drew moths, and soon was busy shaking hands and making conversation. Always he would introduce Hap, and always the person could not avoid staring at Hap's strange green eyes. Hap felt his face turn red. He wished he'd found a way to stay back at the Aerie, or at least that Umber had allowed him to wear his hat.

During a lull in the onslaught of well-wishers, Umber

positioned himself in front of Hap and spoke quietly out of one side of his mouth. "Best behavior now, Hap. You're about to meet one of the princes."

Hap looked over Umber's shoulder and saw a broad-shouldered man approach. The man walked stiffly, hardly moving above the waist. His face was as cold and chiseled as a tombstone, with eyes turned down at the corners. His hair was thinning and tied back from his face, while his eyebrows grew wild. There was a silver cape draped over one of his shoulders.

"Prince Argent! How good to see you." Umber lowered his head, spread his arms, and stuck one leg before him, with the heel on the ground and the toes pointing up. "And may I introduce my young friend, Happenstance?"

Hap performed an awkward copy of Umber's bow. "Good evening, Your Highness," he said. When he looked up again, the prince was staring at his eyes. Argent didn't show surprise or unease like most, and a moment later he turned and spoke to Umber as if Hap were not there.

The prince did not bother with pleasantries. "We have things to discuss, Umber. First, I have reviewed your suggestion for what you call 'fire departments' stationed throughout the city. I think the idea has merit, and would like to see a more detailed proposal. Likewise with your tidal mills; building those on the coastline makes perfect sense."

Umber dipped his forehead. "Absolutely, Your Highness."

"Also, I saw the new device that you sent to the palace. Some sort of press for creating documents?"

"The movable-type printing press, Your Highness," Umber said with an eager smile. "There are only two in the world right now—yours, and the one I will use to reproduce my books. It speeds the production of all manner of printed materials—more than two hundred pages in a single hour!"

Argent's flinty expression never changed. "We are glad to have it for our proclamations. And I have no objection to you using such a thing for those books of yours. But is it true that you plan to make these movable . . . whatever you call them . . . widely available? So that anyone at all might be able to use one?"

"True, Your Highness. It will take time, but a press in every town is my goal. It's for the good of the kingdom, I assure you. Consider what will happen when people throughout your land can share their ideas and—"

Argent abruptly raised a hand. "That is exactly what I am considering. You and I see the world with different eyes, Umber. You seem to think that every man, woman, and child ought to express himself and think freely. But that is not what people really want. They are content to live their humble lives and let the wisdom of kings and princes be their guiding light. Too many ideas flying about will only confuse them. And, incidentally, Umber, those wonderful presses of yours can print foolish and rebellious ideas just as easily as pragmatic and useful ones." The prince's voice had begun to rise, and he paused to temper himself. "I want their production stopped at once."

Umber tried to maintain his smile, but he looked as if he'd taken a bite of something foul. "But really, Your Highness—"

"Another thing, Umber," interrupted the prince. "Many months ago, my father asked you for suggestions to improve the kingdom's defenses. We are still waiting for your response."

Umber tugged at his collar. "I apologize, Your Highness. Unfortunately my talents don't lie in the military direction."

"Be careful that you don't lie in *any* direction," Argent said, as his expression darkened. "Come now, Umber. Don't pretend there are limits to your inventiveness. Surely you know how to improve the reach of our catapults, the strength of our swords, the flight of our arrows. Don't you care to ensure the safety of the nation that you've worked so hard to enrich?"

The thought made Umber's mouth cinch tight. "My prince," he replied, putting a hand over his heart. "Shouldn't ingenuity be spent on higher purposes than a better way to maim or kill a man?"

"Not if that prevents the death of one of *my* people," Argent said. He thrust his jaw forward. "We've allowed many of your innovations, Umber, and we are a stronger, happier kingdom for it. But there are rivals and warlords that look upon our prosperity with jealous hearts. And you are partly responsible, because all the good you've done has in fact made us a target. So the 'military direction' matters. I hope one day you will see the truth of that."

There was a cascade of laughter nearby. Argent suddenly remembered that he was at a party. "One last thing, Umber," the prince said, tugging at his clothes to straighten them. "Regarding this afternoon's incident in the market: I hope this isn't another case of you stirring up magical things that are best left alone." He glanced in Hap's direction, and Hap gulped by reflex.

"I apologize for the mayhem, Your Highness," Umber said.

Argent replied with a single rapid nod, and strode stiffly away.

Umber seemed to exhale for a full minute. Hap heard him mutter something that he probably meant to think to himself. "Slow down, Umber. You're pushing too far, too fast, and it scares them." Umber looked around as if coming out of a daydream and shrugged toward Hap. "Don't get the wrong idea, Happenstance. Prince Argent isn't a bad fellow. He can be reasoned with, and he honestly cares about his people. But he lacks imagination. Trust me, though, there could be a worse successor to the king."

"Is the king here tonight?" asked Hap.

"The king is very ill," Umber replied. He scanned the crowd and scowled. "Where's that waiter with the little sausages? I kept trying to wave him over. . . ."

Hap noticed a man on the other side of the room who glanced Umber's way every few moments. *Another prince?* Hap wondered. This fellow looked like a better groomed version of Prince Argent, with eyes and hair of chestnut brown. He wore a narrow crown with an emerald in its center, and a short green cape held by a golden clasp at his throat.

"Is that Prince Galbus by the fountain?" asked Hap.

When Umber looked that way, the man nodded. Umber smiled in return, but his mouth fell flat when he turned back to Hap. "No. That is Loden, the youngest prince. Third in line from the throne, and we should all be thankful for that."

"Why?" Hap asked, watching Prince Loden talk to a circle of admirers.

Umber whispered his reply. "Loden is a cunning, ambitious schemer with no scruples to speak of. But few people realize it because he is also endlessly charming. I intend to keep you as far from him as possible."

"Oh," said Hap. It was hard to imagine that the handsome man across the room was as bad as Umber believed. "Well, what is Prince Galbus like?"

A blast of horns dulled the chatter and laughter of the guests. All heads turned toward the musicians with their trumpets angled high. When the fanfare ended, a giddy fellow in garish clothes parted some nearby curtains and pranced into the hall. In one hand was a bowl-size goblet filled with red wine sloshing over the rim. He raised it to his lips and guzzled while applause erupted among the guests, and they began to shout his name: "Galbus! Galbus!"

The middle prince did a jig that caused his crown to fall off, and then stopped and raised the goblet high. He wobbled as he waited for the applause and laughter to fade, and finally spoke in a loud, unsteady voice. "My friends, my friends! Welcome and thank you for joining my celebration!"

Galbus was paler, blonder, and thinner than his brothers, and more boyish, with large eyes and red cheeks. Something about his manner—and the dark wine-stains all over his shirt and trousers—gave Hap the impression that Galbus was liable to say something outrageous.

"Before I begin to accept your presents—and you know

how I love presents!—I would like to show you the gift I've.
gotten for myself." A mischievous grin spread over Galbus's
face. The guests chuckled, and a breathless expectation filled
the room. Hap saw Argent staring woodenly with his arms
folded across his chest.

Galbus hiccupped, staggered, and went on. "I said to myself:
'Myself, there is something your brothers have that you do
not!' And do you know what that is?"

"Oh dear, what's he up to now?" Umber said quietly, barely
moving his lips.

Galbus put a cupped hand beside his ear. "I said, people, do
you know what that is?"

The guests shouted back. "No! Tell us, Your Highness!
What is it?"

Galbus stumbled back, nearly falling. He heaved a dramatic
sigh of relief. "My brothers have little armies all their own
to keep their royal persons safe, and I do not! And so, I am
proud to introduce my new royal guard!" He swept his hand
toward the curtain at his back, which was yanked aside by an
accomplice. From the corridor behind it raced two dozen pigs,
all dressed in miniature versions of the uniforms that Argent
and Loden's guards wore, but with yellow capes. The pigs
dashed into the crowd, squealing and slipping on the marble
floor of the hall. The walls shook with the laughter of the

guests, and Galbus roared with such gusto that he fell to his knees and his side, somehow managing not to spill the rest of his wine. In the chaos, Hap saw Prince Argent turn away in disgust and leave the room.

The party returned to some normalcy once the swine had been herded from the hall. Galbus gleefully accepted present after present, admiring each before handing it to a servant to whisk away. Finally the young prince spotted Umber across the room, and his mouth opened with delight. He raced over, careening off other guests along the way.

"Umber, dearest Umber!" he cried when he arrived, out of breath and with his crown askew. "I'm so glad you're here, it wouldn't have been a party without you!"

Umber repeated his formal bow. "Happy birthday, Your Highness. And may I introduce—"

"And look at *you*!" interrupted Galbus, grabbing Hap by the shoulders. "My stars, look at those eyes! You're the boy everyone's talking about!"

"I . . . I guess," Hap said, wishing he'd left with the pigs.

Galbus's breath smelled like wine. "Is it true that you can leap so high? I beg you, show me! Show us all!"

"Your Highness," Umber said quickly, "what Hap did was out of panic, and he certainly could not reproduce the feat.

Now, if I may—will you accept the first gift I've arranged for you this evening?"

"Of course!" cried Galbus, releasing Hap and clasping his hands together.

Umber looked at the musicians at the far end of the room. The conductor had been waiting expectantly for a signal that Umber finally provided: a tap of his nose with two fingers. The conductor nodded, suppressing a smile. He called out to the guests. "A gift for his majesty Prince Galbus: *new music!*" As the people rushed to complete their conversations, the conductor faced his musicians and lifted his arms. He stirred the air with his hands, the last whispers fell to silence, and the music began.

A cello spoke first, beginning so simply that some in the crowd gave one another secret shrugs as if to say "Is that all?" Then violins joined in, echoing the graceful tune. Hap saw heads turn so their ears might better receive the sound. The song grew in complexity and majesty, with the crowd so still that a painter might have set up his easel and captured the scene. Hap looked at Galbus, who stood with his hands pressed over his heart as if to keep it from dissolving. A truth occurred to him: Music was a kind of magic, capable of weaving a powerful spell.

Umber leaned near Hap's ear and said quietly: "Would you

believe that where I came from, this piece was so familiar that many found it trite?"

Just when the music reached the peak of its intricate beauty, the tune settled down again like birds drifting off to sleep. Each instrument fell still in turn. The final note left behind a hush so profound that not a breath could be heard.

It was so quiet for so long that the conductor glanced nervously over his shoulder, wondering if somehow they had failed to please. But every guest was smiling toward Galbus, who stood in a daze. The prince came out of his rapture with a gasp for air. He pried his hands apart and applauded madly, and the rest joined him until the claps and shouts built to a thunderous roar.

"Umber! Umber!" Galbus cried, seizing Umber's hand and shaking his arm from wrist to shoulder. "The finest yet! Magnificent!"

"I dedicate that to you, my good prince, and while the composer is long gone, I'm sure he would be pleased that it found such a happy new audience," Umber said.

"What is this piece? And who was this composer? I have to know his name!"

"That was the Canon in D Major, Your Highness. And the name you seek is Johann Pachelbel." Umber waved to the conductor, and the musicians resumed the livelier waltz they'd played before. "I have one more gift for you, my friend. Will you have it now?"

Galbus's eyes grew huge as his gaze found the gift that Hap was holding. The prince snatched the present and tore off the paper. There was a hinged box inside; he threw the latch and opened it. Hap recognized it as the same box that someone had handed Umber when they first arrived in Kurahaven, with the same long-necked orange bottle nested inside. Galbus giggled as he pulled the bottle from the straw. "Is this what I think it is?"

Umber nodded. "It is indeed. The effect will be delightful, but I recommend you use it *outside*, Your Highness. In fact, I strongly advise it."

"Have no fear!" Galbus said, holding the bottle high. A trio of laughing women rushed up and tugged at Galbus's arms, urging him to dance. "Duty calls, Umber!" Galbus cried, stuffing the gift inside his vest. He grinned at Hap. "But you, young man, I hope to see you soon. A visit must be arranged! I'll show you the gardens, and the Heartspring, and the guts of the great clock that Umber designed for us! Would you like that?"

"Um . . . yes, Your Highness."

"Then it shall be done!" Galbus giggled as the ladies dragged him into the crowd of dancers. For the moment, Hap and Umber stood alone.

"We should leave before long, Hap," Umber said. "There's still time for the hypnosis. The sooner we try that the better, I think. With luck your memory will return tonight."

Hap nodded. He'd met enough new people for one day.

There was a thunderous explosion among the dancers, and a yellow cloud billowed toward the ceiling. People squealed like children and ran from a central spot on the floor, except for a few who fainted. As the crowd parted, Hap saw Galbus, bent over and clutching his stomach, howling with glee. Around him, phantom serpents made of smoke wriggled toward the fleeing guests. The illusion did not last long; the serpents were already losing their shape and dissipating.

Umber groaned. "In fact, we should leave right now."

"Not an entirely successful evening," Umber said, raising his voice over the clatter of the wheels. He pulled his leather-clad notebook from his pocket. "Better make a note about the printing presses. Wouldn't want a furious royalty on my hands."

"Did it bother you, what Prince Argent said about your presses?" asked Hap.

Umber's eyebrows writhed as he considered the question, and then he grinned. "Not terribly. There's one thing the good prince doesn't understand: Once an idea is out and about, it can't be called back, silenced, or erased. You can't contain it, any more than you could put the head of a dandelion back together after the wind has scattered its seeds. People have *seen* the movable-type printing press now, in my print shop and in the palace. They know such a thing is possible. That makes it inevitable. And that is all that matters."

CHAPTER
14

"I think we'll attempt it right here,"
Umber said. "It's such a peaceful spot. Sit, Hap."

They were back on the terrace atop the Aerie, under the
tree of many fruits. Oates was with them for safekeeping, but
Umber asked the big fellow to give them privacy, so he leaned
against the balcony, out of earshot.

Warm air billowed, and hanging chimes played random
melodies. The stars blazed with diamond brilliance overhead,
though fingers of dark cloud had begun to reach across the sky
from the north. Hap lay on the bench with his head propped
on a pillow, and Umber sat on a stool beside him.

"Will this really help me remember?" Hap asked.

"It might," Umber said. "Mind you, I've never tried it before."

"Then how do you know what to do?"

Umber tugged at his nose. "I, er, did some research." He quickly diverted the conversation. "But if this fails, we have other options. We'll go ask Smudge, our archivist, what he might know about you." Hap frowned, remembering the wild man who'd thrown rotten fruit at him and Lady Truden.

"And if that yields nothing," Umber said, "there's someone else we can talk to. But since we both need to stay relaxed right now, I'll say no more about that." He rubbed his hands together. "Let's begin, Hap. First, close your eyes and make yourself as comfortable as you can. Good. Now take a deep breath. The deepest you've ever taken. Hold it for a moment, and let it out slowly."

Hap shut his eyes. His chest rose as he filled it with air.

Umber dropped his voice to a slow, soothing hush. "Very nice. Again, Hap, but breathe with your mouth this time . . . yes. Much better. We'll do ten more, and I'll count with you. One. Two. Three. Four . . ."

Umber kept counting, and Hap kept breathing deeply. Umber told Hap to relax his body muscle by muscle, from his fingers to his shoulders, from his toes to his hips, from his head to his waist. From the moment he'd awoken in Alzumar, Hap had been unsettled, endangered, and hopelessly lost; but now he felt like a rope tied with a thousand knots slipping loose.

Umber whispered, suggesting images that came to life in Hap's mind. Hap walked down imaginary stairs, feeling more at ease with each step down. He envisioned a cask filled with all his concerns, and the spigot opened up and the worries drained away. He pictured a shining candle in a dark room and pretended that nothing else existed. The world faded away. The lids of his eyes seemed to flutter on their own. *Is this what sleep is like?* he wondered.

Umber told Hap his right arm was as weightless as a feather—so light that it would begin to rise. And it did, floating up at Hap's side, until Umber told him to let it fall.

"Wonderful," Umber whispered. Then he asked Hap to remember. He took him back in time.

Remember sailing into Kurahaven.

Remember riding the leviathan barge, and the smell of spices inside.

Remember standing on the beach, watching Mount Ignis erupt. Do you remember?

"Yes." Hap sighed. "I remember."

Now imagine that you take a step backward, and it brings you farther back in time. Remember how we ran through the dark streets of Alzumar. Are you there? Do you remember?

"Yes." Hap remembered it with perfect clarity, down to the clatter of claws as the tyrant worm pursued them. His nose was stung again by volcanic fumes.

Now step farther back. You're in the room where we found you. Right before we found you. Do you remember?

"Yes."

Tell me about it.

"I'm on my back. My cloak feels damp. The stone is warm. I have a cloth over my eyes. A man is with me. I don't know who he is."

Step back again, to the first moment you can remember. The instant you became aware.

"I . . . I open my eyes. I can't see." Hap felt a tiny shiver, deep inside his chest.

Hap. Listen carefully now, and concentrate. I want you to go farther. Before that moment.

Hap groaned.

Focus, Hap. Just step back a little farther in time. An instant before you opened your eyes. What's happening?

Hap gritted his teeth and concentrated. "I . . . wait. Something. It's strange. I still can't see. But someone is holding me. Carrying me."

Who? Is it the same man?

"I . . . I think so. It's him. It's WN."

Where are you?

"I don't know . . . I can't tell. It's strange . . . I'm nowhere."

Nowhere? Umber paused. *What's happening?*

"I think . . . I think we're moving somehow."

How? On a boat? Are you walking? Is he carrying you?

"He's carrying me. But I don't think he's walking. I can't tell!" There was a hitch in his breath.

It's all right, Hap. Don't be afraid. Can you tell me anything else? Do you hear anything, see anything?

Hap shook his head.

Try to go back a little more. Before the man was carrying you.

Hap's face twitched. "It's hard . . ."

Try, Hap. Just one more step. Try.

Hap forced his mind to push back. But it was moving into a fierce wind. With his fists clenched, he tried again.

His back met something hard, smooth and cold, and a chill ran through his bones. A gathering fear urged him to snap out of this trance, but he fought the instinct, sensing that the answer to the mystery was near. He turned around. "There's something in my way. Like a wall."

What kind of wall? There was a new trace of excitement in Umber's hushed voice.

Hap put his palms against the barrier. "It's cold. Like ice, or glass." He stared into it. It was murky gray, with tiny lines and bubbles trapped inside. He looked right and left, and the wall disappeared both ways, into a darkness that even his nocturnal eyesight couldn't penetrate. Some dim instinct told him to follow the wall to his left, and so he walked sideways, keeping his hands on the frigid surface. Before long he came upon a strange pattern in the wall: a series of concentric, imperfect circles, almost like the lines that would form if he dropped a stone in still water. The wall seemed thinner here. He could almost see through it.

What's happening now? What do you see?

"There's something on the other side of the wall. It's dark and blurry. . . . It looks like someone waving his arms."

I don't think the wall is real, Hap. It's there to keep you from remembering what came before. Perhaps you put it there, or someone else did. But you have to get past it if you want to know.

"I can't," Hap said. Something rolled down the side of his face. It could have been a drop of sweat or a tear. He felt Umber's hand close on his shaking wrist.

You can. Imagine the wall breaking. Make it happen. Start with a tiny crack, and make it grow. You are in control, Hap. Nobody has the right to wall your memories away.

Hap drew in a great breath and held it. He put his nose near the wall and focused all his will on the distorted circle at the center of the rings, ignoring the dark blurry shape on the other side that frantically waved. "Break," he said. He put his hands on either side of the circle and pushed.

There was a sound in his mind: *Tik. Tik.* A flaw appeared in the middle of the circle, and it turned into a crack, bending as it spread in a jagged path. The cold stung his hands, but he ignored the pain and kept pushing. His arms trembled, and the cold spread through his wrists and past his elbows.

Hap. Your arm is getting cold. I think—

"Wait! It's working," said Hap through chattering teeth. The crack spread, and the sound grew louder: *TIK. TIK.* The single jagged line spawned a dozen more, radiating outward.

Umber seized Hap's shoulders. Hap could barely feel it, because his arms had gone numb as the cold swept past them and surrounded his heart.

Hap, come out of it. When I count to three, you will wake up!

"Wait!" cried Hap. "It's going to—"

One! Two!

The wall shattered.

CHAPTER
15

Hap didn't know how long he'd been screaming. Long enough for his throat to feel like it was on fire.

A pure and total terror had flooded every pore of his body. It was blinding, deafening, overwhelming. His arms thrashed. His legs kicked. His head jerked.

Powerful arms clutched him around the waist. Umber's voice finally penetrated his consciousness, slipping in between his screams. "Happenstance! Look at us! *Open your eyes!*" When he heard the word *eyes*, Hap realized that his were closed. His lids sprang open, and he saw where he was: still on the terrace of the Aerie. But he wasn't under the fruit tree now—he was straddling the balcony, with one foot dangling over the edge. When he saw the sheer drop below, his screams took on a higher pitch.

"Stop shouting! It's annoying!" bellowed another voice into his ear. It was Oates, who held him from behind. Hap screamed three more times: *Aaah! Aaah! Aaah!* Then he screamed noiselessly until the need for air made him gasp for breath. His arms and legs went limp, and Oates hoisted him up and cradled him in his arms.

"You almost jumped, you idiot," said Oates. "I caught you by the heel."

Hap wanted to say he was sorry, but he couldn't speak yet. Oates carried him back to the bench, where Hap drew his knees to his chest and squeezed them. Umber sat beside him, looking white in the face. He fanned himself with one hand and forced a chuckle. "Didn't expect *that.*"

Hap covered his face with his palms and wept. Umber patted his knee. "There now, Hap. I'm sorry I brought that on. Take your time answering, but . . . did you learn anything?"

Hap choked out a reply. "It was just . . . fear. And darkness, and terrible cold. It was almost like . . ." He clenched his teeth.

Umber spoke in a hush. "What, Hap? Tell me."

Hap gulped. *"Drowning."* He shivered again. "The way water scares me . . . this was like that, but a thousand times worse." He wrapped his arms around himself. It felt as if slivers of ice were running through his veins, piercing him from the inside. "But I'll never do that again. If that's what sleep is like, I'm glad I don't sleep. And I'm glad I don't dream."

An hour later, Hap was back in the tiny room he'd chosen for his own, lying on his bed under a heavy pile of blankets. The glass windows were swung shut and a dozen candles blazed on the wide sills, filling the room with warm light.

"Cozy," Umber said. "I like this place, Hap. You chose well." He sat on a wooden rocking chair that he'd dragged in from another room. It creaked as he eased it back and forth.

Hap sat with his back against the wall. He stared at his hands to see if they'd stopped shaking.

"Feeling better?" Umber asked, still rocking.

Hap nodded. He rubbed a hand under his nose.

"Anything else bothering you?"

Where do I start? Hap thought. The hypnosis had been a disaster. He was still a blank slate, with most of his mysteries intact. He ached to know what the rest of the note said, but it was clear that Umber would reveal its contents only when he was ready. Hap wondered what he could ask to tease out some answers. "I just . . . I don't know what I'm doing here. I don't know what you want from me."

The rocking chair poised in a forward lean. Umber put

his elbows on his knees and made a steeple of his fingers. "Happenstance. Honestly, I don't know what you're here for either. As for what I want—well, all I ask is that you consider this your home, and me your friend. Also, you need to come with me when I want to take you somewhere."

"Because that's what the note says you should do."

"What makes you think that?" Umber asked as he narrowed his eyes and stared at Hap without blinking.

Hap's stomach soured. He opened his mouth to reply, but was saved by a gentle knock on his door. He sat a little straighter when he saw Sophie peering in. She had a basket in the crook of her damaged arm.

"Sophie, dear," Umber said. "Come in."

She stepped inside, keeping her dark eyes cast down.

Umber stood. "How goes the artwork, Sophie?"

"Pretty well, Lord Umber," Sophie told the floor.

"Much better than that, I'm sure," Umber said. "Show Hap what you've brought."

Sophie offered the basket to Hap without looking at him. Hap set it on his lap. It held a half-dozen books bound in leather. Hap read the gold-foiled words on the cover of the topmost volume:

The Books of Umber:

The Rise, Fall, and Rebirth of Kurahaven

"These books are my passion, you know," Umber said. "Here are just a few; there are more in my archives downstairs. This world is filled with amazing creatures and strange histories, Hap. I explore them and chronicle them in these volumes. One day I'll share them all with the world. But for now, they can keep you occupied while the rest of us sleep. Who knows? Maybe you'll find something to prod your memory."

"That would be nice," Hap said.

Umber smiled. "Imagine not needing sleep. You could read all night, every night. I envy you, Hap; all those extra hours to stuff your brain. As for me, I can barely keep my eyes open another minute. Spend the night however you wish. You're safe as long as you stay inside. Good night, young friend."

"Good night, Hap," Sophie whispered, backing out of the room.

"Good night," said Hap.

Umber paused in the doorway. "By the way, Hap, we still have men waiting by the docks to see if Occo turns up at midnight. The trap is set, but I doubt our wounded friend will show."

Hap listened to the Aerie settling down for the night. Umber's steps rose in pitch as he ascended the stairs to his rooftop tower. A door closed somewhere down the hall—Sophie's room, Hap figured. He heard Balfour tell Oates to sleep well. Then it was quiet again, except for the waves scrubbing the foot of the Aerie hundreds of feet below his window. He looked at the other titles in the basket:

The Books of Umber: Origins of the Aerie
The Books of Umber: A History of the Dwergh
The Books of Umber: The Attack on Petraportus
The Books of Umber: The Beanstalk and
Other Londrian Wonders

At the bottom was a volume called *The Books of Umber: Magical Denizens of Celador*. It seemed like a good place to start; he hoped it might say something about green-eyed, far-leaping, never-sleeping people. He opened the book and propped it across his thighs. But when a sharp voice came through his partly open door and startled him, the volume tumbled off and hit the floor with a *whack*.

"Master Happenstance." It was Lady Truden. She pushed the door open and glared at the fallen book. "Those books are precious things. Please treat them with care. How did you get them?"

"Lord Umber had them brought to me," Hap replied, hating the way his voice squeaked.

She turned her head and stared with one narrowed eye. "Did he. And are you only looking at the pictures?"

"What? No, I'm going to read it," Hap said. He picked the book off the floor and wiped the leather cover with his sleeve.

"Is that so?" Lady Tru said, as if doubting that he could read. She folded her arms and leaned against the door frame. "I have heard you never sleep. Surely that isn't true?"

Hap felt his face redden. "It is, my lady."

That answer did not seem to please her. "How *peculiar*," she said. "Well . . . did Lord Umber tell you what is permissible and what is not?"

"No, Lady Truden."

"It probably slipped his mind. But as the one who brings order to this house, may I suggest some guidelines?"

Hap bit his bottom lip. "Of course."

"I think it best that, as a stranger and guest, you stay in your room while the rest of us sleep like normal folk. The Aerie is not a fairground, young man. Unless Lord Umber has explicitly granted you free reign, you might as well remain in here. Do we understand each other?"

Hap understood at least one thing: Lady Truden didn't like him very much, or appreciate his presence. He looked toward the windows. "Yes, my lady."

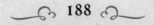

She didn't say anything else. She closed the door behind her, pushing until it latched, and was gone. If she could have chained and barred it, Hap supposed she would have. He heard her steps move briskly away until another door closed down the hall.

After a heavy breath, he started to read.

Encounters have been reported in the sprawling and largely unexplored forest at the heart of Celador. In addition to the notorious witch who once resided near the southern edge by the village of Waldrand, there are tales of animals gifted with human speech and mannerisms, including bears, birds, wolves, and swine. Whether these are beasts under a spell that grants them human intelligence, or human beings under a spell that gives them animal form, is a matter of

CHAPTER
16

Hap sat by his window with the book in his lap, staring at the docks. It was nearly an hour since the clock on the palace tower rang twelve times. His keen eyes saw a lone man pacing on the wooden planks, and from this lofty vantage he also glimpsed more soldiers hiding on the decks of the ships.

He wasn't sure what he wanted to see happen. If Occo fell into this trap, he feared someone might die trying to capture him. Perhaps it was better that the Creep didn't appear. Then Hap could try to believe that his pursuer was gone for good.

As time passed and it seemed less likely that anything would happen, Lady Truden's words began to gnaw at his thoughts. He wondered what he'd done to earn such disdain. Sure, he'd leaped up to Umber's window. But Umber had understood. Why couldn't she? Besides, this was Umber's house. Umber never gave the impression that Hap should be a prisoner while everyone slept. Lady Truden had drawn that conclusion herself.

Hap drummed the leather-bound book with his fingers and whistled out a long, slow breath. "*The Books of Umber*," he said aloud. He wondered if Umber was even now writing a new volume about his latest discovery, a certain green-eyed boy. Hap could just imagine the words: *The boy never sleeps. . . . He can see in the dark. . . . He is capable of great leaps. . . .*

He grunted and slapped the book against his thigh, and looked at the room he'd chosen for his own. With fresh eyes, he noticed the tiny dimensions and the bars on the windows. Suddenly it seemed like a cage, and he felt like a specimen being held for further study. His skin twitched at the notion.

I have to get out for a while, he thought. Nothing was going to happen at the docks, he was sure. And besides, it would be nice to look over the artifacts downstairs. The others didn't have to know; he would do it all in the dark. But when he tried to stand up, he realized that something was wrong.

A deathly cold flooded every corner of his body. His legs and arms stiffened like rusted metal. He flexed his fingers, but even those were hard to bend. *What's the matter with me?* He tried to call out, but his jaw was frozen. All he could do was whine. A terrible thought raged in his mind: *This is death*. Or perhaps a taste of what death was like.

The chills lasted only a minute or two, and then a feverish heat came in its place. It started in his eyes, filled his skull with hot coals, and piped molten lead into his bones. Beads of sweat erupted from every pore of his body. For a moment, the air shimmered around him.

But at least he could move his limbs again—the frozen sensation had melted away. He flexed every joint to make sure. "What was *that*?" he asked himself aloud, and realized that he could speak once more as well.

The fever was gone, leaving his clothes drenched with sweat. He pulled them off and slipped on a simple nightshirt that Umber had left for him. As he stuck his head through the neck-hole and pulled the shirt across his body, he saw something strange in the air.

At first he thought it was a length of spider-silk, floating sideways in the middle of his room. It was directly in front of him, with the near end at his chest and the far end at his door. He leaned over and blew on it, but the thread didn't move. With his brow furrowed, he reached out with a finger. "What?" he said, as his finger passed through the thread without disturbing it. When he looked closely, he could see pulses of colored light moving within the strand. He let the thread pass through his palm, and thought he could faintly hear something: a whispering voice or distant music.

Hap's hands shook. He choked out a quiet, bewildered laugh, wondering what this apparition could be. Was something making it happen, or was it happening because of him? Did it end at his chest, or begin there? His brain buzzed as he recalled the words in the note: . . . *you will observe certain skills arising.*

He followed the thread, intending to walk beside it, but a strange thing happened: It drifted sideways across the room until it pointed to his chest again. He shuffled sideways and the thread moved with him.

Shaking his head, he followed the thread to where it ended on the surface of the closed door. *Or is that really the end?* he wondered. He turned the knob and eased the door open. The hinges made only the slightest squeak. The thread emerged on the other side and drifted to the far end of the corridor, as far as Hap could tell. When he stepped out and turned to close his door, he noticed another remarkable thing: The thread was vanishing behind him as he followed it.

I have to see where it goes, he thought. But curious as he was, he didn't want to get caught breaking one of Lady Truden's rules. He would have to pass her door along the way. *But it's dark, and she won't be able to see me. I hope.*

Hap eased his door shut and padded barefoot down the hall. He stayed on the narrow woolen carpet to soften his steps.

The door to Lady Truden's room was an inch ajar. Hap peered through the gap to make sure she wasn't lurking. He was relieved to see that her side was turned to him as she sat on the edge of her bed. She was holding a painting that wasn't much bigger than her hand. It was a remarkably accurate portrait of Umber. *Something Sophie painted?* Hap wondered. Lady Truden's free hand came up, and she brushed the backs of her fingers across the painted face. Her shoulders heaved, and Hap heard a heavy sigh.

Hap cringed. He didn't know what was worse: the shame of witnessing such a private moment, or the fear of being caught spying. With his breath held to keep the smallest sound from betraying him, he moved past the door.

The thread dipped into the arched opening of the staircase. He stepped off the carpet and moved cautiously down the stairs, feeling cold stone under his feet. As his gifted eyes pierced the darkness, he wondered what it was like for the others, who always needed a candle or lantern to find their way so they didn't blunder into a wall or tumble down stairs.

The steps curled smoothly to the left, and the thread spiraled with them. *It's leading me,* he thought, and the notion made him stop and bite his lip. He wondered if this could be a trap of some kind—if the thread would lure him outside, to where Occo the Creep was waiting to pounce. But when he touched the thread again and heard those distant sounds, he dismissed the idea. *No,* some instinct told him. *This has nothing to do with the Creep. But where is it taking me?*

Hap approached the landing slowly. He edged his head around the final curve. No lanterns burned in the grand hall, but there was a tiny source of light coming from somewhere. He leaned out a little farther.

Next to the hearth, the wall was riddled with fractures. One of those cracks widened at the floor, where a dim glow shined from within. The thread floated across the room, directly toward that crack. *Strange,* thought Hap. He thought he saw a small dark shape move across the glow.

Hap squinted to sharpen his sight as he traced the thread's path. But as he watched, it flickered and vanished. Hap reached for the space where it had hung. He felt and heard nothing. *What just happened?*

Something caught his eye from the other side of the room. A small form, sleek and short-legged, scurried from under a bureau. *The rat,* Hap thought, remembering how Umber released it when they arrived.

The rat craned its neck left and right, pulling its lips back to bare slats of yellow tooth. It moved across the floor in furtive bursts, wriggling its nose before advancing again. The rat saw a crust of bread on the floor and it scuttled over and seized the morsel between its jaws.

The yellow glow in the crack dimmed again, as if something had stepped before it. *Another rat?* wondered Hap. He edged his head a little farther from the stairs to watch. The rat was cramming the bread into its cheeks. It turned to keep an eye on the larger expanse of the room. Hap stopped breathing when he saw a tiny silver point emerge from the crack, a few inches off the ground. As the point eased silently out, he saw that it was a kind of spear. And it was being held over the shoulder of a man.

A man no bigger than a mouse.

Hap covered his mouth with his hand. He watched as the miniature man crept toward the rat.

The bread wasn't left there by accident, thought Hap. *It was put there for bait. And Umber brought the rat here so it could be hunted!*

Some keen sense alerted the rodent to the attack. It craned its neck and spotted its stalker. But before the rat could even poise to run, the spear flew and sunk into its shoulder. The rat squealed, spun, and writhed. It seized the spear in its jaws and plucked it out. With a hiss, it ran back toward the bureau. But its first steps were clumsy, and it slowed to a crawl. The tiny man retrieved the spear and jogged after his prey.

The hunt ended quickly. After two more thrusts of the spear, the rat fell onto its side. The hunter drew a knife from his belt, circled the rat, and crouched behind its neck. Hap closed his eyes for a moment, not wanting to see the fatal slice. When he opened them again he saw the hunter step back, away from the dark spreading pool, and wipe the blade on his thigh as he waited for death to take the rat.

Hap took a closer look, thankful for the sharpness of his vision. The little man was dressed in a leathery coat with a furry collar that looked like the hair of the rat he'd slain. His leggings were black and velvety—moleskin, Hap figured. He had sandals on his feet, and a broad belt at his waist.

The rat twitched one last time, and the hunter prodded it with the spear to make certain it was dead. When it didn't move, he plunged the spear into its side, spat on his hands and rubbed them together, seized the hairless tail with two fists, and dragged his kill toward the dimly lit crack.

Hap saw the cat too late to prevent the attack. A flick of her tail finally caught his attention. It was the black cat that had squirmed out of Dodd's grip earlier that evening. *She must have slipped inside before Umber closed the door,* Hap thought. And while Hap had watched the rat meet its doom, the cat had waited for her turn to kill. She was poised with her chin low and haunches high, on a long shelf above the hearth.

"Look out!" Hap cried as the cat leaped.

The tiny man's head turned toward Hap, and then upward as he sensed the attack from above. He rolled to one side as the cat landed. As he sprang back to his feet, a black paw lashed out. The edge of one claw caught in his shirt and spun him. He pulled the knife from his belt, but another swat of the paw sent the knife flying. The little man grunted and clutched his wrist. The paw swiped again and sent him sprawling. The cat's mouth came down on his shoulder, and her ears went flat as the jaws squeezed.

It all happened in the time it took Hap to cover the distance. He seized the cat by the loose skin on the back of her neck. "Let him go!"

The cat growled in protest and glared at Hap. She brought her back claws up to rake at the little man's gut.

"No!" shouted Hap. He lifted the cat by the scruff of her neck, and the man with her. There was a table nearby, and he carried the cat there and lowered her head to the surface so the little fellow wouldn't fall to his death. "Drop him!" He pushed his thumb into the corner of the cat's mouth and pried the jaws open. The hunter gasped and fell onto the tabletop, pressing a hand on the spot where the jaws had clamped. Hap let the cat go, and she slunk away with her belly scraping the ground, heading for the stairs.

"Are you hurt?" Hap asked. He kept his voice low because he thought it might hurt those tiny ears.

The little man pushed himself to his knees. His chest heaved, and he prodded himself on the shoulders and ribs, searching for wounds. "Go away," he said. The voice was faint, like someone speaking from a distance, but deeper than Hap expected.

"But . . . are you bleeding?" Hap brought his face as close as he dared to the tiny form. He could scarcely believe what he was seeing. It was a perfect reproduction of a man, down to the delicate fingers and the long, fine, straw-colored hair on his head. The leathery coat was thick; it might have kept the cat's teeth from piercing the skin.

The man glared at Hap with his lips pressed together. He stood and straightened himself to his full height. *Three inches, maybe four,* Hap thought.

"Leave me alone," the fellow said, bunching his hands into pea-size fists.

"But . . . ," Hap sputtered. "How will you get down from the table? Let me help you."

The fellow walked to the edge and stared at a floor that must have seemed a hundred feet down. "I'll manage."

No words occurred to Hap. He kept gaping.

"How can you see me, anyway?" the little man snapped. "It's dark. I can hardly see you at all."

"My eyes . . . they're not like most people's eyes."

The hunter cocked his head to one side and squinted. "No. They ain't." He folded his arms across his chest. "You're the green-eyed boy. I've seen you around."

"My name is Happenstance."

"I've *heard* them use your name. I ain't deaf. Well, Happenstance, you're supposed to leave me alone. *Everyone* is. That's the agreement."

"Agreement?" Hap said, blinking.

"Umber's and mine," the little man said. "The big folk leave me alone, and I don't hurt nobody."

Hap started to smile but quickly suppressed it. "But how could you hurt—"

"Deadly spears and arrows, that's how," said the hunter, jabbing a finger in Hap's direction. "Tipped with spider's poison. I don't have any with me, lucky for you, or you'd be screamin' in pain right now. Now get out of my sight!"

Hap took a step back and raised his hands. "Are you sure I can't . . . ?"

The little man rolled his shoulder back and forth, loosening the muscles. His tiny jaw ground from side to side. "Where's that filthy cat?"

"I think it went upstairs. It could be hiding, though."

The little man spat and wiped his sleeve across his mouth. "Fine. I'll allow you to help me down."

Feeling a little giddy at the opportunity to hold the little man, Hap put his cupped palms on the table. The hunter stared at the hands with his lip curled up on one side. He walked past them and jumped onto Hap's forearm instead, straddling the wrist and gripping the sleeve tight. "Go on."

Hap lifted his arm gingerly off the table. With his knees slightly bent, he started to walk toward the crack in the wall in slow, smooth steps.

The little man punched Hap's arm, with surprising strength. "Just put me down, you green-eyed goon! I can walk, can't I?"

Hap dropped to one knee. Keeping his arm as level as possible, he eased it down. The hunter didn't wait for him to get all the way to floor; he hopped off and dropped the last foot, landing on two feet and a hand with an acrobat's grace. Without looking back, he retrieved his knife, grabbed the rat's tail with two hands, and dragged it toward the crack in the wall.

Hap fought the urge to call out, *You're welcome*. Instead, he said, "Wait! Did you see anything strange a few minutes ago—like a thread hanging in the air? It went right toward that crack where you live."

The little man stared back. "Are you sick in the head or something?"

"What? No—I just wondered if you saw anything. I did. At least, I think I did."

The little man shook his head and moved on. He called back over his shoulder. "If I see that cat again, I'll kill it." A few seconds later, he disappeared inside the crack, pulling his prey behind him.

CHAPTER
17

The hulking creature was at least twice the height of a man. It had scaly green skin and stringy hair tangled with bits of seaweed. Tusks curled from the corners of its wide mouth. It was climbing out of a jagged hole in the hull of a wrecked ship. Nearby, an exhausted sailor hauled himself onto a rock as the sea frothed around him. Less fortunate sailors bobbed lifelessly in the waves. There was a chest balanced on one of the creature's shoulders, and for artistic effect the lid stood open to reveal the heaps of pearls inside.

Hap looked at the words engraved at the bottom of the picture frame: COASTAL TROLL. "Lovely," Hap said, frowning to himself. The walls were crammed with images like that one, painted or engraved in myriad styles. There were pictures of stone trolls, mountain trolls, forest trolls, and cavern trolls. There was a barn-size boar with enormous tusks, about to gore a helpless knight. There was a wolf standing on two legs, with hairy arms shaped like a man's, and intelligent, piercing eyes: *The Wolf That Walks*. There was a dragon with its wings spread wide, staring at a misty promontory where a robed figure stood, barely visible in the fog: *The Dragon Lord*.

Hundreds of artifacts cluttered the shelves and bureaus. Hap didn't open any drawers, not wanting to pry—or, at least, to be caught prying. So he looked at the stuff that was there for anyone to see. He picked up a curving piece of bone that ended in a sharp point. DRAGON CLAW. FOUND IN CHASTOR. DATE UNKNOWN, said its tag.

He was still picking his way through the collection when dawn crept into the narrow windows, and he heard someone on the stairs. He stepped into the middle of the room, pretending to stare at the great carved pillars that supported the ceiling. Balfour emerged from the staircase, still in his nightshirt. He was a little more bent over than usual, and when he arched his back it produced a symphony of gristly cracks and pops.

"Woke up more decrepit than normal," Balfour yawned. "Morning, Hap."

"Good morning," Hap said.

"Hungry?"

Hap's stomach rumbled. "A little."

"Not surprised. I've seen the way you eat. Join me in the kitchen and I'll whip something up. But first I've got to start the coffee. Heaven forbid Umber awakes and his precious black stuff isn't ready."

"Good, isn't it?"

Hap nodded. Balfour had toasted an enormous slice of bread and slathered it with butter and honey.

"Umber says too much butter's bad for you," Balfour said, shaking his head. "Says it clogs the blood, if you can believe that. He's got some funny ideas, that Lord Umber."

The corner of Hap's lip turned upward as he chewed.

"Well, look at that!" Balfour said. "You almost smiled. I was starting to wonder if you knew how."

Hap sank in his chair. "I . . . I don't know how to feel, most of the time."

Balfour set a silver pot on top of the stove and brushed his hands. "I suppose you don't. Tell me, Hap: What's it like, not being able to remember anything before a few days ago? I can't imagine."

Hap slid his hands into the opposite sleeves and curled up in the seat. "It's like being lost. I don't know what to think. I wonder if I should be missing someone. I wonder if someone is missing me. I . . . I don't even know what kind of person I am."

Balfour patted Hap's arm. "A perfectly nice one, as far as I can tell."

But I feel like a nothing. A nobody. A blank, Hap thought. He wiped his nose with his sleeve. "What is it like for you—being able to remember? Do you remember some things, or all things?"

Balfour's eyebrows went up, wrinkling his forehead. "What a question! I never considered it before. Well, I've been around for a while. I have plenty to recollect, for sure." He leaned back in his chair. "I'd say that memory is like a book. It's a long story that goes back to when you're just a few years old. When I turn back to the very first pages, I can remember giggling when my dad tossed me up in the air. I can recall how light and dizzy I felt when I saw the first girl I ever loved. And I can remember how numb and heavy I felt on the day she died. Yes, Hap, I think memory is like a book."

"If it's a book, then mine is very short," Hap said. "But it feels like something else to me: a box getting filled up with things. And some of the things, I don't understand."

"That might be a better way to look at it," Balfour said. "A chest of stuff all jumbled together. Sometimes you dig in to search for one thing, but you find something else that was long forgotten. It's strange how even the most trivial stuff can be preserved. A joke someone told; a meal you ate; a game you played. You can hardly believe it's still there."

"My memories were stolen," Hap said. "I can't find them, no matter how hard I try." He licked a fingertip and used it to gather up the crumbs on his plate.

Balfour offered a sympathetic frown. "You're still hungry, I'll toast another. Never fear, Hap. You're so young! Even if you don't get your past back, you have years ahead to write your book and fill that box. All it takes is time."

Hap was going to nod in reply, but the door to the kitchen clattered open and a pale-faced, bug-eyed Umber blew in like a storm. The black cat was in his arms. "How did this beast get inside? I can't believe it survived the night!"

"It won't survive another," Hap said. "At least, that's what the little man said."

Umber's jaw unhinged. "You saw Thimble? And he *spoke* to you?"

So that's his name, Hap thought. He looked from Umber to Balfour. "We talked, but only because I saved him. From that cat."

The cat meowed as if in reply, and her tail twitched. "You saved Thimble from this cat?" Umber said, mostly to himself. The cat squirmed out of his grip, and Umber let her drop.

With the kitchen door closed, she had nowhere to go.

Hap nodded. "The little man—Thimble—killed the rat. He didn't see the cat coming."

Balfour poured some cream into a saucer and put it down for the cat to drink. He winced when he bent his knees. "And you just happened to arrive at that exact moment, to save Thimble?"

"Um. Yes."

Umber and Balfour stared at each other. "What were you doing downstairs?" Umber asked.

"I'm sorry," Hap said, shrinking back in his chair. "I just came down to—"

"No, my boy!" cried Umber, fanning the air. "I'm curious, not angry! Who am I to scold anyone who wants to explore? I just want to know how you came to be there at the right moment, and what Thimble said to you. That little ruffian hasn't spoken to anyone in ages! I want to know everything that happened. But hold on—I think I smell coffee, and the story can wait till there's a mug in my hands!"

When Hap reached the part about the thread of light, he saw Umber's fingers begin to drum on the side of the mug.

"Bewildering," he said when Hap was done. "But you're feeling all right now, after that chill and fever?"

"Yes," Hap said. "It scared me, though. What do you think it was, Lord Umber?"

Umber shook his head. "No idea. But I don't think it's a coincidence that you saw the thread a moment later." He raised the mug for another sip. "And speaking of that, did that thread mean anything to you, Hap?"

The question was meant to sound casual, but Hap saw the avid look in Umber's eyes over the arc of the mug. Hap remembered the note, and its hint of skills arising, and wished again that they could talk openly about it. "I don't know. It seemed like . . . a path or something."

"Hmm. I wonder if anyone else could have seen it," Umber mused. "Something tells me *no*. Hap, if you see another thread, pay close attention. It might be important."

"Seems to me it *was* important," Balfour said. "Thimble would have died if Hap didn't follow it."

"But who is Thimble?" Hap asked. "Where did he come from?"

"Thimble doesn't talk about his origin," Umber replied. "When I found him while visiting the kingdom of Meer, he'd been living in a cage for years, enslaved by a loutish fellow who showed him for profit. I offered that man a fortune to purchase Thimble's freedom. And the cretin refused! So we . . . er . . . *liberated* Thimble through other means." Umber looked at Balfour, who covered his mouth and coughed to disguise a grin. "I brought Thimble here and told him he was free to go where he wanted. He stayed, but he's chosen to keep to himself. By then he was disgusted with big folk, as you can understand."

Umber slapped the mug on the table with gusto, and cracked his knuckles. "But we have other business to attend to now. Are you ready, Hap?"

Hap blinked up at Umber. "Ready for what, sir?"

"Exploration! Illumination! First, I'll show you our caverns. And then it's off to the archives. With any luck, we'll know more about you before the day is done."

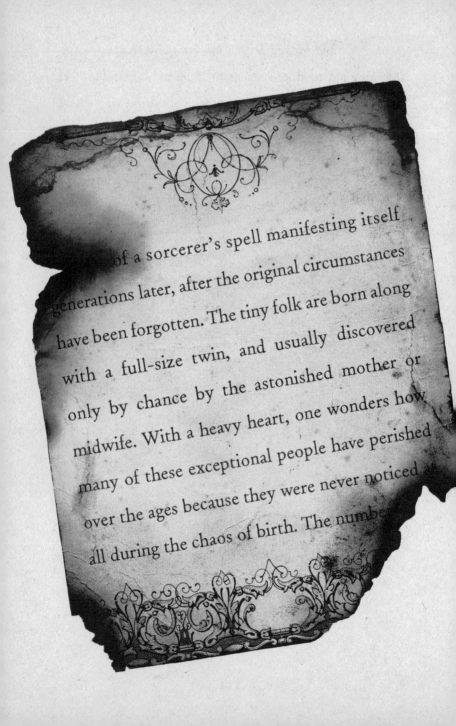

... of a sorcerer's spell manifesting itself generations later, after the original circumstances have been forgotten. The tiny folk are born along with a full-size twin, and usually discovered only by chance by the astonished mother or midwife. With a heavy heart, one wonders how many of these exceptional people have perished over the ages because they were never noticed at all during the chaos of birth. The number ...

in every way except for their miniature size. In proportional terms, they are far stronger and faster than their normally sized counterparts. They also have the enormous appetites one associates with voles, shrews, and oth

CHAPTER
18

With a lamp held shoulder-high, Umber led the way down a corridor that plunged deep into the rock behind the Aerie. Oates trudged behind them. This time he bore a battle-ax that looked too big for Hap to lift.

They veered right as the passage divided and came to a great door that blocked the corridor. It was barred on the near side by a thick beam. Umber put the lamp on the ground and pushed his sleeves past his elbows. "Don't trouble yourself, Oates. I can handle this." He put his hands under one end of the beam and heaved up, straining every modest muscle in his arm and grunting with the effort. Oates smirked and shook his head.

"Got it!" Umber said, staggering under the weight before the beam slipped from his hands and clattered onto the floor.

He danced back to keep his toes from getting mashed. "That was as light as a feather to me."

When he followed Umber past the open door, Hap was amazed by the vast space on the other side. The corridor widened into a natural cavern with a high, arching ceiling crowded with mineral fangs. There were thousands of tiny lights around and above, clinging to the stone and twinkling like stars in pale shades of every color. A closer look showed what they were: glimmer-worms, like the ones Umber had in Alzumar.

"The glimmer-worms thrive here," Umber said. "We breed them throughout our caverns to light the way."

"This is dull. Can we go back now?" groused Oates.

"Charming, Oates. Come along, Hap," Umber said. He led them down a path between pillars of rock, bypassing smaller lanes that angled into adjacent chambers.

They soon arrived at an unexpected sight: a wide subterranean pond, filled by a steady and musical rain of drips from the rock above. In the middle of the water, something silvery-white leaped and plunked. "Crystal-fish," Umber said. "Brought here by the dwarves—excuse me, by the *Dwergh*—who built the Aerie centuries ago. They're blind, transparent, and delicious. The fish, I mean, not the Dwergh. Never call them dwarves, by the way, Hap, if you happen to meet them. They take great offense."

A sharp slapping sound made Hap and Umber turn their heads. They saw Oates staring at his palm, which was covered with brightly glowing jelly. A similar smear was on his neck. He cast a sullen, guilty look at Umber. "I felt it crawling on me."

"Don't squish the glimmer-worms, Oates," Umber said with a sigh. "They're harmless and beneficial."

"Says you," Oates grumbled. He wiped the goop on his shirt, and they moved past the lake.

"Ah, this will impress you," Umber said as they rounded a corner.

Just ahead, the throat of the cave was sealed with enormous blocks of stone. An opening in the center, wide enough for a wagon to pass, was barred. Hap had seen the stout portcullis in the Aerie's gatehouse, and a sturdier one at the palace, but both were flimsy compared to the one before him now. An unsettling question formed in his mind. He opened his mouth to ask, but Umber anticipated his question again.

"You're wondering what on earth is on the other side, that calls for such a barrier?"

Hap nodded.

"Nasty things," said Oates. He had walked with the ax slung casually across his shoulder, but now he held it sideways with both hands gripping the handle tight.

"That's the truth," Umber said. "Those caverns plunge deep

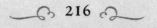

under the mountains. And there are some foul creatures down there. Hobgoblins. Cavern trolls. Other monstrosities." There were sinuous pillars of stone on the other side, and the passage that twisted out of sight looked like a throat ready to gobble down whoever walked that way. Umber's face turned grim, and he went on in a hush. "Sometimes if you stand here and are very quiet, you can hear noises from deep within. Grunts. Whispers."

Oates exhaled loudly.

"Have you ever . . . gone down there?" Hap asked quietly.

"No need," Umber replied. "I know what's there, and I don't care to see it again." A smile replaced the shadow on his face, and he winked at Hap. "But there's a winch in that alcove that we can use to raise the portcullis—would you like to take a stroll?"

Hap whipped his head from side to side.

"Ha! That's quite all right, Hap. We have more important things on our agenda. It's time to meet Smudge in the archives. Though once you've met him, you might decide that exploring that cavern was a better idea!"

CHAPTER
19

Hap had been to this spot before. He and Lady Truden had been splattered by fruit when they showed their faces at this door to the archives.

"Don't forget to ask," Oates urged Umber.

"It's easy to remember with you hovering like a thunderhead," Umber replied.

Umber took a trio of old books from his pack. He pressed his back against the wall, reached sideways, rapped on the door with his knuckles, and called out, "Smudge! Smudge, good fellow! Can you hear me?"

Papers shuffled on the other side of the door. A froglike voice called back: "I'm busy! Leave me be!"

Umber rolled his eyes. He whispered to Hap, "Smudge is

an odd bird, for sure. He burrows so deep into the archives that he never wants to be disturbed. Hard to handle at times, but he certainly knows his way around the collection. It's almost worth the aggravation."

"No it isn't," said Oates.

Umber cleared his throat and shouted toward the square opening in the door. "You're always busy, Smudge! But I'm coming in, anyway. And I'm bringing someone new with me, so you'd better behave yourself!"

There was a furious slam. *"No strangers!"*

"If you meet him, he won't *be* a stranger!" Umber reached sideways, lifted the latch on the door, and poked his head into the room. He peered left and right, and motioned for Hap and Oates to follow.

Hap had only glimpsed the room before. Now he could see the seemingly endless rows of bookshelves extending into shadow. There were cluttered desks and tables near the door, lit by dozens of jars where glimmer-worms munched on mushrooms and leaves.

Smudge was nowhere to be seen. Umber huffed out a breath, folded his arms, and called aloud, "We need your wisdom, Smudge. Where are you?"

"Not over here," came a sour reply.

Umber shook his head and walked to where he could peer

between two of the shelves. He groaned and covered his eyes with a hand. "Smudge! Put on some trousers, man! How many times have we spoken about this?"

High-pitched giggles cascaded from behind the shelf. It was hard to believe that a voice so low could laugh so high. Hap heard feet padding on the floor and a scuffle of material. Smudge's voice croaked again. "*She's* not here, is she?" he asked, as if referring to a species of viper.

"Lady Truden? She is not," Umber replied.

"Good. Can't stand her," the archivist said. His voice approached the end of the shelf.

"Not to break your heart, but she isn't fond of you, either," Umber said, brushing something off his sleeve. "Smudge, I want you to meet Happenstance. He has some unusual abilities, and I wish to know if our archives tell us about others like him."

"What strange eyes he has," the froglike voice said.

"Smudge, please stop spying from between the books and get out here," Umber said.

"If you've got trousers on," Oates added.

A moment passed, and then fingers appeared, curling around the end of a shelf. A shaggy head poked out next, with dark eyes set wide. Smudge was small and wiry, with wild dark hair and a tangled beard that partially covered his sunken, bony chest. He squinted at them, sniffed with contempt, and crept across the floor. He'd put trousers on, Hap was grateful to see, but they were filthy and torn.

"Your trousers have holes in them," Oates said, pointing.

Smudge sneered back. "Of course they do! How else would I get my legs in them?"

"And you smell like compost," Oates said, pinching his nose.

"That stuff between your ears, you mean?" growled Smudge.

"Oates is tactless but truthful, Smudge," Umber said. "Your odor would offend a hobgoblin. You'll need a bath after this."

"No bath! Too busy!" howled the archivist, staggering back.

"You can pry yourself away for an hour, my friend," Umber insisted. "But look, Smudge: See what I've brought you!" He held up the three moldy, ancient books.

Smudge's eyes gleamed. "Books for me?"

"If you behave yourself," Umber said, tucking them under his arm. Smudge turned his head sideways, trying to read the titles. Umber hid the words with his other arm. "First, I want to know—"

Oates tugged at Umber's sleeve. "You said you'd ask about me first."

Umber furrowed his brow. "And the question would be

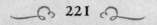

out already, if you didn't interrupt. Smudge, have you turned up anything about Oates's curse?"

A wicked grin oozed over Smudge's face. "What, is the big brute tired of telling the truth all the time?"

"Yes," Oates said.

Smudge chuckled and wiggled his fingers inside his beard. "Sorry! Nothing yet. But there are still so many texts to read and scrolls to decipher. It would help if the brute knew *who* cast the spell—"

Oates opened his mouth to speak, but Umber raised a hand. "We've been through that, Smudge. Oates has no idea." Umber turned to Hap to explain. "Oates was a bit of a liar and a thief back then, and he probably aggravated some sorcerer in disguise."

Oates's shoulders slumped and he stared at the floor. Umber reached up to pat his back. "Don't lose hope, my good man. Sure, Smudge despises you, but there's nothing he likes better than digging up lore. And you know I'm making other inquiries far and wide. You trust me to cure you some day, don't you?"

"Not really," Oates mumbled.

"Nevertheless," Umber said. "Smudge, kindly keep searching on Oates's behalf. Meanwhile I have a new mystery for you."

Smudge was already inspecting the new mystery. He stepped close to stare into Hap's eyes. The stench of unwashed flesh and hair was so strong that Hap craned his neck back. "What strange thing has Umber found now?" Smudge said, fiddling with his beard.

"Mind your manners, please, and call him Hap," Umber replied. He recounted what they knew so far: the discovery in Alzumar. The unseen stranger who was there when Hap awoke. Hap's unusual abilities. The creature, Occo, who pursued them across the sea. Umber said nothing about the burning note except the initials of its author: WN.

Hap held his breath with anticipation, because Smudge was nodding at a faster and faster rate as Umber spoke. He blinked madly, and his fingers twiddled inside his knotty beard, causing it to ruffle as if a strong breeze was blowing. It seemed that, at last, they were on the verge of getting some answers.

"This is what we want to know, Smudge," Umber finally said. "Who is WN? What is Occo, and what does he want? And most importantly, can you shed any light on Hap himself? I'm counting on your knowledge, Smudge. Can you tell us anything right now?"

Hap leaned forward with his fingers digging into his thighs.

Smudge licked his lips and finally spoke in a halting croak.

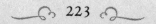

"Brother Caspar had a . . . special interest in the green-eyed folk. Didn't want me to talk to others about it."

Umber's eyes seemed to double in size. "Caspar never told *me*, that's for certain. Why, Smudge? Why didn't he want you to talk about it?"

Smudge tucked his shaggy head between his shoulders. "Brother Caspar would be angry if I said."

Umber groaned and clasped his forehead. "Really, Smudge. Do I have to remind you that your brother left like a thief in the night, taking some of my archives without permission and leaving you behind? You owe him nothing. But now I need your help and your trust. This is more important than you can imagine, Smudge. Tell me!"

Smudge's lower lip quivered like jelly. "Brother Caspar . . . he wanted to be powerful and important. Like you, Lord Umber. He was forever looking in the archives for hints of great treasures. Or spells of power. Once he found scrolls that told of green-eyed folk. He told me to look for more, but keep it secret."

It was a good thing, thought Hap, that Smudge was staring at the floor as he spoke. If he'd seen the fury gathering on Umber's face, his mouth would have clapped tighter than an oyster. Even Oates took a step back.

"I assume he took all those scrolls with him," Umber said

through gritted teeth. "But what did Caspar learn, Smudge?"

"Well . . . Brother spoke of magical men with bright green eyes. They were called many things. *Hoppers. Tinkers.* But mostly *Meddlers.*"

Hap's head felt light with excitement. *Hoppers* made sense, considering his ability to leap. He'd kept quiet until now, but he had to speak. "What's magical about them? Why did your brother want to know about them?"

Smudge peered at Hap through narrowed eyes. "The green-eyed ones turn up when momentous things happen. Great disasters and great victories. Years apart, sometimes. Perhaps there are many of them, or a few. Perhaps they never die." That thought sent an icy shiver through Hap's bones.

"These green-eyed people—are they heroes or villains?" Umber asked.

Smudge squirmed, as if it were painful to remember his brother's words. "Both. Or neither," he said. "Brother Caspar said they're never at the heart of history. Only lurking around the edges and bending the path of destiny the way they desire. They come and go quickly . . . people only notice them because of the eyes." Smudge stole another sideways glance at Hap.

Umber's anger faded, displaced by a look of burning curiosity. "Bending the path of destiny?" he asked. "How can they do that?"

"Brother told me a story," Smudge said, while using his pinkie to scrape something from his ear. "Long ago, two armies lined up to battle. Their generals met on the field between them and agreed on a truce. But one general saw a serpent on the ground and drew his sword to kill it. When both armies saw the raised sword, they thought the battle was on and rushed at one another. A kingdom fell that day. Brother said, 'Who do you suppose lured that serpent to the field? A Meddler,' he said. 'Tinkering with the fates of men.'"

Umber nodded. His thoughts seemed to be racing. "But how do the Meddlers know what to do? And why do they meddle? What do they want?"

Smudge's shoulders rose and fell. "Nobody knows. Brother always wanted to learn how to find one, or summon one. . . . He thought one could steer his fate to give him what he desired." He turned to stare at Hap with a forlorn look in his wide-set eyes. "If he only knew one would come to his door, he would not have left."

Hap tried to keep his breath from heaving out of control. *This can't be. . . . Is that really what I am? A Meddler? But I don't care about changing destiny. I don't care about any of that!*

"And what about this WN, Smudge?" Umber asked. "Do you know of a Meddler that goes by those initials?"

Smudge shook his shaggy head. "I don't know any names. Brother Caspar might have."

"Brother Caspar," Umber muttered. "I've got a name or two for him. Well, how about Occo, Smudge? Can you tell us anything about him?"

"I know nothing of that creature." Smudge averted his eyes. "But there is someone else who might know."

Umber's face went pale, and he sighed heavily. "I hoped that could be avoided."

"Who does he mean, Lord Umber?" Hap asked.

"The guest," Umber said. Hap remembered the terrible sorceress who once ruled the Aerie.

"If it concerns the wicked and murderous, she is the one to ask," Smudge croaked.

"If we must, we must," Umber said. "In the meantime, Smudge, I want you to scour the archives for whatever you can find about the Meddlers and this nasty fellow who's after Hap. Maybe there's a scrap of information that your brother forgot to steal."

Smudge nodded. "I will begin at once."

"I appreciate that, but first things first," Umber said. "Oates, see to Smudge's bath. Smudge, you can have these books once you're cleaned up."

Smudge squealed and ran for the maze of shelves. But Oates

expected the attempt, and he seized Smudge by the arm. He lifted the thrashing archivist and tucked him sideways under his arm.

"Wait!" howled Smudge, trying in vain to grab the books away from Umber. "At least show me the titles!"

"Fair enough." Umber held the books up, one by one. "This one's about the Death Boars of Gomar. This one's about Chastor; perhaps we'll learn about the Dragon Lord from this. This one's written in Dwergh, and I don't know what it's about."

Hap read the silver words embossed in the leather cover. "It says 'A Chronicle of the Terrible Reign of Khorgon.'"

Smudge's struggles ceased at once, and Umber gawked at Hap. "You can *read* that?"

Hap shrugged. "Well . . . yes."

Umber looked at Smudge, and back at Hap. He dropped the books on the nearby desk, raced to a shelf, and plucked out some volumes.

"You put those back where they belong!" shouted Smudge, still sideways in Oates's grasp. "I have a system!"

Umber ignored Smudge. He opened a book and thrust it under Hap's nose. "What does this say?" he asked, nearly shouting.

The writing on those tan, wrinkled pages looked strange, and far different from the language that was commonly used, but Hap could still decipher it. "It's about a queen who was turned into a fox by a witch, and the king didn't know what happened to her, so he consoled himself by going on a hunting trip, and—"

"Never mind!" Umber said, clapping that book shut. He shouted to Smudge, "The boy just read a language that's been dead for three hundred years!" He opened another book and held it wide. "Now this! Read this!"

Hap stared at the odd writing. The characters looked more like pictures than letters. But still, he understood the meaning. "There dwelled in these lands great birds of prey, so large that even a horse might be plucked off the ground . . ."

The eerie silence that followed made Hap look up. Umber's smile was as giddy as ever, and his eyes looked ready to spill tears.

"You know the languages of this world, even the ancient ones," Umber said. He hugged the book to his chest. "I don't suppose . . . Hap, tell me what this means: *Cogito ergo sum.*"

Hap had to wait for a heartbeat, but the answer came. "That means, 'I think, therefore I am.'"

Umber uttered another phrase in another strange tongue. *"D'où êtes-vous?"*

Again, Hap put it into the common language. "'Where are you from?'"

"Chi trova un amico trava un tesoro."

"Um . . . 'He who finds a friend finds a treasure.'"

Umber smiled. "How very true."

"What kind of ridiculous languages are those?" cried Smudge, still horizontal. "You made those up!"

"No, Smudge. Those are the tongues of a lost world. Lost to me, at any rate," Umber said. He grinned again at Hap and tousled his hair. "My dear boy. You're a polyglot!"

"A baby frog, you mean?" Oates asked. Smudge guffawed and slapped his thigh.

"A poly*glot*, Oates," Umber said. "A speaker of many languages. Hap, will the wonders of you ever cease?"

CHAPTER
20

As he followed Umber down another subterranean corridor, Hap had to ask. "Lord Umber . . . about your archivist. Why do you—"

"Put up with someone so obnoxious, unkempt, and malodorous? Because he is also supremely talented in his own way," Umber replied. "Of course, it was better when his brother was here to rein him in. Bloody Caspar! Here I am, trying to become the authority on everything magical and monstrous, and now I discover a cavernous hole in my knowledge, thanks to him."

Magical and monstrous, Hap thought. He knew Umber didn't

mean any harm with the words, but still they stung his heart. *Am I one, or both of those?*

The passage was blocked by a wall with a locked iron door in the center. There was a wooden rack beside it, with pegs for five cloaks of heavy brown fur, lined with wool on the inside. Umber handed the smallest cloak to Hap. "Put this on. Please."

It was cool inside the caves, but the cloak seemed better suited for a frozen winter's day. Hap was going to ask why he needed to wear it until he saw the look in Umber's eye: grim, determined, and perhaps even frightened.

"It won't really be colder in there. But you'll swear it was," Umber said. He rubbed his hands across his face, mashing the flesh. "Hap, I'll be honest: I'm not sure that bringing you here is the right move. Meeting a sorceress is not for the faint of heart. But Turiana's knowledge is vast, and she may know something about Occo, or even about these Meddlers. If Caspar were here, this wouldn't be necessary. I could wring his neck for that!

"It's likely that Turiana won't respond to us at all, because lately she's slipped into a deep slumber. But if she awakens and her mood is foul, it can get . . . *intense*. Also, she has a knack for picking thoughts out of one's mind. She won't know precisely what you're thinking, but she may seize on a scrap of a notion that's floating around in your head. That can be unsettling too." Umber smiled weakly. "I think that covers it. Do you still want to go through that door?"

Hap's hands shook. He clasped them together. "Yes, I'm sure," he said, wiggling his shoulders into the cloak. If there were answers inside, he wanted to hear them.

Umber swallowed audibly. There was a chain on his neck that held a key. He slid it into the keyhole, turned it, and paused.

"One more thing," he said with his palm flat against the door. "I told you once that Turiana was beautiful. Remember?"

Hap nodded.

"That's no longer the case," Umber said. The door groaned as he pushed it open.

An icy gust washed over Hap as they stepped inside an oval chamber. Halfway across the space, iron bars reached from floor to ceiling, making the far side a prison cell.

The cell wasn't cruel. Its furnishings would have comforted a king. Against the bars, close enough for a visitor to reach, was an oaken table with cheese, bread, a bowl of fruit, and a decanter of wine upon it. None of it had been gnawed or touched. There was a bed with silk sheets, a gold-embroidered rug, handsome tapestries on the walls, a bureau, a sofa, and finally a chair in the darkest corner, occupied by a ghastly form.

Hap let out a croak of dismay. At first he thought a corpse

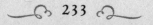

had been left there to mummify. Then he remembered what Umber had said: that the sorceress had fallen into a deep slumber.

Umber put his fists around two of the bars and pressed his forehead between them. "Turiana," he said quietly. And then, a little louder: *"Turi."*

Hap forced himself to look at the sorceress. It was hard to believe that life still coursed through those limbs. She looked as if she'd been frozen for a millennium. The sorceress was clad in a faded yellow-white gown that reached to her bare feet. The yellowed toenails had grown wild, curling like wood shavings. Her hands, with skin drawn tight over frail bones and dark veins, clutched the wooden arms of the chair. Her head was bowed, and her face was obscured by a gray veil. At least, Hap thought it was a veil at first. Then he noticed the tiny multilegged creatures crawling over it, and saw it for the sheet of cobwebs that it truly was.

His teeth began to chatter. *The cold is in your mind,* he told himself.

Umber cleared his throat and spoke louder. "Turi. It's me. Umber." Hap watched, but saw no reaction.

"I brought someone with me," Umber said. "A boy who has come into my keeping. We found him in Alzumar. He's a remarkable young man with some peculiar abilities. And he has the most amazing, sparkling green eyes. It's possible that he is something called a Meddler."

Hap folded his arms tight, trying not to shiver. The figure in the chair still didn't move. "I don't think she can hear you," Hap whispered.

"She hears everything," Umber replied.

Hap stared again at the still form of the sorceress and frowned. He dearly wanted to know more about his origins and the Creep who stalked him. A vivid memory of Occo sprang into his mind: the hissing voice and strangely jointed legs. And that was when he saw the cobwebs that covered her face gently flutter. A spider dropped on a thread and scrambled into a fold of the faded gown.

It was hard to perceive at first, but the sorceress was in motion. Her head turned, as slowly as the moon, until it faced Umber and Hap. Hap's kneecaps knocked against each other. He heard a papery crackle as her withered fingers uncurled from the arm of the chair and rose to her veiled face. One yellowed nail tore a peephole in the web. Hap saw a tiny glimmer where a dark eye peered out.

The veil fluttered again when the sorceress spoke. Hap expected a brittle, ancient voice, and so the whispery beauty that he heard jarred his senses. "And there is something else you haven't mentioned," the sorceress cooed. "The thing that pursues you."

Hap's mouth sagged. He stared at Umber, who mimed a plucking gesture at his temple. *She took that thought out of my mind,* Hap thought.

"How nice to hear your voice again, Turi," Umber said. Hap was struck by the name Umber used. *Turi.* It sounded affectionate.

"Never mind your flattery," she replied. "I won't fall for that again."

"I meant what I said those many years ago," Umber replied quietly. "I hardly expect you to want to help me now, but I need your wisdom, Turi. You know something about this boy and his pursuer—you wouldn't have spoken otherwise."

She shifted her veiled head. Hap knew her eye was focused on him. He *felt* it. The sensation of cold stung his skin and iced his blood.

"Truly, Umber," she said. "Of all the things you've collected, this is the rarest and finest. And a *child*, no less. I did not know there were such things among his breed. If only I'd caught one. I never would have fallen. Never."

Umber pushed away from the bars and raised a hand, palm

out. "Stop it, Turiana. Hap is not something I've collected or captured."

"Study him while you can, Umber. You won't have this pet for long. He'll fly away when he discovers what he is. If his stalker does not get him first."

Umber put a hand on Hap's trembling shoulder. "That *stalker* tried once and was grievously wounded, Turi. If he even survived, I think he's learned his lesson."

Turiana's laugh was as cold as sleet. "If you did not kill him, he only waits and heals. He will return before long. He cannot resist. The boy has something he desires above all things."

"What do you mean? What does he want?" Umber said, his voice rising.

The sorceress pressed her skeletal hands on the arms of the chair and stood, moving as if under water.

"What do you know about this stalker, Turiana? His name is Occo. What is he?" Umber said, insisting.

Turiana's head turned. Her veil of spider-silk drifted sideways, and Hap saw the corner of a bony jaw and skin stretched tight over a sinewy neck. She took a smooth step forward, almost floating over the ground. "Set me free and I will tell you everything you wish to know, Umber."

Umber closed his eyes and shook his head. "You know I can't."

"But I have learned my lesson," she said, drifting closer. "After all these years in this dungeon, I have found my soul again. The wickedness is gone. Set me free and I will show you."

"The king wanted you put to death, Turi," Umber said. "You live only because I promised to hold you here."

"Forget your fool of a king," the sorceress said. "*You* could rule here, Umber. Isn't that what you want? You talk of progress, and freedom and knowledge for the common folk. But the king and the princes will never let you have everything you wish for, and you know it. So you settle for tiny, meager steps. But all the obstacles would be swept away if you ruled."

"Turi, stop," Umber said, turning his face away.

"I could help you, Umber. I would serve you. And I could show you how to use this boy!" A long finger with bulging knuckles pointed at Hap, and his skin twitched from his face to his toes.

"Enough, Turiana!" cried Umber. "After the evil you did, I could never set you free. You know this."

The ghastly figure crossed her arms. Hap could see every bone and tendon under the taut skin. "Then I will tell you nothing. Not even what Occo is. Or how to save yourselves from him."

Umber's shoulders sagged, and he lowered his head. "I'm sorry you feel that way, Turiana. Come, Hap." He turned to walk away.

"Wait," the sorceress said. Her veiled face came to bear on Hap. "There is one thing I will tell the boy. If he dares to hear it."

Umber narrowed his eyes. "What do you mean, *dares*?"

The veiled face floated toward the bars, nearly touching them. Hap stepped back. "But he may not like what he hears," the sorceress said.

"If you're trying to frighten the boy, I don't appreciate it," Umber said. "Come, Hap."

"No—I want her to tell me," Hap said. Umber looked at him, questioning. Hap bit his lip and stared back. He was tired of all the questions, and the secrets Umber was keeping. If the sorceress could solve any part of the mystery of whom or what he was, he needed to know. Still, his limbs shook, and not just from the cold.

"Fine," Umber said after a moment. "Say it, Turiana."

"Leave, Umber," the sorceress said. She pointed toward the door. "I will tell the boy alone."

Umber leaned toward Hap and spoke quietly from the side of his mouth. "I don't think it's a good idea."

Hap stared at the sorceress, who stroked the bars of the cell

with her skeletal hands. He sensed a cruel grin behind the veil. "I'll be all right, Lord Umber. Just don't . . . go too far."

Umber gave a deep breath a slow escape. "I'll be right outside. If anything seems amiss, get out. Or give a shout." Hap nodded. Umber backed out of the room and swung the door closed. Hap imagined Umber on the other side with the knob in his hand, ready to spring back inside.

He faced the sorceress, pulling the cloak tighter across his chest. His mouth felt like a desert. "What . . . what did you want to tell me?"

The sorceress whispered, as if to be sure that Umber would not overhear. "First, I want your help."

Hap edged backward. "I don't think I can do anything for you."

"It is the smallest of favors. Umber has things that belong to me. Rings and bracelets. Pendants and amulets. All my pretty things. Trinkets, really—of no value, but I miss them so much. Umber keeps them among his other treasures. They would comfort me while I spend my lonely years behind these bars. You seem like a good boy. Would you find them and bring them to me?" Her ancient hand reached through the bars, beckoning. "Surely you wouldn't deny a poor prisoner this tiny favor?"

"I don't think Lord Umber would—"

She wagged a bony finger. "Umber would not have to know! This is our secret. And I do not ask without offering in return. I will give you the answers you seek."

"What . . . what answers? What do you know?"

"What you are. The powers you might wield someday, if you learn to use them. But first you must escape this pursuer. He will surely come back for you, I promise you that! And if you knew what he will do when he catches you, you would scream until your throat caught fire. I will tell you how to save yourself, if you do as I've asked!"

Hap clasped his hands over his mouth. He wanted those answers desperately, but he could sense how poisonous this sorceress was. She brushed her ragged nails across the bars of the prison, making hollow clacking sounds.

"I can't do that without asking Lord Umber," Hap said. "It wouldn't be right. I can't."

Turiana bent her head forward at a predatory angle. "Of course you can. And aren't you curious to see what happens if you do this for me? It's in your nature."

"My nature? What do you mean?"

"Fetch what I have asked for, and I will tell you."

"I won't," Hap said. "I'm sorry."

"Horrid child! Then you won't hear what you need to know—only the words you'll wish you never heard!" With one hand, she tore off the web that hid her face. Hap saw transparent skin threaded by dark veins, stretched drum-tight over a bony skull. Her eyes were shriveled like raisins in their deep sockets. Like a viper she spit out two terrible words:

"You're dead!"

CHAPTER
21

Hap barely remembered leaving the
room where the sorceress was imprisoned. He fled in a senseless
panic, flinging off the fur cloak along the way. His sight was
lost to a blinding fog, and all he heard was a dull, surging roar
that had to be the racing of his heart.

He recovered his wits on the other side of the door with
his face crushed against Umber's chest. Something hurt, and
he realized that he was biting the knuckles of the hand he'd
crammed between his teeth.

"Come with me," Umber said, and with a hand around
Hap's shoulders he steered him through the tunnels, into the
Aerie, up the water-driven lift, and into Hap's own room
where he collapsed in his chair.

When Hap was able to speak, he told Umber what had happened.

"Turiana is cruel, Hap," Umber said. "You wouldn't do what she asked, and so she decided to frighten you. Look, you are obviously not dead. You breathe. You eat. Your heart beats. You bleed, too, as I recall."

Hap leaned against the wall and took a deep breath. He remembered the terrible cold feeling that had swept over him just before he saw the strange thread of light. *I told myself it felt like death,* he thought. He tried to banish the notion from his mind. "Maybe she meant that I'm *going* to die," he said, although that alternative wasn't pleasant either.

"Well, that goes for all of us, if you think about it," Umber replied. He tried to smile at his own joke but failed. Something seemed amiss with Umber. His complexion had turned ashen. His features sagged, and dark crescents cradled his eyes. The grin that always came easily was nowhere in sight. Umber pressed his fingers to his temples and ground them in circles.

The sight was enough to shake Hap out of his own misery. "Lord Umber—are you feeling all right?"

Umber ignored the question. "And it's a good thing you didn't do what she asked, Hap. Those *trinkets* she wanted are the source of her powers. She'd have freed herself in minutes,

and what a disaster that would be." He stared at the floor with glazed eyes.

"Lord Umber?" said Hap. Umber grunted.

"If . . . I may . . . I wanted to ask about something you said to Smudge," Hap said. "When you told him that I can speak languages, you said something about this world . . . and *your* world. What did you mean?"

Umber didn't respond right away. At first Hap thought Umber didn't hear him. Then Umber's head rose from his hands and he glared at Hap. Hap edged back, astonished to see such a wild-eyed look directed at him.

"How many times do I have to say it? I can't tell you everything yet! Can you let an hour pass without one of your blasted questions?" Umber pinched the bridge of his nose. His voice fell to a mumble. "Sorry . . . just . . . just leave me alone for a while, will you?" He stepped out of Hap's room and closed the door behind him.

CHAPTER
22

Hap could spend only so many hours alone in his room. He peered down at the harbor to see if the Creep's vessel was anywhere in sight. It was not, but it didn't make him feel much better, after what the sorceress had said: *He will surely come back for you. . . .*

He wished he could visit Umber on the terrace, but Umber clearly wanted solitude. The sudden change that had come over him was strange. His energy, humor, and exuberance had wilted like a flower in the frost. All that remained was a dim shadow of the man he was.

Hap wandered downstairs, looking for a friendly face. He was pleased to see Sophie come out of the kitchen with a bowl of fruit. She lowered her eyes as usual when she saw him, and tucked her damaged arm behind her back. But the corners of her mouth also turned up.

"Hello, Sophie. I haven't seen you around."

"I've been working on engravings for Umber's books," she replied. "It takes a lot of time, and Lord Umber wants me to finish while it's fresh in my mind. Not that I could ever forget that tyrant worm." She paused to bite her bottom lip. "Hap, would you like to see the room where I make the art?"

"Of course." Hap was about to mention Umber's strange transformation, but an angry shout cut him off.

"You! Happenstance!" It was Lady Truden. She swept into the room with a fiery glare focused on Hap.

Hap didn't know what to think as she strode toward him. He clutched the front of his shirt and tried to guess what he might have done wrong—something grave, by the look on her face, but he couldn't imagine what. Just when he thought he might be trampled, she stopped abruptly a foot away.

"What's the matter with Lord Umber? What the devil did you do?" she said, leaning over him with her teeth bared.

"I-I didn't do anything," Hap said.

"Is Lord Umber sick?" Sophie asked in a barely audible voice.

Lady Truden's eyes darted toward her. "The sadness is back. Bad as ever."

Sophie stared down at the fruit in the bowl. "But why do you think it's Hap's fault? This has happened before and Hap wasn't even here."

Air gusted out of Lady Truden's nose. "I wasn't speaking to *you*, young lady. Don't you have work to do?" Sophie seemed to shrink to half her size as she bustled out of the room.

"Well?" Lady Truden growled. "He was fine before he spent the morning with you!"

Hap melted under her glare. "I don't know what happened. We went to talk to Smudge. And then he took me to see . . . the guest."

Lady Truden gasped. "The sorceress? Why?"

"He thought she might know—"

"This *is* your fault!" she said, jabbing her finger an inch from Hap's nose. "I told him not to talk to her. It always upsets him! He never would have if *you* hadn't come. . . ." She clenched her fists so tight that Hap heard the knuckles crackle.

Hap felt his face turn crimson. "But . . . Lord Umber will get better, won't he?"

"You'd better hope so," Lady Truden said. "I've never seen him so low! You just keep away from him so you don't make it worse. Keep away, you hear?" She stared at him with nostrils flaring, waiting for some sort of answer. Hap felt a sour taste in the back of his throat. He didn't know what to say.

Rescue came in the form of Balfour's gray-haired head poking out from the kitchen door. "Hap! Give me a hand in here? Right away, please."

Lady Truden had the same expression that the cat had worn when it lost Thimble as its prey. "Excuse me, my lady," Hap said. He trotted into the warm sanctuary of the kitchen.

Hap stared into the mug of hot milk and cinnamon that Balfour provided. "How long do you think the sadness will last?" Hap asked.

Balfour shrugged. "Hard to guess. These episodes—that's what Umber calls them—can be as short as a few days or as long as a month."

"It is my fault, isn't it?" Hap asked quietly.

Balfour rapped the table with his knuckles. "Listen, Hap. You're a fine young man, so I'll be honest with you. Umber *has* been troubled since we found you. But it's not about you. I think something in the note that was on you has made Umber think about the place that he came from, years ago."

Hap remembered the strange words that he'd spied in the note from WN: *I know where you came from, Umber. I know too what happened to that world of yours. . . .* "I've heard Lord Umber talk about his world. What does that mean? Where did he come from?"

"I couldn't say. Umber doesn't like to talk about it, I can tell you that."

Something in Balfour's tone told Hap there would be no more discussion of Umber's other world. He swirled his milk inside the mug. "But do you think seeing Turiana made Lord Umber sad, too?"

"Could be. It's upsetting for Umber, seeing her."

Hap nodded. *It's upsetting for anyone,* he thought.

"Of course, it's not just that she's hideous and cruel," Balfour said. "There's another reason. Do you know how he defeated her, and became the Lord of the Aerie?"

Hap shook his head. "No. Does Umber have a book about it?"

"No—he would never write about that. But I can tell you. I should begin a little farther back, though." The oven door squealed when Balfour opened it. As he told Hap the story, he raked the simmering coals into a pile and stacked fresh wood on top. "Umber showed up in Kurahaven about ten years ago, confused and bewildered. I was the first person he met—did you know that? I ran a little inn near the harbor back then. I gave him a place to stay, introduced him to the Merinots, and showed him around. He started earning a reputation right away—it was one invention after another—and soon I was working for him. Before long the king caught wind of this fellow. With Tyrian's blessing, it didn't seem like there was anything Umber couldn't improve. Our ships, buildings, medicines, farms, universities . . . the man was a genius.

"The other remarkable thing was how brave he was, and how curious about anything supernatural or extraordinary. If there was a wizard on a far-off island, he'd go make friends. If there were goblins in the mountains, a serpent in a swamp, a ghost in a village, or an ogre in the forest, he'd rush out, as giddy as a puppy, to take a look. And he'd usually drag me with him.

"It's funny, Hap. I always had the sense that he was looking for something out there . . . an answer to some problem that I could not imagine. And I wondered if maybe, when he found you, he'd discovered what he'd been looking for.

"But let me finish my story. Finally, Umber couldn't resist the biggest challenge of all: Turiana. You've met her, but how much do you know about her?"

"She was the sorceress who ruled the Aerie," Hap said. "At first she was good, but she turned evil."

"Evil is an understatement. Many of our folk fell victim to her spells, and it took a handsome tribute to keep her from doing worse. Gold, diamonds, pearls . . . anything she demanded, the king gave her. There was little else he could do, because the Aerie is such a stronghold—it would have been madness to attack. It was Umber who finally put an end to Turiana's reign. Can you guess what he did?"

Hap shook his head. Balfour laughed as he spoke, as if he could hardly believe the tale himself. "Umber walked right up to the Aerie—with a bouquet of flowers, if you can believe that—and asked to meet her. People thought he'd lost his mind. I stood as close as I dared, and watched as the black door opened and Umber stepped inside. *There goes my employment,* I said to myself.

"Not a word was heard for forty days. Then, wouldn't you know it, the black door opened and Umber strolled out. 'The reign of Turiana is over,' he said. Somehow, he'd broken her. What's more, all the tribute the king had paid over the years was still inside, waiting to be reclaimed.

"Tyrian was so delighted that he asked Umber to name his reward. Umber wanted two things. The first, the king gave happily, and that was the Aerie itself. And so Umber became Lord Umber of the Aerie. The second, the king was not so willing to grant. Umber asked that Turiana's life be spared. He promised to keep her safely imprisoned in the Aerie. The king finally relented, with one condition: Umber's own life would be the price paid if Turiana ever escaped."

Hap's neck stretched high. "Wait—if Turiana escapes, Lord Umber will die?"

"That was the bargain." The fire in the oven was blazing. Balfour shut the door and used a cloth to clean the ash off his hands.

"But you didn't say *how* he defeated Turiana," Hap said.

Balfour talked over his shoulder while he selected a pan from a shelf and put it on the stovetop. "What's the last thing you'd expect to defeat a hateful being such as Turiana?"

Hap dropped his head into his hands. "Please, Balfour, my life is already full of unanswered questions. I can't take any more."

"Very well," Balfour chuckled. "It was love, Hap. Love did her in."

Hap wasn't sure he'd heard Balfour right. "He . . . she . . . *what?*"

"Hard to believe, if you see Turiana now. But keep in mind: This was before her powers were stripped away. One of her spells made her the most beautiful woman you could imagine. And that is what Umber saw when he was led to her throne."

"So Lord Umber fell in love with her?"

Balfour untied a sack and dug a scoop into the pale green beans inside. "Just the opposite, Hap. It was Turiana who fell for Umber. Not immediately, though. The first thing she did was lock him in a cage that she set beside her throne, probably intending to let him die there. Now, I don't know much about what happened next. It's another thing that Umber doesn't talk about. But I think she became fascinated with Umber as the days went by. She'd never met anyone like him—who has, really? And considering her ability to peer into the mind, I'm sure she learned more about him than any of us knows.

"As weeks went by, she *did* fall in love, or as close to love as such a wicked thing can come. I think Umber finally convinced her that he loved her as well. She trusted him, and freed him. And when her guard was down, Umber took away all those things—the rings, the amulets, the charms—that gave her those dark powers. He even used those talismans long enough to banish all of her foul creatures into the caves below the Aerie. And that is how the serpent was defanged."

Hap nodded. "He tricked her."

"Indeed," Balfour replied. "And though she richly deserved it, I think he feels bad about it. Nobody likes to betray another person. It's also possible that he returned her feelings in some small way. Turiana wasn't always wicked, you know—the dark power that she pursued corrupted her. Umber might have seen the good inside, and hoped to bring that out and save her from herself. If you ask me, that's why it bothers him to see her."

Hap looked at the kitchen ceiling. Somewhere a few stories above, Umber sat with his mind befogged by a dark cloud. "I wish I could do something for him."

Balfour scooped the beans into the pan and covered it again. "There's a small thing you can do, if you give me a few minutes to roast these coffee beans."

CHAPTER
23

Hap crept upstairs with the silver tray, praying that Lady Truden wouldn't intercept him. He peered around the third-story landing at the closed door to her room, hoping she was inside, preoccupied with her miniature portrait of Umber. Holding his breath, he hurried up the last set of steps.

Umber was on the terrace in his favored spot under the tree of many fruits. Normally the man couldn't keep himself still, even when sitting. His knees bounced, his head bobbed, his fingers drummed on any surface, and his eyebrows flitted up and down. But now he looked as grave and still as a statue, slumped on the bench with his elbows on his knees and his fingers pressed against the corners of his eyes. He didn't seem to see Hap approach, or hear the rattle of the mug on the tray, or smell the delicious, earthy scent that steamed out of the pot.

Hap had to talk past the lump in his throat. "Lord Umber?"

Umber replied with a soft grunt.

"I thought you might like some coffee," Hap said. "Balfour made it. He's teaching me how. I can roast the beans and everything."

Umber put his hands on his knees and straightened slowly, as if all of his joints had fused. He looked at the tray with its pot of coffee, tiny pitcher of cream, and the thick-rimmed mug that he favored. With a heavy hand, he gestured at the lip of the planter. "There," he said.

Hap put the tray down. There was another tray there already with a barely touched meal, and a third tray with a cup of brewed herbs. "You should eat, Lord Umber."

"Please," Umber mumbled. "I hear enough of that from Tru."

"I'm sorry." A warm breeze washed over them, bearing the scents of a hundred blossoms from the tree of many fruits and the other flora on the terrace. It was hard to believe a person could be sad on such a perfect day in such an amazing garden. "Lord Umber, I hope it's not my fault you're feeling this way."

Umber stared at nothing. "It's not. This has always happened to me. Even before."

"Before?"

"Before ... all this," Umber said, gesturing weakly at the city and the sea. "I'd feel this way now and again in my old world. But I could ... take something to help me then. Medicine."

Hap clasped his hands behind his back. "Is there anything I can do for you? There must be something. Is it better if I stay or go?"

"Doesn't matter," Umber said. His voice fell to a mumble. "Nothing matters. None of you, none of this. It's not real anyway, is it? How could it be?"

Hap's head angled to one side. "You don't think this place is real?"

Umber shook his head.

"But ... how could that be? I'm real," Hap said. "It's like that phrase you asked me to translate. *Cogito ergo sum*. I think, therefore I am. Thinking makes me real. All of us are real."

Umber spoke with his hands over his eyes, rambling. "Too strange to be real. Magic abounds ... laws of nature and physics ignored. No, it's a fever dream, a delirium. I'm lying somewhere badly wounded, and all this is the hallucination of a dying brain ... only logical explanation. This place, these people ... you exist in my head, as long as you're in sight.

Walk down those stairs and you'll cease to be, until I imagine you walking back up."

Hap stared, wondering if one of them had lost his mind. "Lord Umber, I promise you, if I go downstairs, I'll still exist. I'm not going to disappear."

Umber sniffed. "That's what I *think* you think."

"It's true," Hap said. "Watch, I'll do it." He walked across the terrace, took a deep breath at the top step, and descended out of Umber's sight.

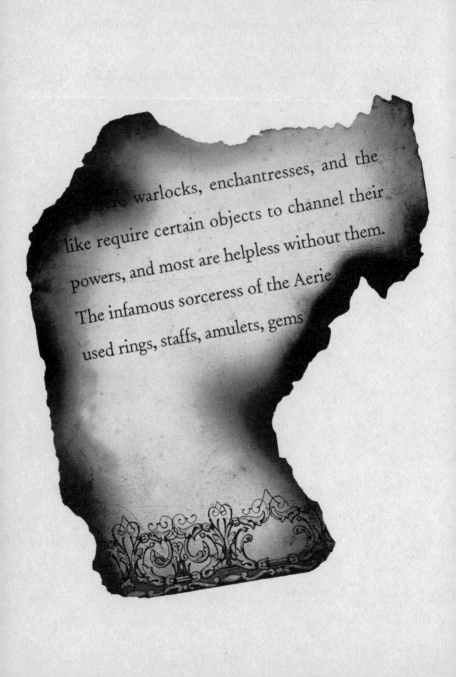

...ere warlocks, enchantresses, and the like require certain objects to channel their powers, and most are helpless without them. The infamous sorceress of the Aerie used rings, staffs, amulets, gems

CHAPTER
24

"I went down the stairs," Hap said a minute later, when he had returned to the terrace, "and I was there all the while. I didn't cease to be."

Umber shrugged. "Just the sort of thing I'd imagine you would say."

Hap shook his head. It was pointless to argue, if that's what Umber wanted to believe. "I wish you'd try the coffee."

Umber looked with heavy-lidded eyes at the silver pot. He lifted it and poured steaming black liquid into the mug. Without bothering with cream, he raised the mug to his lips, took a joyless sip, and set it down again. "Tried it." His gaze returned to a meaningless point in the afternoon sky.

Hap twisted his lips. "I've been thinking about what

Smudge said, Lord Umber. About the Meddlers and steering fate. And then I remembered that strange thread of light I saw. Do you think those things are connected somehow?"

Umber only grunted again in reply.

Hap sighed, wondering if there was anything he could say to rekindle Umber's enthusiasm. "I've been reading your books," he finally said.

Umber didn't respond, but Hap pushed on. "They're amazing. I can see why you want to share them. That's what your new printing press is for, isn't it? So you can make copies of them, and everyone can know what you know." As he waited to see if Umber would reply, a sound came from behind: a displeased huff of air.

"Did I not tell you to leave Lord Umber alone?" Lady Truden said. She was at the top of the stairs with her arms crossed and her fingers tapping her elbows. It was obvious to Hap that she'd prowled up quietly. He would have heard footsteps otherwise. Most likely she wanted to catch him here, just so she could scold him.

Hap glanced at Umber, hoping for words in his defense. But Umber's thoughts were still adrift. He'd plucked a leaf off the tree and was tearing it into tiny pieces.

"I was just trying to help," Hap said.

Lady Truden pointed toward the stairs.

Hap left the terrace with his hands crunched into fists. As he departed he heard her snap at Umber: "You haven't touched the tea I made. How do you expect to get better? And the food, do you mean to starve yourself to death?"

After that, Lady Truden made it her mission to know where Hap was at every moment and to keep him from seeing Umber. Hap had to find other ways to spend his time in the days that followed.

At first most of his hours were devoted to absorbing Umber's books. He read about giants, ogres, goblins, gnomes, faeries, elves, witches, warlocks, serpents, and other things too strange to believe. Not once, though, did he read about people with eyes or unusual abilities like his.

A boy who never slept had many hours to spare, and he soon sought other pastimes. He observed the habits of the nameless fisherman and his wife who dwelt in Petraportus, the crumbling castle: Every morning they tossed their nets into the harbor; every afternoon they rowed their tiny boat to the Spout for fresh water; and every night they lit their driftwood fires. He wished he knew their names and their stories. Balfour said they had simply sailed into the harbor on a rickety craft years before and taken residence in the old castle, refusing to speak to anyone.

Hap inserted himself where he could into the routines of the Aerie. He made himself Balfour's apprentice in the kitchen, which suited him well, since he enjoyed learning to cook and could better satisfy his own remarkable appetite. Balfour was amazed by the quantities of food that Hap could ingest.

Hap spent time with Sophie as well. In another room of the Aerie devoted solely to her craft, he watched her produce the illustrations for Umber's books. Before Umber, she explained, engravings were done by carving wood. Umber introduced a new process that delivered a far more detailed result. Hap watched her work on an exquisite print of the tyrant worm. With her sketches pinned to the wall to guide her, she painted her design onto a smooth slab of limestone, using a brush dipped in greasy ink. When that was done, she treated the stone with a solution of Umber's invention. This, she explained, ate away the areas of the limestone that were not protected by the ink. Next she would put the etched stone into a press to create her prints.

While Sophie was busy, Hap wandered around the room, looking at her other sketches and color studies. They reminded Hap of what he saw the night he crept past Lady Truden's room. He hesitated, wondering if his question was better left unspoken. "Sophie, did you ever paint a portrait of Lord Umber?"

The brush Sophie had been holding clattered on the floor. "What? No!" She reached for the brush and wiped it on her smock. "Well, why do you ask?"

"It's just that I saw a painting . . . it was very good, and I wondered if it was you that—"

"She *showed* it to you?"

"Lady Truden, you mean? Um . . . not exactly. Her door was open, and I—"

"Hap! Don't ever speak of this again!" Sophie dropped her voice to a whisper. "Yes, I painted it for her. I didn't want to without asking Lord Umber, but she begged me, and she made me swear not to tell. She'd be furious if she knew you saw it. Especially *you!*"

"But why did she want it? Why would she be angry that I saw it?"

"Oh, Hap," Sophie said. "You seem so smart in most ways. But so dim in this one way. Can't you see how she feels about Lord Umber?"

Hap stood with his mouth hanging open. *That explains some things,* he thought. Her fierce loyalty to Umber, and her protectiveness. "But why does she hate *me* so much?"

Sophie glanced at the door before answering. "When you first came, I heard her arguing with Balfour. She said she had a bad feeling about you, and that Lord Umber was too quick to trust you. Then, when that . . . *Creep* attacked, and people got hurt, she was sure she was right. She thinks something might happen to Lord Umber because of you."

Hap slumped into a chair. "And now that Lord Umber is . . . not well . . . she blames me."

He looked at Sophie. She turned her head away and bit her lip.

Hap felt hot moisture in the corners of his eyes. "Is that what everyone thinks? That I did this to Lord Umber?"

Sophie sat beside him. "Oh no, Happenstance! It's not like that at all! Don't worry. He'll get better soon, and Lady Truden will see that she was wrong about you. She's really not so bad, you know. You just seem to bring out the worst in her." She shrugged and smiled, and Hap smiled back, glad that she was getting comfortable around him. When she spoke now, it wasn't the bashful whisper she'd used before. Once or twice, she even looked him in the eye before dropping her gaze. But she still kept her damaged hand out of sight whenever she could, under her smock or behind her back.

Days later, while Hap was walking with Oates, Smudge popped his head out of the archives and called to him. "You there! I need you!"

Hap froze in his tracks. "Me?"

"Who'd you think I meant, the ignorant hulk beside you?"

Oates shook his head and brushed past the sneering little man.

"What do you want me for?" Hap asked.

Smudge scowled. Whatever the favor was, he wasn't happy that he had to ask. "I . . . er . . . have a scroll or two in a language I've never seen," he muttered, scratching at the floor with toes that poked from torn stockings. "Thought you might be able to . . . you know. Tell me what they say."

And so Hap took on another responsibility, as a translator for Umber's library. Smudge guarded his archives jealously and only gave Hap a precious few documents to decipher. But Hap was thrilled—here was a chance to delve beyond *The Books of Umber*. Each time he got hold of another ancient text, he hoped to discover some secret about himself or Occo. But it never happened. Most of the books and scrolls were dull histories of ancient lands.

The passing days might have been pleasant except for the pall that Umber's mood cast over the Aerie. The despair did not lift. If anything, it grew worse. At night, when Lady Truden slept, Hap would climb to the terrace. Sometimes Umber was locked inside his rooftop tower. More often, even in the darkest hours, Hap found him slumped on his favorite bench with his face turned toward the starry sky and a barely gnawed piece of fruit at his side.

When Hap first met him, Umber floated through the world as if buoyed by his relentless good cheer. Now he moved like a man whose clothes were lined with lead. His slender body thinned until he looked frail. A sparse beard grew on his usually shaven face, and Hap was surprised to see gray hair amid the sandy brown.

Umber's gloom began to infect the others. Lady Truden took it hardest of all. If a book or package arrived for Umber—and they did, on a regular basis, brought by ships from the far corners of the world—she'd rush up the stairs, hoping it might be delightful enough to propel Umber from his miserable state. But each time, she'd plod back down with her mouth clamped in a thin grim line. Grief pooled inside her, fermented, and bubbled up as fury. If she couldn't catch Hap doing something she considered wrong, she'd find someone else upon whom she could unleash her temper.

Hap met Thimble a second time, late one night when the others slumbered. While Hap was looking through bureaus for artifacts to ponder, the tiny voice drifted up from ankle-high. "Is Umber better yet?"

Thimble stood near the crack in the wall that Hap supposed led to his home. Hap was several steps away, so he walked over to close the distance.

"Stop there!" Thimble commanded, thrusting a pen-size spear forward. "Or you'll be in more pain than you can imagine." He must have seen the smirk that flashed quickly on Hap's face, because he lifted the spear over his shoulder and poised to fling it. "What, you don't believe me? One nick from this and you'll be thrashin' on the floor, screamin' for your mother!"

Hap winced at the reference to a mother he did not know. He narrowed his eyes at the little man. "Why? Does your little spear have that spider venom on it?"

"You'd better believe it," Thimble said, shaking the spear.

"If you say so," Hap said, pursing his lips.

"Don't give me that look!" snapped Thimble. "I'm happy to stab you if you doubt me. But know this: There's a spider you see every day, and you think it's harmless. And it is, but only because its little fangs can't pierce your skin. But that poison is deadly, and it's all over the tip of this spear!"

Hap let his head tilt to one side. "And how do you get the poison from the spider? Does he lick the spear for you?"

Thimble's pinhole nostrils flared. "Idiot. You catch 'em and lash 'em down. Then you have to know where to stick 'em." He jabbed his spear at an imaginary spider.

"I hope you're careful," Hap said.

"Still alive, ain't I?" Thimble said, puffing himself up to his full height of just a few inches.

Only because of me, Hap thought. "Well, to answer your first question: No, Lord Umber isn't better yet. But you obviously know that something is troubling him."

Thimble rested the spear across his shoulders, behind his neck. "I've heard people talk. And I've seen him, mopin' in his garden."

Hap leaned back in surprise. "*Seen* him? How could you possibly get all the way up there?"

Thimble glared up. "I know my way round this place. There are ways I can take that others can't."

Hap was impressed. He couldn't imagine being Thimble's size and venturing all the way to the terrace. He wondered what path the little fellow took to get there. Did he mount the stairs? Did he climb the chains of the water-lift, or the tapestries on the walls? Or were there fissures in the stone behind the walls that he could squeeze through? Hap wondered, too, exactly how far Thimble had explored.

"So you've been all the way to the terrace," Hap said.

"And what if I have?" replied Thimble, rocking the spear across his shoulders.

"I just wondered if you've been inside Lord Umber's

tower," Hap said. He was thinking about the secret thing he accidentally saw when he leaped up to Umber's window: the sleek silver box that glowed with unnatural light.

Thimble shook his head, disgusted. "You're pokin' your nose where it don't belong."

"I just—"

"*You just* mind your own matters, you nosy whelp. I know what you're askin' 'bout. It's Umber's secret, and I'll keep what I know to myself. That's how I repay him for what he done for me."

And what about what I did for you? Hap wanted to ask, but he held those petty words inside. "But you *have* seen it. And you know what it is."

"I've seen it. And I got *no idea* what it is," Thimble said. He turned and vanished in the crack in the wall.

CHAPTER
25

On the eleventh day of Umber's great despair, the weather turned. Sun changed to gloom, and gentle breezes to stiff winds that made clothes snap. Hap found Balfour staring wide-eyed at a device with glass tubes and dials, mounted on the wall. Balfour had both hands against his cheeks. "Maybe this is why my bones ache more than usual," he said.

"What is that thing?" Hap asked.

"Umber invented this. Or *introduced* it to us, as he prefers to say. He calls it a weather glass. See the liquid in that tube? It's dropping like an acorn. So unless this thing is broken, it's telling us that there will be a storm. But . . ."

Hap waited. "What, Balfour?"

Balfour rubbed a hand across his forehead. "I've never seen it fall this fast. Not even close. We have to tell Umber."

Hap reached the terrace without Lady Truden spotting him. Umber wasn't in his usual seat. He'd wandered to the edge, where he leaned heavily on the balcony.

"Lord Umber," Hap said.

"Mmm," Umber replied.

"Balfour says a storm is coming. A bad one." Hap looked at the long hill beyond the city. At the horizon he saw a thin band of blue, the only sky not yet engulfed by the gathering storm. Hundreds of gray-white gulls chased the blue as clouds swept inland.

"Storm. I can see that," Umber mumbled.

"What should we do?"

Umber's reply was barely audible. "Nothing. Harbormaster has a weather glass. So does the palace, and all my captains. They've spread the word."

Hap joined him at the balcony. In the harbor below, the smallest boats had been dragged ashore, and men hurried to secure the larger craft. More ships sailed in from the open sea with sails stretched to the breaking point. "Look—your weather glass is saving lives, Lord Umber. That must make you glad," Hap said. Umber didn't respond.

The surface of Kurahaven Bay was churned by the wind into a million foaming peaks. For Hap, this was infinitely worse than the sight of calm waters. His fingers hurt, and he realized it was from gripping the rail with all his strength.

The first drops of rain spattered his face. "You should go inside, Lord Umber. Would you like to come down to the kitchen? Balfour will make us something to—"

"Just leave me alone," Umber said.

"But—"

"*Alone,*" Umber repeated, raising his voice. He rubbed one temple with the heel of his hand.

Hap backed away. He wiped the rain from his eyes and trudged toward the staircase landing, where he heard someone else's feet on the stairs, rising quickly. As Lady Truden rushed onto the terrace, he ducked behind a vine-covered trellis. After she passed, he slipped downstairs unseen and went to his room. There he stood by his window and watched the storm. What made its gathering power worse was that the wind blew straight into the mouth of the harbor. The tall peaks on either side of the bay gave no shelter.

Hap's door was open, so he heard clearly when Lady Truden came down the steps and slammed her door. Though the wind whistled loud through a seam in Hap's window, he still heard her wailing cries.

The tempest frightened Hap but also amazed him, and so he left his window open despite the slashing rain. He pulled a chair to the sill and watched as darkness fell. There was genius in the way his windows served as the eyes of the face carved into the Aerie. The rain was channeled past the corners of the eyes, so that the face seemed to weep.

The wind and waves pummeled Petraportus. He hoped the nameless fisherman and his wife would be all right. Nobody was in sight at the docks and in the streets of Kurahaven. He saw a canvas tent in the marketplace take flight, and wondered if the merchants, including the clothier Poncius, had taken good care of their wares.

By midnight the storm doubled in strength. Hap gazed at the water, knowing that, with his nocturnal sight, he was the only one who could see the new peril amid the churning waves: a small boat trying desperately to reach the safety of the harbor.

He pressed his face between the bars of the window to get a better look. Two were aboard: a man and a boy. Father and son, most likely. There was a single mast, but only the shreds of a sail were left, and even those tore away and fluttered inland as Hap watched, blinking away the driving rain. The boat yawed wildly as the man fought with a single long oar to keep the

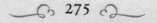

bow pointed at the docks, an unreachable salvation still a half-mile away. The boy clung to the man's waist and buried his face in the shirt. Not a thing could be done for them, Hap knew. No ship could venture out to rescue them.

A frothing gray wave reared up, loomed over the boat, and collapsed. For a moment the craft vanished, and then it bobbed up with sheets of black water streaming off. The man had lost the oar or let it go, because he held the boy by the wrists as they sprawled across the steep tilt of the deck.

"No!" Hap screamed aloud, as another wave rose up, curled high, and slammed down, pushing the craft deep into the sea. It vanished, as if it was never there. Hap shoved himself away from the bars and put his back to the window. He seized his hair and pulled. *No,* he screamed again, inwardly this time, dumbstruck by horror at the thought of the poor man and boy, lost to the very fate he feared the most.

CHAPTER
26

Hap pressed his hands against his face,
hating the unnatural eyes that had let him see such a thing.
And then he heard a sound that somehow cut through the
roar of the storm. It was booming, sonorous, and familiar. He
whirled to look outside once more, daring to hope. Where the
boat had been lost, something enormous rose from the brine.

"*Boroon!*" Hap shouted. "*Oh, Boroon!*" He leaped so high,
his head thumped against the stone ceiling.

The leviathan broke the surface with the fishing boat
cradled inside the railings of the barge. Water poured away,
baring the deck. The father and son were there, rising on their
hands and knees to gawk, dumbstruck, at the miracle from the
deep that had saved them. Nima ran from Boroon's back onto

the deck. She opened the hatch and waved them over, and they crawled into the safety of the cabin.

"*Nima!*" screamed Hap, rubbing the bruise atop his head. She couldn't hear him, of course, but it didn't matter. He shouted both names again, just for the joy it brought: "*Nima! Boroon!*"

Hap's conscious life was only a few weeks old, but he wondered if he would ever love a pair of beings more than he did the leviathan and the web-fingered captain at that moment. *There's a memory for the book of your life,* he told himself as the rain mingled with his own happy tears.

Boroon's mighty tail propelled the rescued folk away, seeking shelter elsewhere. Hap stripped off his rain-dampened clothes and threw a nightshirt over his head. He plucked a book from the basket and sat on his bed, still smiling.

Before he could start to read he felt the symptom he'd known before: the crippling stiffness that froze every joint in his body. He squeezed his eyes shut. In his mind he saw Turiana, and heard her saying those terrible words, and he forced his mind away from that memory. *This will pass,* he thought. And it did pass, faster than the first time, driven away by a sweltering fever that also quickly faded.

He stood with his chest heaving like bellows, still

wondering what caused the brief affliction, and annoyed that it interrupted his moment of joy. Umber had told him that, if the chill and fever came again, he should watch for another thread of light. And there it was, hanging in the stormy air just outside his window. *Just like the one that led me to Thimble.* But this thread hung vertically, and didn't point to him.

He approached it cautiously, as if it were a wary bird he might frighten away. *Pay close attention,* Umber had advised him. *It might be important.*

Whatever it was, it was unaffected by the ferocious wind. The thread just rippled with a sinuous motion. Hap reached the window and stared at it. There was something ominous and frightening about its color—a bruised, infected purple. But like the first thread, it had tiny pulses of light moving through it, originating from some point below. He reached out and touched it, expecting to hear the same faint whispering or music. He yanked his hand back an instant later. There was a sound—but it was cold and unpleasant, and his nerves jangled.

This thread is different, he thought. *The first was mine. But this belongs to someone else.*

He pushed his head between the bars—there was just enough room to squeeze through, though it hurt his ears to try—and looked down. And there, climbing like a spider, reaching up to slide his daggerlike fingertips into a crevice in the walls, was Occo the Creep.

Hap pulled his head back so fast that it felt like his ears had been sheared off by the bars. He stumbled and fell, and pushed away on his palms and heels until his back was against the door.

He's coming for me! His mind paralyzed him with too many jarring thoughts to process: *Run! Hide! Fight! Don't move! Scream! Be quiet! Call for help!*

The glimpse had told him that Occo was climbing swiftly. Soon hands would rise up and seize the bars. But then what? The bars made it impossible for Occo to enter. Was he strong enough to wrench them right out of the stone?

He doesn't know I saw him, Hap thought. All Hap saw was the top of his uncovered skull as he searched for a grip. His head was hairless and smooth, ghastly white, and slick with rain. And Hap had noticed something else in that momentary glimpse—something coiled around the Creep's shoulder. *Never mind that—do something!* his instincts screamed.

Next to the door was one of the countless artifacts that cluttered the Aerie. It was a small figure of a gnomelike creature, made of iron. It was there to prop the door open on windy days. But as Hap's eyes fell upon it, he saw neither a statue nor a doorstop. He saw a weapon. He seized it by the neck. *I'll throw it as soon as he shows his face,* Hap thought. *He'll lose his grip and fall.*

As he crept toward the window, padding softly with the heels of his feet off the ground, he pictured the craggy rocks at the foot of the Aerie. *That will be the end of him.* He stood close enough to strike but far enough to stay out of reach, held the statue over his shoulder, and waited. His legs shook and his heart knocked against his ribs.

The thread of light had disappeared.

Where is he? Hap inched closer. *You should have gone for help right away,* a voice inside told him. His muscles twitched, and he sensed the metallic taste of blood—he'd bitten the inside of his cheek without realizing it.

Occo should be at the window by now. Hap wondered if the howling wind had pried Occo off the wall and sent him plummeting to his doom. He edged closer, and darted his head to the window and back. Nothing reached for him, so he stuck his head out for a better look. Occo was not on the wall above or below or lying dead on the rocks. A terrible possibility leaped into his mind.

The terrace. Umber!

He raced for his door, threw it open, and tore down the hall. "Oates! Oates!" he screamed, even before he slammed Oates's door open with his shoulder.

The big fellow lurched up in his bed. "Who? Huh! What?"

Oates couldn't see in the pitch-black of his room. Hap tugged his arm, shouting with his words blurring together: "Get up, get up! The Creep is back! Climbing the wall! Heading for the terrace—Lord Umber, Oates, *Umber!*"

Oates erupted from the bed and reached blindly for a stack of weapons he kept leaning in the corner. His grasp fell on a long-handled battle-ax, and when he seized it up, the rest clattered to the floor. Hap saw a short, light spear that he could wield. He caught it as it fell and carried it with him.

They ran into the wide corridor, which was lit by a lantern with a candle inside. Other doors flew open. Sophie raced out of her room with her bow and a quiver of arrows tucked under one arm. In her good hand she clutched the hooked instrument that had to be strapped in place before she could shoot. For the first time, Hap glimpsed the pale stump at the end of her damaged arm.

Balfour hobbled out of his room, and a shrieking, wild-eyed Lady Truden burst out of hers. "What is it? What's happening!" She and Balfour collided, and they fell to the floor in a heap of tangled limbs.

Hap didn't wait to help them up. He seized the lantern by its ring-shaped handle and led the way up the stairs, bounding five steps at a time on his powerful legs. He heard Oates thump after him.

The wind nearly knocked Hap off his feet when he raced onto the terrace. The rain stung his cheek like needles. The first time he tried to shout, the wind choked him. He turned his head and cupped his hand, shouting, "Lord Umber! Look out! Occo is here!"

Oates charged forward. His deep voice took up the cry: "Umber! Umber!"

Sophie arrived beside Hap, dropped her bow and quiver, and fumbled to strap the instrument onto her bad arm. "Hap, do you see him?" she shouted.

Hap's head whipped right and left. Umber's favorite bench was unoccupied. Above it, the branches of the tree whipped about like tentacles.

"Where did you see the Creep?" Oates shouted. Hap pointed toward the wall that faced the bay. Oates ran to the spot with the battle-ax poised over one shoulder.

Maybe we got here first, Hap thought, hoping with all his heart that it was true. A clatter reached his ear, and he looked toward Umber's tower. The howling wind blew the door open and sucked it closed again. "His door is open!" Hap cried.

He saw a crack of light between the closed shutters of the window above. *He can't hear us,* Hap thought. He put down the lamp—the others needed it, not him, and he wanted both hands on the spear. Leaning into the wind so he wouldn't fall, he bolted for the opening.

Sophie shouted something after him, but the wind tore her words away. The door blew open again, as if to let Hap in, and when he raced inside it slammed shut once more. Hap whirled and pointed his spear, fearing that Occo had closed the door and not the force of the storm. Nobody was there. "Lord Umber!" he cried again. There was no reply.

Hap looked frantically around. Despite his alarm he was keenly aware that he'd never set foot in here before. His gaze flashed over the scene: Curved walls inside a round tower. A jar of glimmer-worms hanging from a crossbeam. A chair and footstool beside a fireplace with cold ashes. A dining table for one with an undisturbed meal and a crystal glass filled with wine. A small stove.

No Occo. And no Umber.

A staircase hugged the wall. Hap heard something clatter above. His voice cracked as he called again. "Lord Umber?" The spear shook in his hands.

The door flew open and Sophie came in. Her bow and arrow were ready.

"Upstairs!" cried Hap, bounding five steps at once.

"Hap—you can't go there!" Sophie shouted, but Hap was already at the top. Two rooms were there, with a landing between them. The smaller room, a quick glance showed Hap, was filled mainly by a large bed surrounded by gauzy curtains. "Lord Umber, are you here?" he cried. And then he heard the clatter again, in the other room.

It's the room I'm not supposed to see, Hap realized as he leaped inside. He heard the clatter a third time. It was only the wind hammering against the shuttered window. His eyes danced madly across the scene, searching for Umber or the enemy.

There was a desk in the room, with stacks of parchment sorted into piles. And in the middle of the desk was the thing Hap knew he was never, ever supposed to see.

CHAPTER
27

Hap recognized the object by the strange
metal it was made from: smooth as the surface of a pond.

He'd seen the other side when he leaped up to Umber's window. That was the side that glowed with strange, flickering light. This side was different. Its entire surface was that polished metal. It was hinged at the bottom, and opened like a case. And there was a word, Hap realized, engraved in tall letters on the vertical surface that faced him. But it was not a word that meant anything to him:

REBOOT

A jolt ran through Hap as he realized that he'd just done the one thing that was expressly forbidden by Umber.

Besides, Umber was still missing. *Get out of here! Now!*

His feet were a blur as he raced for the stairs. As he rushed down, Sophie stared with her mouth tightened into a disbelieving circle. He jumped the last seven steps, desperate to put his trespass behind him. Before his feet touched the floor, Lady Truden rushed into the tower. Her head reared back, and she pointed a trembling finger. "Where were you?"

"Nowhere—I thought he needed help!" Hap pleaded.

"You came in here! And you went *upstairs*?" Lady Truden asked in a scream. She turned to Sophie. "Did he?"

Sophie staggered back. She looked at Hap and her jaw trembled. "I . . . I . . . ," she sputtered.

Lady Truden didn't wait for an answer. "Get out, boy! We'll deal with you later!"

"I heard something," Hap said in a rush. "I thought Lord Umber was—"

"*Out!*" Lady Truden shrieked.

Hap bit his lip and ran. The wind slapped his face as he left Umber's tower. Balfour had arrived and was turning in every direction, shouting for Umber. Oates was coming back from the balcony.

"Did you see anything?" Hap called to Oates. Oates shook his head.

Where's Umber? Where's Occo? Hap's mind was frantic. Something round and red, the size of a fist, rolled across the stone terrace, blown by the wind. It came so close that Hap could stop it with the side of his foot. It was an apple, with a single bite taken from it. The bite was fresh, Hap saw when he picked it up, because the flesh inside was still white. *Umber was outside. He picked an apple off the tree.* Hap looked toward the place where Umber liked to sit, under the tree. Balfour was there on one knee, reaching under the bench for something. He lifted the small thing and held it between his thumb and forefinger. *Umber's black ring,* Hap realized. He clutched his stomach.

"I think he took Umber!" Balfour said, choking on the last word.

"But . . . how could he?" Hap called back. From his brief glimpse, he was sure it was no easy task for Occo to climb up the sheer wall in this storm. He felt sure Occo couldn't have carried Umber down the way he came up. *Unless . . .* Something tugged at Hap's thoughts. He remembered what was looped around the Creep's shoulder. *A rope?* His gaze followed the balcony at the edge of the terrace. He saw nothing on the side where Occo had climbed up—but at another corner, he spied a dark cord tied around the rail. "Over there!"

Oates arrived at the spot a moment after him. They stared

down. The rope dangled to the foot of the Aerie, whipping in the wind far below. It led to a narrow rocky space on the shore.

"We're too late," Hap said, in a voice too weak for anyone to hear.

Oates stepped over the railing and gripped the rope. His eyes met Hap's for a moment. "Umber is gone because of you," he said. He slid over the edge and lowered himself swiftly, hand under hand.

The words stung Hap like hornets. He slumped to the floor of the terrace and his spear clattered on the stone beside him. Oates always spoke the truth. *He's right,* Hap thought. Umber was lost, and it was his fault.

Balfour had built a fire in the hearth of the main hall, where the stone walls muted the storm's ferocious howl. Hap sat on the floor with his chin on his knees. Sophie jabbed at the fire with a poker. Balfour slumped in a chair, and Lady Truden paced endlessly across the room.

Heavy feet squished on the stairs, and Oates and Dodd came in, mournful and rain-soaked.

"Anything?" Lady Truden said, clutching her throat. She groaned as Oates shook his head. "What about you and the others, Dodd? Did you see what happened?"

"No, Lady Truden," muttered Dodd, staring at the water dripping from his shirt.

"Useless idiots!" Lady Truden snapped.

Hap pushed himself to his feet. "I want to go look for him."

"No," Balfour said, rubbing the bridge of his nose with his little finger.

"Why not?" Lady Truden shot back. She glared from Balfour to Hap. "If anyone should risk their neck to find Lord Umber, shouldn't it be him?"

"Yes," Hap said. It felt strange to agree with her. "It should be me. Besides, I can see in the dark."

"That's right! Now get out of here and find him," Lady Truden said. Her long arm pointed.

Balfour thumped his fists on the arms of his chair. "No! What's the matter with you, Tru? You want to send this boy into the night with that demon on the loose! What if it gets him?"

Lady Truden's face trembled with fury. "What if it does? Lord Umber might be hurt. He may have minutes to live! We have to find him!"

"Calm down, Tru. And sit, Happenstance," Balfour said. There was a command to his voice that Hap hadn't heard before. "Listen, all of you. There's no point trying to find Umber now. Occo got away with him—by sea, for sure, on that strange horse of his. If Occo wanted to kill him, he'd have left him dead on the terrace. Besides, Umber was alert enough to take off the ring that opens the black door, and leave it for us to find. So Umber must be alive, correct?

"Now, I don't know what we should do next, but I know what we must *not* do: allow Hap to fall into the hands of that wicked creature. Hap is what Occo wants. If you ask me, he only took Umber because Hap is too hard to catch."

"You're right," said Lady Truden. Her eager gaze fixed upon Hap. "We need Happenstance! We'll trade him for Umber . . ." Her hands rose as if she planned to seize him.

"We'll do no such thing," Balfour said.

Lady Truden bared her teeth at Balfour. "Why not?"

"He's just a boy, Tru," Balfour said quietly.

"A boy, you say! What sort of boy never sleeps? What boy has strange green eyes that see in the dark? What boy—"

"Enough!" shouted Balfour. "There's more to it, Tru. Umber told me the boy is important, and that he must be kept safe at all costs." Hap looked at Balfour, who stared back and nodded.

"And you expect us to believe that?" cried Lady Truden.

Balfour pushed against the arms of the chair and stood, straightening his usually bent form. "Are you suggesting that I'm not telling the truth?"

"I'm suggesting that you're more concerned about this child than the lord of this house!" Lady Truden said. "But now that you mention truth—Oates, did Lord Umber say the same thing to you, about the boy?"

Oates furrowed his brow. "No. But that doesn't mean—"

"And isn't it Lord Umber's command that I rule the Aerie when he is not here?"

"Yes, it is," Oates grumbled.

Lady Truden lifted her chin. "Well, Lord Umber is gone. And my first order is to keep a close watch on the boy. Dodd, you or one of your men, go to the shipping offices and tell the captains what has happened. Make sure Sandar knows. As soon as the storm abates, they must put to sea and begin a search."

Hap watched out a window as poor Dodd, wearing a long coat against the storm, trudged down the causeway on foot. Fortunately for Dodd, the causeway was elevated. Even the biggest waves couldn't wash over the road and sweep him away.

Hap was still watching an hour later when Dodd trudged back up to the Aerie. This time the wind was in his teeth, and Dodd had to lean into the gale to make any progress.

When Dodd was halfway up the steep road, something came out of the raging water. A tall wave dashed against the side of the causeway, and when it withdrew, a dark creature with a gaunt rider remained. *Occo and his horse!* Hap thought. In seconds, the ridged tail at the rear of the horse divided at the end and transformed into powerful equine legs. The creature stood, shook off the water, and clattered across the stones after Dodd, bearing Occo on its back.

Dodd drew his sword and paused, as if considering whether it would be wiser to stand his ground or run for the safety of the gatehouse. He chose flight.

Hap had hesitated when he saw Occo climbing the walls of the Aerie. He knew he couldn't do it again. He ran for the main hall, screaming, "Occo is on the causeway! He's after Dodd!"

Oates rumbled down the stairs, and Hap followed. Balfour came behind, faster than Hap would have expected for a man with so many aching parts. Oates threw open the door to the gatehouse and charged outside.

Balfour called after Hap, "Happenstance, wait! You're not to venture outside!" Hap pretended not to hear him and rushed after Oates. The wooden doors of the gatehouse were open, but the portcullis had been lowered. Hap looked out between the iron bars, afraid of what he might see. He felt one of Oates's strong hands close over his shoulder.

Dodd was on the causeway, a stone's throw away. Occo and

his horse were nowhere in sight. *Thank goodness,* Hap thought, until he saw the way Dodd staggered toward the Aerie. His sword lay in the road behind him. Dodd wobbled and dropped to his knees, and started to crawl.

Wilkin and Barkin had already charged out the narrow door beside the portcullis. They put their elbows under Dodd's arms, dragged him back to the gatehouse, and propped him in a chair. Wilkin's face was purple with rage and anguish. "We didn't see what was happening, Dodd—so sorry!"

Dodd's teeth chattered and he struggled to breathe. Hap saw bruises on his neck. Streams of blood flowed from four punctures on one side. He imagined Occo's long, sharp nails piercing the flesh.

"His . . . face . . . ," Dodd said hoarsely. "I pulled his mask to one side . . . saw another eye . . . like a cat's eye . . . horrible . . ."

"Easy, Dodd," Barkin said. "Don't try to talk. Wilkin, get that medicine kit Umber gave us!"

Wilkin bustled away. Dodd looked at the faces peering down, and his gaze lingered on Hap for a moment before turning to Balfour. "He said . . . if we want Lord Umber back alive . . ." Dodd's hand went inside his coat, probing, and came out clutching a folded parchment. With a trembling hand, he thrust it at Balfour. He coughed before he could speak again. "He told me . . . do as this says, or Umber dies."

Balfour took the parchment and opened it. His gaze swept back and forth across the message. When he was done he shut his eyes and rubbed his palm across his face.

"What does it say?" Oates asked.

"Hap, come inside with me," Balfour said.

They stood inside the Aerie's first floor, where the rush of water turned the creaking paddle wheel. The note was at their feet, where Balfour had let it drop after reading aloud. The words were scrawled in a spidery hand, and the smudged, flaking ink was a color somewhere between red and brown. A lump formed in Hap's throat when he wondered what Occo used for ink.

"What on earth can we do?" mumbled Balfour.

Lady Truden circled them, stomping. "Exactly what the note tells us to do." She stabbed toward the note with her finger. "And soon! Within the hour, or Lord Umber will be thrown from Petraportus, onto the rocks!"

Hap looked up at her. Her mouth was clamped so tight that the color was driven from her lips. Over Lady Truden's shoulder he saw Sophie watching from the bottom of the stairs, blinking back tears.

Balfour spoke with his eyes closed. "Tru—Umber would never let us surrender the boy. I can assure you of that."

Lady Truden squeezed her hands, turning the knuckles white. *"How else can we save Lord Umber?"*

Oates's voice boomed out. "Let me go. Let me try to rescue him."

Lady Truden glared. "Read the note, you fool! Occo will be watching. If anyone but the boy comes, he'll kill Lord Umber. And of course he'd see you—that's why he chose Petraportus for the meeting place!"

Hap stared at the parchment. Lady Truden was right. There was no other way. Umber was being held in the crumbling ruins of Petraportus, in the last tower standing. Even now, a dim light could be seen at its pinnacle. There was only one way to get there: across the bridge of rubble that reached from the old castle to the foot of the Aerie. The bridge was in plain sight of the tower. Occo would see if anyone but Hap tried to cross. And with the storm raging, there was no way to use a boat to sneak someone over. It was a perfect trap.

"I have to go," Hap said. "There's no other way." Balfour slowly opened his eyes. The others stared. Lady Truden sighed with relief and leaned on the table.

Balfour pushed his chair back and stood. "Happenstance. You can't—"

"Please, Balfour," Hap said, standing as well. "I haven't been around here for long. Well . . . actually, I haven't been around *anywhere* for long. I don't know who I am, or what I'm here for. I know that Lord Umber's important, though. I've seen all the good things he's done. I know for sure the world needs him. I can't say that about me."

Sophie made a choking sound and stumbled up the stairs. Balfour looked like he wanted to speak, but no words came out.

"Who knows," Hap said. "After the Creep lets Lord Umber go, maybe these legs of mine will help me get away."

"I don't believe that," Oates said.

The last drop of moisture in Hap's mouth evaporated. "I guess I should go now."

"Wait—I'll get you some of Umber's trick bottles," Balfour said suddenly. "Like the one he used on the tyrant worm, and the one he gave to the prince. They might give you a chance."

"No!" cried Lady Truden. "No tricks. You're risking Lord Umber's life, you old fool!"

"And you're trying to doom Hap's," Balfour snapped. His face darkened with a fury Hap had never seen. "He's taking the bottles, Tru, like it or not."

Lady Truden cried out in disgust. "What does it matter, anyway? It's hopeless. How do we even know the boy won't run off as soon as he's outside, to save his own skin?"

Balfour gave Lady Truden a cold stare. She crossed her arms and turned away.

"I guess you'll just have to trust me," Hap said to her back.

There was a small door made of oak and iron in a corner of the first floor. Lady Truden had the key that opened it, and Oates heaved the door open. Behind it was a short tunnel through solid rock. It emerged outside the Aerie, where a narrow staircase descended to the foot of the pillar, and the bridge to Petraportus.

Hap turned before leaving. "Good-bye, everyone." Lady Truden looked away, Oates squeezed his shoulder, and Balfour gathered him in a hug. Hap breathed deeply and stepped into the tunnel. Halfway through, he stopped. Sophie was calling, shouting his name. It was by far the loudest he'd ever heard her speak.

CHAPTER
28

Hap stepped into the howling gray blur of the storm, onto the slick stairs that were etched in the pillar of rock. The steps were barely two feet wide and slippery from rainwater cascading across them. A chain was the only railing, and he gripped the cold wet links, moving hand over hand.

The gale blew steady and strong down the mouth of the bay, and the waves obeyed it with a rhythmic assault. They rushed at Kurahaven like brigades, crashing thunderously on the shore. The harbor was crumbling under the attack. Piers tilted and splintered planks bobbed in the foam. Two of the largest ships had torn free of their moorings and hammered wildly against the docks.

At the bottom of the steps the crude breakwater that

connected the Aerie to Petraportus was under the same assault. On a calm day it would be an easy stroll across those rocks, the remains of a fallen tower. But now the waves rose up to bow before engulfing the jumbled stone in tons of churning black sea. Foam and water hissed and drained into the gaps, just in time for another monstrous wave to pounce.

Sometimes there was scarcely one second between waves; sometimes there were a few. Hap started to gauge the timing, noting with a grimace that a longer delay between waves led to a bigger, more lethal wall of water. *But I might be able to make it,* he thought. Nobody else could, he knew; his grasshopper legs gave him a chance. Of course, Occo the Creep must have been thinking the same thing. He didn't want any helpful friends coming along. *Especially not Oates,* Hap figured.

He stood at the end of the bridge. With his clothes soaked by rain, he felt twice as heavy. Petraportus loomed, with its remaining tower listing at a frightening angle. The dim light still glowed in its topmost windows.

Across the span stood the broken foundation of the fallen east tower. There was a wide crack in the center where the wall had shattered. He'd be safe if he could make it that far.

Hap watched the incoming waves. The next two were close together. After that came a larger gap. *That's when I go,* Hap thought. *Before the third wave.* His ribs clutched his heart.

He imagined himself caught under one of those crushing waves, with tons of water driving him into the depths and holding him there until his mouth opened and black water filled his lungs.

The first wave shattered against the breakwater. The second rose and toppled heavily onto the rocks. *Now!*

Hap ran as fast as he could without slipping on the wet stone. He jumped for a large rock, landed with two feet, and hopped again. Pools of black water were everywhere, filtering into the crevices. One of his feet came down in a puddle and slipped between two stones. He pried it out, sensing a new mountain of water rising at the corner of his right eye. *Don't fall,* screeched a voice in his head. And he knew he must not fall—another life beside his own was at stake.

The wave rose with a *whoosh.* When it reached full height, it seemed to pause. The wind ceased, and the storm fell strangely quiet. *Because that wave is so big that it's blocking everything,* Hap realized. The crack in the foundation seemed a mile away. In the momentary lee of the wave that was about to drown him, he jumped. He soared across the wet stones. The wave toppled. Hap could have reached out with his right hand and touched it. His foot came down on another stone, and he pushed off again.

The wave slammed onto the breakwater. Everything was

lost in a roar of inky water and gray foam. Hap flew through the crack in the keep, feeling the spittle of the wave lash his shoulders, and came to rest with his hands and feet on the floor. He felt every frantic thump of his heart. His hands went to the pockets of his coat, feeling for the precious items nestled within. Everything was still there.

He was in a round, roofless space surrounded by ragged walls. The rain still hammered down, but he was safe from the waves. Across from where he'd entered, he saw an archway that led into a larger space. He clambered across piles of stone and went through, into the legendary keep of Petraportus. Here, he knew, was the wonder of its age: a castle for a maritime empire, with a hall so vast that a ship could sail inside to the great pool under its dome.

The pool remained, but the dome had partly collapsed and littered it with blocks of stone. The marble columns that once supported the roof were shattered and broken. Still, the remaining walls offered some shelter, so the pool was surprisingly calm as the storm shrieked across the gaps overhead. Hap heard waves pounding at the other side, trying to complete the demolition. The stones grumbled against one another. Even as he stood there, a chunk rolled out of the walls and splashed into the pool.

As the ripples spread, something else sloshed in the water.

Hap saw a dark thing just under the surface. The water bubbled, and a head emerged. It was a horse's head, but with hard, plated skin and a spiny fin instead of a mane. Hap's teeth pressed together. *Occo's horse,* he realized. The beast's neck craned sideways, and a brown eye stared. Beyond that, Hap saw something even more ominous: the prow of Occo's ship, sticking out from behind a fallen pillar.

He put a hand to his cheek to stop his teeth from chattering and looked around the keep. The archway to the west tower was on the opposite side. He could get there by picking his way around the pool.

The sea horse swam in place, watching him. He grimaced at it, and then started his journey. A terrible fate seemed moments away. Either the rest of the dome would collapse on his head, or Occo would dart out and seize him. *This is insanity,* part of his mind screamed. *How do you know Umber's really alive? Get out of here!* He ignored that voice. "Be ready," he said aloud.

In a sheltered alcove halfway around the pool, he saw a pair of water barrels on the stone floor. There, too, were the ashes of a fire, a pair of hammocks suspended from the stones, a little stove and a few other meager belongings. *The fisherman and his wife,* he recalled, and at the same moment he saw their cold and lifeless bodies on the ground.

Hap didn't know what had happened to them, but he was

certain Occo was responsible. They were side by side on the rocks. Their faces were masks of terror, with eyes staring and mouths open in petrified screams. Rain spattered their waxen cheeks. Hap turned away and covered his eyes, but the faces remained inside his mind. *Those poor people,* he thought. He remembered his glimpse of Occo. All he'd seen was the top of the pale head.

What on earth did they see?

CHAPTER
29

Hap heard a splash in the water behind him. Occo's horse had swum closer. He reached for a stone and flung it at the creature. It tilted its head to let the rock sail by and snorted at Hap. Jets of mist shot from its nostrils.

"I hate you. And your master, too," Hap said.

The horse shadowed him as Hap leaped from stone to stone until he reached the tower. The room at the base was intact, except for some gaps in the walls where stones had fallen. A staircase curved up and out of sight. It took all his will to raise his foot to the first step. "Here we go," he said aloud, and began his strange journey up the sagging tower.

Streams of water flowed down the stairs. There were rooms along the way. He'd enter one and cross to another flight of steps on the other side. The rooms had been stripped of furnishings long before, and now all he saw were nests in the cracks of the walls. The birds couldn't see Hap, but they knew something was passing by. His gifted eyes saw them ruffle their feathers in the dark.

Occo must be crazy, Hap decided. Or, at least, the Creep did not understand what a precarious state the tower was in. Hap could feel the whole structure rocking in the wind.

A block of stone the size of a barrel fell inward. Hap had to press his back against the wall to keep from getting crushed. It tumbled down the stairs and smashed into the curving wall below, pushing another stone six inches outward.

"We're all going to die," Hap said. Before he could move on, he had to take three deep breaths of wet, salty air. He thought the top must be near because there were new sounds above. They were hard to understand at first, with the storm whistling through gaps in the walls. But the higher he went, the clearer the sounds became. And what he heard was completely unexpected.

Umber was talking. That alone was a surprise, but what astonished him was the tone of Umber's voice. It sounded like the old, exuberant Umber, not the sad specter who haunted the Aerie for nearly two weeks. Hap smiled in spite of his fear.

"Come on, Occo!" he heard Umber say. "You can tell me. How did you follow us across the sea? It won't do any harm to let me know."

Occo's icy voice replied. "I sent my steed to wound the leviathan. She could smell the blood in the water, and we followed the scent."

"Clever," Umber replied. "I should have guessed! Now, what sort of being are you, anyway? Are there many like you? And what is it you want from me? The curiosity is killing me!"

"*I* will be killing you if you do not hold your tongue."

It sounded as if they were just a half curve of the stairs away. Hap wondered if he might be able to approach unseen and surprise the Creep. But that hope was dashed as another sound rose up from below, echoing through the walls: a whinny from Occo's horse. *A signal,* Hap thought.

"Now, silence!" Occo hissed. "He is coming."

"Who is?" Umber asked brightly. Hap heard a metallic whisper, like a blade being drawn from its sheath. "Absolutely, I'll be quiet now," Umber said next.

Hap curled his fingers into fists, steeling his nerve for whatever would come next. He pressed his back to the outer wall and crept up the remaining steps. The teetering was more pronounced near the top of the tower. Bits of mortar fell from the walls and bounced down the stairs, *tick tack tick*. Something far below shifted and crashed, and the whole tower shuddered.

"Doesn't feel safe, does it? Perhaps we should leave," he heard Umber say. "Sorry," Umber added as Occo snarled.

Hap saw orange light ahead. It grew with every step. Finally, he spied the edge of the threshold that led to the top. Two steps later he saw Umber's legs, bound tight with cord. Another step revealed the rest of Umber, sitting with his back against the wall. Umber's arms were lashed to his sides, and he had a cloth around his eyes. The tip of a saber hovered at his neck.

Hap paused while he was still out of Occo's sight. There was something he had to do before he went farther, if he was to have any chance to save Umber and himself. When that was done, he took the final step, arriving at the threshold.

From there he could see the entire room. The space was round—or had been round, at one time, before a quarter fell away, leaving a sheer drop off a jagged edge. Beyond that gap, the elements raged.

Occo stood near Umber, holding the saber. His head was covered once more by the sack of gauzy material. A bright blue eye peered out from the single hole. "At *lasssst*," Occo whispered when Hap appeared in the glow of the lantern.

"At last what? Who's there? Wait—it's not Happenstance, is

it? Hap, tell me that's not you!" Umber said. There was a hint of panic in his voice.

"It is me," Hap said.

"Do my orders mean nothing?" Umber cried. "Get out of here!"

"I can't," Hap said. "Occo will kill you if I don't do what he says." He didn't want Occo to know how frightened he was, but his quivering voice betrayed him.

"You're too important, Hap!" Umber said, wriggling and leaning forward. "Don't fret about me. Run, as fast as your legs can—"

"Enough," Occo said, putting his blade under Umber's chin and forcing his mouth closed. "Step into the room, child. Or I will put an end to this Umber right now."

Umber shook his head and mouthed, "No!" But Hap wiped his sweaty hands on his coat and stepped into the room.

"Halt there," Occo said. Hap froze.

"If you vanish, I will kill him," Occo said.

"Vanish?" Hap said. "I don't know how to do that."

"Good," said Occo. The awful slurping came from inside the mask. "Take everything from your pockets. *Now!*" He wiggled the blade against Umber's flesh.

Hap's shoulders slumped. He put a hand in the right pocket of his coat, and then the left, and took out the bottles that Balfour had given him. "That's all I brought. These are medicine, if Lord Umber needs them," he lied.

"Throw them away." Occo gestured to the window by Hap's shoulder. Hap looked at the blade against Umber's neck and tossed the bottles into the storm.

"Now your coat," said Occo. Hap took it off and pushed that out the window as well. The wind tore it away. Occo looked him up and down, satisfied that nothing else was hidden. He stepped away from Umber and circled toward Hap, striding like a bird on those long legs that bent backward at the knee. Waving his blade, he forced Hap to the far side of the room. There was a rusted iron grate leaning against the wall near the stairs. Occo lifted it with one hand and jammed it into the threshold, blocking the way out. *So strong,* thought Hap.

"What's happening? What's going on?" asked Umber.

"We're trapped," Hap replied. There was no other way out, except the windows or the gaping hole behind him.

Occo shoved the saber into the sheath at his waist. He stared at Hap with his eager blue eye.

"Let Lord Umber go," Hap said. "That was your bargain."

"What bargain?" cried Umber. "Happenstance, you'll do no such thing!"

"I will let him go when I have what I want," Occo said.

"What *do* you want?" Hap said.

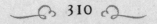

"I want to *see*," Occo said. He reached for the top of his head, pinched the gauzy material, and ripped the sack away from his face. Hap gasped. The face was smooth and pale, and studded with gray, wrinkled lumps. *No, not lumps!* Hap screamed inwardly. *Eyelids!* There were seven or eight at least, scattered in a senseless pattern across Occo's cheeks, temples, and forehead. Only the blue eye was open, but the other lids began to twitch. A second eye high on the forehead revealed itself. It was utterly different from the first, yellow at the edges and brown in the center. *An animal's eye,* Hap thought, pressing his palm against his mouth.

The rest of the wrinkled lids flipped open, one after another, and a menagerie of eyes bulged from deep oozing sockets. The soulless black orb of a shark. A glittering bird's eye. The silvery eye of a reptile, with a vertical slit for an iris. There was even a rodent's red eye on Occo's pointed chin. Each set of lids blinked to a different beat.

"I want to see what *you* see," Occo said, dropping the sack to the floor. Hap understood why the fisherman and his wife had died with terror frozen on their expressions. Occo's entire face horrified, not just the eyes. His mouth was a cruel crescent, arcing down at the corners. His teeth were yellow needles, and his tongue was a wiggling wormy thing.

Hap's stomach was trying to turn inside out. A sickening

truth dawned on him, and he forced it into words. "You . . . steal . . . *eyes!*"

Occo's long fingers traced the bulging orbs on his face. "I pluck what I need. A fish's eye, to see under the water. A falcon's eye, to see what is far. A cat's eye, to see in the dark. . . ."

"Are you serious? This is *fascinating!*" Umber said, wiggling his bound feet.

Hap's voice was a strangled croak. "And now you want *my* eyes . . ."

Occo edged toward him. Hap saw all the stolen eyes swivel and blink faster. For the first time he noticed the pink tendrils that were rooted in the sockets and gripped the orbs, holding them in place.

"*Yes.* I want to see what your kind can see," Occo said, still advancing. "For a lifetime, I've searched. I came close so many times . . ."

"So many times? But I've only seen you once."

"Not you. I was after the other one when I learned of you."

"The other one?" Umber said. He was trying to use his shoulder to push the cloth away from his eyes, and not succeeding. "Do you mean WN? Do you know what that stands for, by any chance?"

"His name doesn't matter," said Occo. "I have this one now. He is the same kind."

"What do you mean *the same kind*?" Hap asked, backing away.

"Don't you know what you are?" Occo said, moving closer and raising his hands. Hap stared at the terrible nails on the ends of those fingers, shuddering to think of what they might do. "You're a *Meddler*, child. You can *see* them."

"See what?" Hap croaked.

Watery drool spilled from Occo's mouth, and he slurped again. "The *filaments*! Fortune! Doom! Destiny! Fate!"

"You mean—those threads of light? But I barely see them at all. I don't know what they mean."

"They mean *everything*." Occo feinted right and left to force Hap straight back toward the ragged gap that led to oblivion. Hap felt the wind tugging the back of his shirt. Hard rain lashed his neck.

"What's happening?" Umber cried. He rubbed the side of his face against the floor, determined to scrape the cloth from his eyes. "Hap, you can't let him get you! Run, boy!"

"You are freshly made, aren't you?" Occo said. "The sight takes time. Your eyes will grow stronger. Before long they will see. But not for you. For *me*." Occo spread his long arms wide. All Hap could do was move back until his heels were at the precipice. The sea pounded insanely on rocks hundreds of feet below.

"I will need room for your eyes," Occo said. Hap felt a lump rise in his throat as the Creep's blue eye bulged out of its socket, pushed from behind by the quivering tendrils. With his forefinger and thumb, Occo plucked the eye from their grasp. He dropped the orb, and it plopped wetly on the floor. The tendrils opened wide and crooked like fingers, eager to hold a fresh eye.

Hap screamed into his palm.

"What was that? Hap, are you all right?" Umber shouted. He crawled toward them blindly, wriggling like a caterpillar.

Occo laughed as a second eye quivered out of its socket. "And I won't need this cat's eye, either. Your eyes will see in the dark for me, won't they, little Meddler?" He plucked out the eye and flicked it over Hap's shoulder, into the storm.

"I could use some help right now," Hap muttered thickly.

"You are beyond help," Occo said. He crouched, ready to spring. And then all of his remaining eyes bulged at once. He lifted one foot off the ground and shrieked so loud that Hap clapped his hands over his ears.

There was a tiny silver spear driven deep into Occo's ankle. He pulled it out and flung it aside. Spittle flew from his mouth as he screamed with rage. He drew his saber and slashed at the air. His eyes swiveled in all directions, searching high and low to see who had given him such pain.

"What's happening? Hap, are you there?" Umber shouted.

And then all of Occo's eyes turned toward the tiny form of Thimble as the little hunter sprinted across the open floor.

... are only a few recorded instances of those tiny folk, perfect in form in every way, but only a fraction of the size of ordinary human beings, so small that they could fit easily in the palm of one's hand. Despite their miniature size, they often demonstrate incredible courage, as when the one named

CHAPTER
30

When Sophie had called to Hap just before he left, she relayed remarkable news: Thimble had come to her and offered to help. He owed his freedom to Umber and his life to Hap, he'd said, and he hated the thought of being indebted to either of them. Besides, only he could go with Hap undetected and perhaps save them from the Creep.

The others had caught only fleeting glimpses of the reclusive fellow over the years, and they were astonished by his offer. Still, they were skeptical of what effect Thimble's weapons—a spear and dagger tipped with spider's poison—might have against the mighty Occo.

But the tiny wound in the Creep's ankle was clearly causing

agony. A pink sweat erupted across Occo's exposed skin, and his limbs quaked. Rage drove him to the brink of madness.

Thimble looked like a frantic mouse as he ran for a crevice in the wall. Occo hobbled after him, shrieking so loud that he drowned out the storm. *"What is this pain? What did you do to me?"* He flung his saber at Thimble. Hap was sure that would be the end of the brave little fellow, but the blade struck the floor and bounced over Thimble's head, clattering down on the other side.

Umber had finally managed to push the blindfold away from one eye. "Thimble?" he cried. "Hap, you brought Thimble to help you? Brilliant!"

Even hobbled by the poison, Occo bore down swiftly on Thimble. The tiny man slipped between two of the stones just as Occo reached to grab him. The Creep plunged his hand into the crevice. *"I'll crush you! I'll mash you to a pulp!"*

Occo threw his head back and howled again. He pulled his hand from the crack. A miniature knife—tainted, Hap knew, by the same venom—was driven to the hilt under one of the long fingernails. Occo shook the hand madly to dislodge the blade. Then he threw himself at the wall. He seized the edges of the block where Thimble had vanished. With awesome strength he shoved it from side to side, intending to crush Thimble inside the crevice.

"Bad idea," said Umber.

The stones in the wall above began to shift. Occo was too wild with rage to notice. The block in his hands loosened more from his effort, and he rocked it with even greater fury. Hap hoped that Thimble had somehow managed to escape.

At last there was a wrenching sound loud enough to capture Occo's attention. He looked up at the unstable wall and finally perceived the danger. Before he could pull his hands away, the blocks shifted and Hap heard the crunch as Occo's wrist was pinned inside. Occo shrieked again and writhed, trying to pull loose. Over his head the wall sagged inward and came apart. Occo gaped back at Umber and Hap as if looking for help.

A stone that must have weighed three hundred pounds hit Occo's shoulder, hammering him to the floor. Five more landed on his legs. Hap turned away, plunging his fingers into his ears to muffle the awful sounds. The rest of the wall tumbled onto Occo, stone after stone.

When Hap dared to look again, he saw just a twisted foot sticking out from one end of the rubble.

"Thimble!" Hap cried. He ran to the pile of rocks and called through cupped hands. "Are you there? Tell me you're all right!"

"I ain't dead," came the faint reply. Thimble stepped out

from another crack farther down the wall. "I climbed along the outside and came back through here." He pointed toward Hap's leg with a tiny hand. "Watch behind you, though."

Hap looked down and froze. A shaking long-fingered hand inched toward his boot from the pile. But it couldn't come any closer; the arm was trapped under enormous chunks of stone. Hap gasped, because he saw the Creep's horribly damaged face staring up from between two blocks. The lids of the remaining eyes fluttered shut, one by one. All Occo could manage was a hoarse whisper. "Hate . . . your . . . kind . . ."

"Why?" asked Hap. In spite of what Occo had done to the fisherman and his wife, in spite of what Occo wanted to do to him, Hap felt the hot sting of pity in his heart. The Creep was finished, his broken body beyond the help of any healing powers.

"The sight you have . . . and you fritter it away . . . on foolishness . . ."

"Me? I don't know what you're talking about," Hap said.

Umber had wriggled closer. "You there! You said Hap was made. What do you mean? Made how? Made by who?"

Occo's clutching fingers uncurled. The last eyelid closed. His only reply was a final hiss that faded into nothing.

Hap bent low and rested with his hands on his thighs, feeling his whole body tremble.

"Hap?" said Umber. "If you don't mind, could you cut me loose? The Creep's blade is over there. That would do the trick."

"Of course," Hap said. Before he took a step, another rumble, ominously loud, shook the stones under his feet. Something cracked, loud as thunder, and the section where the Creep lay parted from the rest of the tower and fell into the night. Hap caught a glimpse of Occo's broken body slipping away.

A deep vibration rattled the tower. Hap heard Thimble's tiny voice from below. "We need to go!"

"The legs! Legs first!" Umber shouted, lying on his back with his feet in the air. Hap slipped the blade under the cords and sawed furiously. Umber kicked the cords away and rolled over, struggling awkwardly to his feet with his hands still bound to his sides. "Forget the rest," Umber said as part of the roof caved in nearby. Blocks of stone tumbled like dice. One smashed into the grate that Occo had used to block the stairs, tilting it and leaving a narrow gap below.

"There's some luck!" Umber cried. "Can we squeeze through?"

Hap scooped Thimble up, and at the top step, bent to pick up the box that he'd used to carry the little fellow. It was padded with cloth and straw to keep Thimble safe.

* * *

Hap thought the journey down the crumbling tower would never end. He and Umber pounded down the steps, hopping over rubble, leaping across widening gaps. The partial collapse at the top had unbalanced the tower even more. It rocked and shuddered so violently that it was hard to keep their balance as they ran. By the time they were halfway down, Umber was puffing for air. When they reached the last flight of steps, he was wheezing. Hap heard stones tumbling down behind them.

They emerged from the tower moments before tons of rubble choked the stairwell, pushing a billowing cloud of dust ahead of it. There was a roar and splash outside—it could only be an immense part of the tower toppling into the sea.

When the world stopped shaking, Umber dropped to his knees inside the safety of the domed keep and gasped for air. Hap cut the cords that bound Umber's arms to his side. "Well—hah! That's one for my books," Umber said, laughing as he rubbed one arm with the other hand. The familiar twinkle had returned to his eyes. "Oh—there's the Creep's ship! Clever of him to hide it here in the storm. And look who else is with us."

Hap turned and saw Occo's horse in the water, watching them.

"I wonder if it can understand me?" Umber said. "I think it might." He stood and tugged the hem of his shirt. "Your master Occo has been destroyed," Umber called out. The horse tossed its head and chuffed. Hap wondered if that meant *I know.* "You are free to go," Umber said. "Or you can stay here and join our company, if it pleases you. I won't blame you for his wicked deeds."

The horse stared for another moment. Then it turned and swam out of the dome and vanished under the waves.

Umber shrugged. "That's that, I suppose. Now we just have to—"

"They're dead, Lord Umber," Hap blurted.

"They?" The skin between Umber's eyebrows wrinkled. "Who?"

Hap pointed. "The fisherman and his wife. Occo killed them."

Umber walked slowly to the spot where the bodies lay. "Ah. Poor folk. I had no idea." He stared down for a while with his head bowed. "Whoever they were, we'll give them a decent burial, Hap. A mausoleum right here would be proper, I think."

"They're dead because of me," Hap said, blinking fast and looking away.

Umber came back to grip Hap's shoulders. "Don't you *dare*, Happenstance. Not for a moment can you blame yourself for the things the wicked do. Yes, Occo was after you. But it was just poor fortune that put those two in his path."

Hap bit his bottom lip. *But was it really poor fortune?* he wondered. *Or is this what happens to some who cross paths with a Meddler?*

"Come on," Umber said. "Let's wave to the others and let them know I'm alive."

"Wait," said Hap. There were things he needed to say before he dared return to the Aerie and face Lady Truden again. "Before I came here . . . after you disappeared . . . I saw it, Lord Umber."

Umber narrowed an eye. "Saw *what*, Hap?"

"The thing I wasn't supposed to see. When Occo came for you . . . I thought you were in danger, in your tower. I ran in to help. And I saw it." Hap remembered Thimble, still inside the box in his pocket, and he lowered his voice to the faintest whisper: "The silver case. With that word on top."

Umber tilted his head to one side, waiting.

Hap winced. "You know. REBOOT."

Umber didn't bother to whisper in reply. "That's all you saw? The case, and that word?"

"Yes."

Umber took a deep breath and held it. He put his hands on his waist and let the breath whistle slowly out his nose. "First of all, there's no need to whisper. I'm certain Thimble saw it

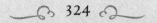

long ago; that little sneak pokes his nose into everything."

A tiny indignant voice, muffled by cloth and the wooden box, cried out from Hap's pocket. "You don't know that—you never caught me!"

Umber rolled his eyes. "Do you know what *reboot* means, Hap?"

Hap shook his head. "It doesn't mean to get a new boot, does it?"

"It means *start over*. Does anyone else know you saw it?"

"Sophie." Hap's head shrank toward his shoulders. "Lady Truden."

Umber wrinkled his nose. "Ooh. I imagine Tru's head nearly exploded."

Hap dropped his gaze. "She wants me to leave."

Umber waved off the notion. "Well, I assure you *that* isn't going to happen. You're part of our company now, Hap. I am deeply grateful for what you and Thimble have done. But I suppose Thimble owed me that much."

Thimble called out again. "I saved you. You saved me. Now we owe each other nothin'!"

Umber grinned. "Only thanks, my brave friend. As for you, Hap, you had no debt to me, but you risked your life, anyway."

If there was ever a time to ask forgiveness, Hap knew it had

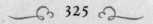

arrived. "There's one more thing I need to tell you."

Umber arched an eyebrow. "There's *more*?"

Hap cleared his throat. "Remember the note from WN? I . . . read part of it."

Umber's head snapped back. "*What?* But how? I've had that locked away since . . ." His eyes nearly closed, and he scratched his emerging beard. "Aaaah . . . when I fell asleep in the barge, and woke up in the darkness. I had the feeling someone was there! That candle didn't go out by itself, did it?"

Hap stared at the stones under his feet. "It was wrong, I know it was, but I wanted to see it so badly. I am so sorry, Lord Umber."

Umber looked sideways at Hap. "So. How much did you read?"

"To where it said, 'I know from where you came, Umber. I know too what happened to that world of yours.'"

Umber's jaw slid from side to side. "Well . . . who am I to blame you for trying to see the note? You were scared and confused, whisked away by strangers. And I withheld the only clue to your identity. Frankly, I'd have done the same thing.

"But don't worry. First thing tomorrow, I'll show you the whole note. Please give me until then—there are other things I have to explain first, and I need time to gather my thoughts. I wish I could say this will answer all your questions and put your mind at ease. It won't, I'm afraid. But there's one thing that we know for sure now: Happenstance, you are a Meddler."

The storm began to fade hours later. Oates appeared outside the Aerie and heaved a rope across the bridge. Umber secured it on their end, and he and Hap gripped it tight as they crossed with waves washing around their knees. Lady Truden nearly fainted with relief when Umber walked into the Aerie again—not only because Umber was safe from the Creep, but also because he'd clearly emerged from his dark mood. Still, the return of Umber's buoyant spirits couldn't keep him from collapsing onto a sofa in the main hall and falling into a deep slumber.

Hap took the padded box from his pocket, put it on the floor by the crack in the wall, and opened the lid. Thimble climbed out.

"Thank you," Hap said. "You saved us."

Thimble puffed out his tiny chest. "Don't forget it," he said, and disappeared into his hole.

CHAPTER
31

Dawn broke slowly, as if reluctant to reveal the damage of the storm. The last tower of Petraportus was a fraction of its former height, a shattered fang that stabbed the sky. The city's docks were smashed. Ships were half sunk or run aground. Roofs were sheared off, chimneys toppled, and the tents of the market were shredded and flattened. But as soon as the light allowed, people emerged to begin repairs, as numerous and industrious as ants.

When Hap stepped out of his room, he found Lady Truden waiting for him in the middle of the corridor. "Happenstance," she said.

All his muscles tensed. "Good morning, Lady Truden."

Her jaw hardly moved as she spoke. "I wanted to tell you

that . . . I mean to say . . . you are forgiven for trespassing into Lord Umber's tower. It was understandable, under the circumstances. Of course you will not be asked to leave. You will always be welcome here."

Hap leaned to one side, trying to see behind Lady Truden. Surely, someone was pressing a sword into her back, forcing her to say these words. But she was alone.

"Thank you, Lady Truden," Hap said.

"I also want to say that . . ." A long pause followed. She groped the air with her fingers as if she might find the words she wanted there. "The things I said . . . I didn't mean . . ." She put a clenched hand to her mouth. "Lord Umber is a great man. I can't imagine losing him. *All* of us losing him, that is."

Hap nodded. "Yes, Lady Truden."

"Also," she added with the corner of one eye twitching, "Lord Umber wishes to see you in his tower."

"Um . . . all right," Hap replied.

Lady Truden nodded curtly, went to her room, and closed her door a bit too hard.

Hap walked up to the terrace, glad to end the conversation. The door to the tower opened before he could knock, and a smiling Umber, with a mug of coffee in one hand, beckoned him inside. "There you are, Hap! Follow me."

For the second time, and the first by invitation, Hap stood inside Umber's study. The silver case was out of sight.

Umber sat at his desk and Hap took the chair on the other side. Umber leaned forward, with his fingers interlaced. "I'll show you the rest of the note soon, Hap. But first there are some other things you should know. About me, and where I came from. Are you ready to hear my story?"

Hap nodded.

"Good." Umber thumped his desk with his palms, and offered a lopsided grin. "So . . . by now you know I'm not really from around here, don't you?"

Hap's leg was bouncing up and down. He stilled it with his hand. "I guess so. But where did you come from?"

"How do I explain? It's a different world altogether. A separate time and place, disconnected from this one. That's a slippery idea, Hap, can you grasp it?"

Hap tried and failed to understand. "But how can you know that? This world hasn't all been explored, has it? Maybe your land is just far away, across the sea."

Umber shook his head. "This world may not be fully mapped, but mine was. And while the two have some things in common—some language and history, and the stars above—there are undeniable differences. For one thing, if you find an old map here, and it says, *'Here there be dragons,'* well . . . there really *are* dragons. You see, there was no magic where I came from, Hap. No tyrant worms, sea-giants, sorcerers, trolls, curses, or spells. But we had something just as amazing. We had technology."

Hap angled his head, questioning.

"Hap, what would you say if I told you that my people could fly to the moon inside a metal tube? Or that we could speak to anyone in the world, no matter how far they went, whenever we liked? Or that we had a device that could kill a million people a thousand miles away?"

Hap felt his face turn white. "I . . . I would say you had magic. Some of it wonderful, and some of it terrible."

"I suppose you would," Umber said. "But there was nothing magical about it. It was technology, always marching forward, and not always for the better.

"But I'm getting ahead of myself. Where should my story begin? You don't need to know much about my youth. I'll leave it at this: My name is Brian Umber. I was born in a place called New York, in a nation called America. I was a prodigy with an all-consuming curiosity, and by the time I was twenty I had mastered a multitude of subjects at our finest universities. The only question I couldn't answer was: What was I supposed to do with the rest of my life? Every option seemed so dull.

"A wonderful answer came out of the blue when a rich man named Doane called on me. He was inspired, he said, by something called the Doomsday Vault, in a country of my world called Norway. They were gathering millions of seeds from every crop known to man inside a cave in the frozen north, to ensure that those plants could survive a global catastrophe."

"A *what?*" Hap asked.

"Global catastrophe. A disaster that reaches every corner of the world. A collapse of civilization."

"How, Lord Umber? How could something that terrible happen?"

"You underestimate our inventiveness," Umber replied grimly. "But this was Doane's idea: Instead of the seeds of agriculture, he wanted to preserve the seeds of *civilization*. He assembled a brilliant team to gather information on art, music, literature, science, architecture, engineering, medicine, philosophy, and more. Like those crop seeds, the information would be kept in a safe place. If something awful happened, people could remember all the good things that existed, and learn how to restore them.

"So Doane invited me, with my command of so many diverse subjects, to supervise the project." Umber rubbed his hands on his desk. "Does this make sense so far?"

"That sounds like an awful lot of information," Hap said.

"More than you could imagine. Millions upon millions of pages."

"And all the books would go into a vault?"

Umber leaned forward. "There were no books at all."

"But . . . then . . . where was all that information kept?"

Umber stood, walked to the wall beside his desk, and pulled the tapestry there to one side. Behind it was a round metal door with a keyhole in its center. He took a key from his pocket, fitted it into the lock, swung the door open and reached inside. Hap watched with widened eyes as Umber removed the silver case. There was that word again, engraved on the smoothly polished surface: REBOOT. Umber ran his fingers across the letters.

"I told you what this word means, didn't I?" Umber asked.

Hap nodded. "It means *to start over.*"

"That's right. Project Reboot was the name of Doane's venture. Helping civilization start over."

Umber opened the lid, hiding the far side from Hap's view. There was a *click* and a sound like the faint buzz of insects, and then a cold light was reflected on Umber's face. He looked at Hap over the top of the case. "It's all in here, Hap. All of it."

Hap's neck craned forward. "In *there*?"

Umber spun the case around, and Hap saw what he'd only

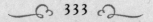

glimpsed before. The part that was flat on the desk was covered by buttons, each with numbers, letters, words, or symbols. The underside of the lid, which now stood straight up, was a rectangle of light. "This is the Reboot Suitcase. It's a machine we called a *computer*. The most powerful one of its size ever built, in fact. It was made to last a century or more. And it gets all the power it needs from sunlight."

Computer, Hap repeated inwardly. He stared at the thing, trying to comprehend. There were words within the rectangle:

PROJECT REBOOT
TYPE OR SPEAK TO BEGIN

"Hap, do you remember the music at the party for Prince Galbus?"

Hap nodded.

Umber spoke toward the computer. "Reboot: Show the music for Canon in D Major by Pachelbel."

Hap jumped back, startled, as the rectangle filled with musical staffs and notes.

"Reboot: Play this composition," Umber commanded.

Suddenly there was music, as if an unseen band of musicians had begun to play. Hap looked around, trying to find them, before realizing that the pure, clean sound came from the silver case. "This *is* magic," he whispered.

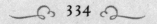

"Depends how you look at it, I suppose," Umber said. "Reboot: Stop music. Show the instruments used in this composition."

The music ended. Hap gasped as tiny, perfect images of stringed instruments filled the screen. Umber pressed his finger against one. "Reboot: Show a schematic of this instrument."

The instruments vanished and a diagram of a violin appeared, with its parts disassembled and labeled: *Scroll, pegs, fingerboard, bridge, purfling* . . .

"Reboot: Explain how to make one of these."

New diagrams and words appeared. Hap read the beginning: *Steps in the construction of a violin. Part 1: Selecting the wood. Step 1, 1* . . . But before he could read more, Umber rattled off a dizzying series of commands, and the computer responded instantly with new words and pictures:

"Reboot: Show the diagram of a sixteenth-century schooner sailing vessel. Reboot: Show the best-known works of the artist Picasso. Reboot: Display a fifteenth-century movable-type printing press. Reboot: Explain how to make the medicine penicillin. Reboot: Show a diagram of an early steam engine. Reboot: Show planet Earth as seen from space."

Hap's brain whirled inside his head. He didn't understand many of the images, including the last one, a wondrous blue-white marble floating in a sea of stars. He tried to make sense of everything Umber had said. "So . . . people gathered information . . . about everything . . . and it's all in here?"

"The project wasn't finished, by any means. But we gathered a lot, until the . . ." Umber hesitated, and his mouth twitched. "Global catastrophe." He slumped in his chair.

Hap watched Umber's darkening expression with alarm. "Lord Umber—maybe you shouldn't talk about this. I don't want you to—"

"Suffer another bout of soul-crushing despair?" Umber forced a smile. "I don't think so. Not so soon after the last. That's why I should get this out now. And who knows—spilling it may do me some good. It's festered inside for many years.

"When Doane recruited me, he insisted the project was urgent. He was convinced our civilization was in jeopardy. To him, every technological breakthrough was another step toward disaster. We'd cure an illness, but also learn to create a more dangerous disease. We tapped new forms of energy, but also astonishing powers of destruction. We found better ways to communicate, but they also meant better ways to share the doctrines of hate and fear. Technology was all well and good, Doane said, but some people were not well and good. He thought all our advances would one day be turned against us by misguided people with narrow, hateful philosophies."

Umber winced and rubbed the back of his neck. "I have to confess, I was enthralled by the challenge of Project Reboot, but I didn't agree that disaster was around the corner. Doane was right, though. Trouble came. Faster than I dreamed possible. Everything went wrong at once."

Umber drank the rest of his coffee in a gulp. "There were acts of cruelty all over the world that you couldn't imagine, followed by terrible acts of revenge. The horrors escalated. Armies clashed, and people panicked. Sickness and famine followed. A civilized world turned barbaric overnight. Even the earth itself was ruined—poisoned and plunged into a cruel, endless winter." Umber's chest hitched. "I'll spare us both the details. But we made a mess of it, all right. A stinking, awful mess."

Hap heard a thumping sound. It was his own foot, bouncing nervously on the floor. "But how did you get out? How did you get *here*?"

Umber puffed his cheeks and shook his head. "I don't know. But I've started to think it was the same way you did, Hap. I was *brought* here."

Hap clutched his own knees. "By WN?"

Umber shrugged. "Maybe. I certainly didn't get here on my own. You see, Project Reboot was headquartered in a remote place, far from where Doane expected the trouble to start, in a kind of fortress that was half underground. We were safe for a while when it all went bad. But eventually the riots spread, and people found us. A mob blasted their way through our heavy doors, looking for food and shelter from the poisoned skies. That caused a fire, but they came inside, anyway. I ended up locked in a room by myself, clutching the Reboot Suitcase with the mob hammering on the door. And then, suddenly . . . it was over."

"Over?"

"All I remember is coughing from the smoke, feeling dizzy and passing out. I don't know why, or how long I was unconscious. I just opened my eyes, and I was *here*. On that hill above the city, with all Kurahaven sprawled out below me. My clothes had been changed, and there was a pack next to me. It had two things inside: a gold coin, and this." Umber tapped the silver case. "My first thought was that I was dead and this was what came next! But I certainly *felt* alive. And a minute later, as fate would have it, Balfour came along on his one-horse cart. That gold coin was good for a month's stay at his old inn. And that was how my new life began."

For a while, all Hap heard was his own breathing. "Have you ever told anyone else about this?" he finally asked.

"Nobody. They'd think I was crazy, unless I also showed them this." Umber put his hand on the computer. "And

I don't want a soul to be aware that this computer exists. If you haven't guessed already, this is the source of all my innovations. But it's better if everyone thinks they come out of my head, because this world isn't ready for everything this computer could show. There is good progress and bad progress; I prefer the good."

"But now you've told me."

"I had to," Umber said. "You had to know what happened to my world. Now that you do, I think you'll understand why I hesitated to show you this note."

Umber opened a drawer in his desk and pulled out two familiar sheets of parchment. "Are you sure you're ready?"

For the first time since he had known the note existed, Hap wasn't sure he wanted to see it. But he nodded, and Umber slid the parchment across the table. Hap wiped his palms on his pants to dry the perspiration. Then he turned the parchment around and lifted it carefully. His eyes raced over the words until he neared the part he hadn't yet read.

By now you must be wondering: Why? Why do what this stranger asks? The reason is this: I know where you came from, Umber. I know too what happened to that world of yours. Quite a mess you folk made of that. I was there; I saw.

What if I told you there was a chance, even a small one, to undo the damage, to save those billion lives? But perhaps that thought has already crossed your mind. Surely it has. And surely you don't think it a mere coincidence that you found your way here, where magic lives. You must have considered the possibility that you might somehow find the key to saving your world.

I tell you this: Such a thing is possible. But it all depends upon the boy. Without him, there is no hope for the world you left behind.

That is all I can tell you for now. You'll know more in time. For now, follow your instincts. That is why I have chosen you.

—WN

Hap laid the parchment back on the table, feeling numb. He looked at Umber, who was watching him closely.

"Do you understand?" Umber said.

"I . . . I think so."

"Please don't run away. Or vanish on me."

"I . . . why would I do that?"

"That note says you're the key to saving a world. A billion lives. More, really. That's why I didn't want to show you the note right away. It seems like too much to ask.

Too much to heap on such young shoulders."

Hap covered his face with his hands. "But . . . how could I save a world? I don't know how to do that."

"Not yet, you don't. We'll figure this out as we go along, I suppose. It has something to do with those threads of light, that's for sure. There's no doubt now: You should do your best to not only see those filaments, but also understand their meaning. That will be your true power.

"Happenstance, the only thing that matters is this: Are you willing to try? As your skills arise, will you master them? Will you become everything you are meant to be? You can trust me to help you however I can—it will be you and me together. But *will you try?*"

Hap didn't say anything for a long time. With his hands over his face, he thought about what Umber was asking him to do. It sounded like madness. And if he hadn't just seen the astonishing machine, he wouldn't have believed the existence of another world was even possible.

The question awed and frightened him. He wished the idea of it would simply go away. But he knew that ideas could never do such a thing. It was as Umber had said many days before: *Once an idea is out and about, it can't be called back, silenced, or erased. You can't contain it, any more than you could put the head of a dandelion back together after the wind has scattered its seeds.*

Hap thought about his life. It may have been brief, but it was surely eventful. Balfour was right when he'd said that memory is like a book. Already, Hap's existence bound many pages. Now those pages added up to something: an identity. *I was nobody when it started, but I'm somebody now,* Hap realized, and his heart swelled to think of it.

He flipped back to the first pages of his remembrance, when he became conscious in an underground city. Strangers found him. But they weren't strangers anymore. They had helped one another, saved one another. There were words for such people, he knew, and words rich with meaning sprang into his mind:

Family. Friends.

He heard Umber take a breath, and remembered the question: *Will you try?* He slid his hands down to his chin, revealing his bright green eyes.

A billion lives. A world in jeopardy. It was a flawed and crazy world, a civilization with a capacity for astonishing achievements and cruel destruction. But it was a place that Lord Umber—his friend Umber—thought was worth saving.

Will you try?

What else could he say?

HAPPENSTANCE AND UMBER'S ADVENTURES
CONTINUE IN BOOK TWO OF THE
BOOKS OF UMBER, DRAGON GAMES.

The boy gripped the railing tight.
He watched the leviathan's enormous tail rise from the brine until it almost broke the surface and then sweep down again in a powerful and dreamlike rhythm that propelled the barge through a rolling black sea. The port city of Kurahaven, storm-battered but still glorious, was far behind, and the sun's fire had been doused hours before on the horizon ahead.

Happenstance eyed the dark waves uneasily. He'd hoped his dread of water might fade as he spent more hours plying its surface. *But it's as bad as ever,* Hap thought, with a little twist at the corner of his mouth. His shoulders rose toward his ears.

There was an open hatch on the deck of the barge, with stairs leading down to the spacious central cabin. A giddy sound drifted up the stairs and into the night. Hap recognized the particular laugh of his guardian. Lord Umber was in his usual high spirits, which were always at their loftiest after a satisfying meal and a hot mug of his beloved coffee, and with the prospect of some thrilling discovery ahead.

Hap walked to the railing at the square prow to see what might lie before him. His extraordinary eyes pierced the darkness and found Nima, the barge's captain, sitting cross-legged on the back of the leviathan, Boroon. Perhaps sensing that someone was watching, she turned to look back at the barge that was strapped to Boroon's immense back.

"Hello, Nima," Hap called. He wasn't sure that Nima could see him in the gloom of night, with tatters of cloud shrouding the moon, but she waved. She stood, walked across the bony plates of the leviathan's back, and climbed the stairs to stand beside Hap.

Nima was clad in black sealskin. As she ran her hands through her long hair, Hap stole a glance at the translucent skin that bridged the space between her knuckles. He pulled his gaze away in an instant; he knew better than most how it felt to have someone stare at a physical oddity.

"Why aren't you below with the others, Happenstance?" she asked.

Hap shrugged. "I felt like coming up here." That was hardly true. What he'd really felt like was not setting out on this adventure at all. He wished Umber could be content to stay home in the Aerie. It was a fine place to dwell, with wonders and mysteries galore inside its crammed archives. Those were the kind he preferred: adventures in ink, which couldn't crush you in their jaws or under their feet. But, sadly, Umber liked the real thing. And to make matters worse, running off to a new land always exposed Hap to more strangers who would point and gawk at his strange green eyes.

"I'm glad to find you here alone," Nima said. "There's something I've been meaning to give you." There was a silver chain around her neck. She lifted it over her head, and Hap saw a fat locket dangling, shaped like halves of a seashell. She held it out, and Hap opened a hand to accept it.

"It's beautiful," Hap said. "But . . ."

"Why am I giving it to you? Because I heard how you risked your life to save Umber. And Umber is my friend. You have spared me an ocean of grief."

Hap clamped his jaw as he thought back to that terrifying night when he'd climbed a crumbling tower to confront the awful, eye-stealing creature that had taken Umber hostage. "It wasn't just me who saved Umber," he said.

"I know that. But Hap, you haven't seen the true gift yet. Open it."

Hap brought the locket closer to his eyes and saw a tiny clasp at the seam of the two shells. He pried it open with a fingernail, and the shells parted. Inside was an enormous pearl. It was as round and lustrous as the moon, which chose that moment to emerge from hiding and shine down on its little cousin. Hap goggled at the orb. He'd seen pearls in the jewelers' tents in the marketplace at Kurahaven, but none so large or stunning. "How can I accept this? It's too much!"

"You land folk value pearls more than I do. And do you really think it is so hard for me to find such a thing?" Nima asked. Hap supposed it wasn't. Nima was amphibious, and she could breathe under the waves as easily as above them. Of course she could dive down and bring up all manner of wonders. Balfour had told him once that the leviathan barge was built and paid for by the fortunes she'd found in sunken ships.

"It may be useful in a difficult spot someday," Nima said. "Or it might help a friend in need. Your heart will tell you when to use it."

Hap snapped the locket shut and put the chain around his neck. "It's wonderful. Thank you."

"It was Boroon's idea, in fact," Nima said.

Hap stared at the leviathan's broad head, cutting the waves before them. "Really? Boroon?" He knew that Nima communicated with the leviathan, but he had no idea that they discussed matters so . . . specific. "Would you thank him for me, please?"

Nima nodded.

A minute passed, silent except for the hiss of water along the leviathan's side. "Where are we going?" Hap asked.

Nima smiled. "Umber wanted it to be a secret. You know how he is about these things."

Hap sighed. If he could change one thing about Umber—besides his constant need for the thrill of exploration—it would be his obsession with secrets and surprises.

Before long everyone else was asleep, even the great leviathan, who bobbed in the water like a breathing island. Hap kept watch for the others, because he needed no sleep. That was another one of the great mysteries about him, the boy with no memory of who he was or where he'd come from.

Boroon's fins swirled in the water, holding the barge in place an arrow's flight from the coast. Hap, like the others, shielded his eyes from the rising sun, staring at the spot where Nima pointed. He looked at Oates, who frowned and shrugged.

Umber thumped the railing with both hands and laughed. "I can see why nobody's discovered this before! Why would any ship come close? It's just a craggy sea cliff, unremarkable and uninviting. Still, Nima, I don't see the opening you mentioned."

"Watch when the wave hits the shore," Nima said. "There."

A crest of water rolled toward the cliff. Hap watched, expecting it to slam against the rock and throw up an explosion of foam. But something else happened: The wave collapsed, as if its foundation had vanished.

"I see it now!" Umber cried. "A cave, under the surface! But how can we get inside?"

"Boroon can take us," Nima said.

Umber's eyes gleamed. "It's *that* big in there? And we won't . . . you know . . . disturb them?"

Nima nodded. "It's large enough. And I have done it once before."

"I'm so glad you discovered this!" Umber cried, with his knees wiggling.

"It was Boroon who saw the cave from underwater. He is a curious soul," Nima replied quietly. "But sometimes I feel I never should have told you about it."

"Hold on, Umber," said Oates, raising a thick hand. "What did you mean, 'disturb them'?"

"Let's not wait another second!" cried Umber, ignoring the big man. "Do we need to douse the fires?"

Nima shook her head. "We'll be under only for a moment," she said.

Under, Hap thought. *Not again.* He crossed his arms to suppress the shivers that ran through his body.

Umber rubbed his hands together and laughed. "Everybody, down the hatch. Boroon is going to dive!"

Hap followed the others down the stairs into the central cabin. Only Nima, who was in no danger of drowning, stayed above. Oates pulled the hatch shut behind him and sealed it, then came muttering down the stairs. He held on to one of the beams in the middle of the room and stared at the ceiling as the barge lurched forward.

This was the second time Hap had been aboard when Boroon took the craft underwater, and it terrified him as much as the first. He sat beside Balfour, Umber's elderly friend and trusted servant, at the dining table that was anchored to the floor, his bloodless fingers clamped on the table's edge. Sophie—the girl who was just a few years older than Hap and was valued for her skill as both artist and archer—was across from him, and she gave him a reassuring smile despite her own obvious nerves. There were round windows of thick glass in the walls, and the water rose past them as Hap watched. The light changed from pale daylight to the dim, shimmering green of the sea and then vanished as they passed into a space where little sun could reach. He felt the squeeze of pressure deep inside his ears, and when he worked his jaw, his eardrums popped.

Umber stood at the bottom of the stairs, bouncing in place and humming. "Listen, everyone—it should be safe to go up in a moment, but I think we should keep as quiet as we can."

"You make more noise than anyone," Oates pointed out.

"Do I?" Umber asked, narrowing one eye.

"With all your squealing and clapping."

Umber glared. "Nothing wrong with a little enthusiasm."

Balfour cleared his throat. "Umber, would you mind telling us why we need to be quiet?"

Umber raised a hand, palm out. "Patience, my friends! We're

almost there!" The barge's bow tilted upward again. Boroon brought them to the surface, but the ascent was slow, as if the leviathan was trying to be as stealthy as such an enormous creature could be.

"It's so much better if you see for yourselves," Umber said. Hap could measure his guardian's excitement by the diameter of his eyes, and they looked now like a pair of dinner plates. Umber dashed up the stairs and threw the hatch open. "Bring the lamps," he called in a half whisper. "And walk softly!"

Hap waited for Oates, Balfour, and Sophie to ascend before him. When he followed, he heard Umber telling them: "Give your eyes time to adjust to the dark." But Hap, of course, needed no time.

Boroon had swum into a great cave that must have been bored out over eons by the endless undermining of ocean waves. The entrance was behind them and underwater. Hap could see a glimmer of dim sunlight filtering through, as if passing under the threshold of a door.

The sea cave was immense. The ceiling of stone was a hundred feet above the top of the barge, and Boroon fit easily in the pool of water that washed up against a broad stone ledge in the interior. When Hap saw the monstrous things that occupied the ledge, his breath was snared inside his throat. For a moment he thought they were toppled statues or mummified creatures—anything but living beings. But then he heard the air rushing in and out of enormous mouths and nostrils, and he saw the subtle rise and fall of the vast chests.

They all stared, grasping the rail. Even the leviathan raised his head from the water to eye the five slumbering things.

Boroon was still the largest creature Hap had ever seen, but these titans were not far behind. A grown man could disappear under one of their feet. Two might have been female, but it was hard to tell with faces so monstrous: warty and craggy, with blunt horns sprouting from chins, cheeks, and foreheads. Their filthy hair had the coarse texture of a horse's tail. The skin on their limbs was etched with countless lines as deep as the bark of ancient trees. Hap noticed, with some alarm, that their ragged garments seemed to have been made from the hide of a beast much like Boroon.

The creatures were sprawled on the ledge in almost drunken poses. Two slumped against the wall of the cave with legs splayed. One lay flat on her stomach with a hand dangling over the ledge and fingers in the water. Two more curled on their sides like babies.

"What are they?" asked Sophie, almost too quietly to hear.

The answer suddenly came to Hap. He'd read about them in Umber's books. "Sea-giants!" he said, hissing the words. More than two hundred years before, the sea-giants had invaded the great city of Kurahaven and smashed it into ruins. The sorceress Turiana had somehow driven them away, and the sea-giants had stalked into the sea, vanishing under the waves, never to be seen again. *Until this day,* Hap thought.

Umber's giddy smile was so wide it threatened to divide his head. "Exactly! We've found their den. Their resting place."

"Resting place! Are you a crazy man, bringing us here?" cried Oates. "What if they wake up?"

"Kindly lower your voice," Umber said, patting the air with his hands. He gestured for the others to gather close, and spoke in a hush. "I don't think we have to worry about waking them."

"We don't?" Balfour asked quietly. "Why is that?"

"I think they're waiting for something," Umber said.

"Waiting? What kind of nonsense is that?" scoffed Oates.

Umber could barely keep still. He rubbed his hands together and shifted his weight from foot to foot. "Do you know why they came to Kurahaven, all those years ago?"

"To crush and plunder," Balfour replied.

Umber shook his head. "They didn't come to crush the city. They came to crush the hubris of its king."

"That must have hurt," Oates said.

Umber pinched the bridge of his nose. "Hubris means arrogance, you great buffoon. Now listen carefully, Sophie and Hap—I don't think you know the entire legend."

Hap and Sophie stepped closer so Umber could keep

his voice low. "These days the kingdom of Celador is a peaceable place, friendly to neighbors and interested mainly in trade. But in that age the kings were growing in power and bent on conquest. They declared themselves the lords of the sea, and their pride grew as fast as their fortunes. They made Kurahaven the wonder of its age, with the greatest fleet ever seen. Then came King Brinn, the fiercest and most ambitious ruler of them all. No ordinary castle was enough for him. And so in the harbor he built Petraportus, the ultimate symbol of his kingdom's might and mastery of the sea: a castle so grand that a ship could sail through its gates and into the man-made harbor in its great hall. Petraportus was quite a statement—so loud that it finally reached the ears of those who did not appreciate man's challenge to their dominion." Umber jutted his chin toward the sleeping giants. "And so the sea-giants roused themselves and put an end to Brinn, his fleet, his city, and his castle. Not to mention his hubris."

Umber's face lost its color for a moment. His gaze wandered to some distant, imaginary point. "It was a message to all humanity, come to think of it: Don't get too big for your britches. There are always forces bigger than you can imagine, ready to put you in your place. If your ambition burns too hot, they'll snuff you out."

For a moment Umber looked ready to plummet into one of

his episodes of despair. "But Lord Umber," Hap asked quickly, "how do you know these are the same sea-giants?"

Umber gave his head a shake, and his eyes came back into focus. His smile was resurrected. "Why, I believe that's the famous Bulrock, right there. Hap, do you remember the story of Brinn's leap?"

"He jumped from the top of Petraportus, swinging his ax, and cut off Bulrock's nose," Hap said. Beside him Sophie, who had brought a pad of paper and charcoal, began to sketch the amazing scene. But she suddenly gasped and pointed at the largest of the giants, who was leaning against the wall of the cave. The tip of his nose was clearly missing.

"Nima," Umber quietly called, "do you think you could have Boroon paddle us a little closer to the ledge?"

Hap looked down. At the moment just fifteen or twenty yards of water separated them from the rocky shelf where the giants slumbered. The idea of getting nearer seemed like madness.

He wasn't the only one who felt so. Sophie's eyes looked like they might pop out and fall onto the deck. Balfour said, "I'm not sure that's a good idea, Lord Umber."

"I agree," Nima said, folding her arms. "It would invite disaster."

Umber waved a hand. "Come now, my friends. They won't

be roused easily—they've hibernated for centuries. I'd love to get a closer look. Touch one, if I can."

Oates glared at Umber. "You *are* a crazy man," he said.

"Because I'm not afraid of my own shadow?" Umber said. "Come on, Hap, you'll join me, won't you?"

Hap shifted his weight from foot to foot. "But . . . Lord Umber . . . if they awaken . . . you know what they could do. We could all get killed. And what if they went back to Kurahaven?"

Umber glowered and worked his jaw from side to side. "What's the matter with all of you? You're as meek as mice." He lifted his feet, one after another, and hopped as he pried off his boots. When they fell to the deck, it sounded like thunder. "Stay here if you like. I'll swim over. Be back in a minute or two, that's all."

"For heaven's sake, Umber," Balfour said. He fired a look at Oates, and Oates nodded back. Just as Umber hooked a leg over the railing, the big man stepped closer and wrapped a powerful arm around Umber's waist.

"What's this?" Umber cried, thrashing in Oates's grip. "I'll decide what I can and can't do! Let go of me, you insolent, muscled mor—" He froze abruptly with his mouth hanging open, staring across the water. Hap turned to look, and his blood turned to cold sludge in his veins.

One of Bulrock's eyes was open.

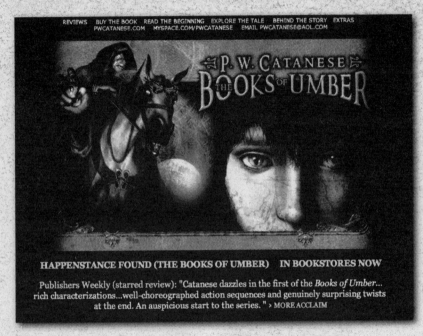

Magical Books
By P. W. Catanese

Classic tales of magic and adventure like you've never heard them before!

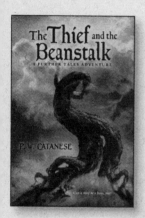

From Aladdin
Published by Simon & Schuster

BE SURE TO CATCH
FABLEHAVEN

Available from Aladdin

FROM ALADDIN · PUBLISHED BY SIMON & SCHUSTER

NOW AVAILABLE FROM ALADDIN

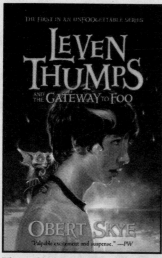

The world of Foo is in chaos, and only Leven has the power to save it.

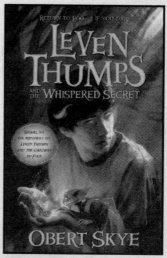

Leven and his friends travel across Foo to restore Geth as the rightful king.

The war to unite Foo and Reality has begun, and Leven is in for the adventure of a lifetime.

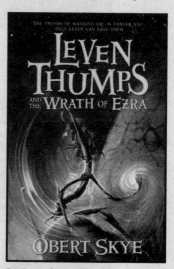

Can Leven discover his new power before the Dearth finds him?

Beyond Fablehaven lies
A WORLD WITHOUT HEROES. . . .

BEYONDERS

A WORLD WITHOUT HEROES